A Healer's Sin

BRYCE GREEN

ISBN: 978-1-963749-62-5 – E book

978-1-963749-63-2 - Paper Back

978-1-963749-64-9 – Hard Cover

Dedication

I want to dedicate this book to my friends and family who have supported me along the way. My parents were both supportive, and I want them to know I appreciate their support. This book started as a fantasy tabletop game, so I wanted to ensure that my friends who helped start the adventure were credited. The adventuring party was played by:

Christopher *as the Game Master*

Devon *as Lana*

Nell *as Thalia*

Craig *as Drulynn*

Noah *as Zee*

Zachary *as Omehk*

Most importantly, I would like to thank my Marvelous wife, Marvellous, for supporting me through thick and thin. Marvellous was there at my best and my worst, and I wouldn't have made it this far without her. She was my first fan and was always there to hear my newest story ideas. I've said it before, and I'll repeat it: I love you now and always.

Acknowledgments

Several team members have helped me with the project. Still, the most significant was my Fiverr book editor, Camile Pen, who did a terrific job helping me edit and provide her opinions on the chapters.

For finding book agents, I had the help of Seraphina O and Verdle K, who were also both on Fiverr. For creating my book proposals, I received help from Panagiotis Kanellis, Denise L., and Tash, all of whom I found on Fiverr.

For beta readers, I had the help of Fiverr beta readers Luna and Jonas, who were both exceptionally helpful.

Several artists were also involved in bringing my idea of character designs for Wallace and Isabelle to life. This includes X (formerly known as Twitter) artists, @MattPainte, and @Yellow_Py. And finally, thank you to Leon N from Fiverr for creating the book cover, spine, and back.

Thank you all for your support!

Table of Contents

A Healer's Sin

Starving, freezing, and left to die, Wallace roams the streets of Elton, a city rotting with corruption, clinging to survival alongside his found family, twins Michael and Melena. Bound by love and desperation, the three steal, scavenge, and kill to endure another winter.

When a fatal illness threatens to end him, Wallace is saved by Abigail Kreila, one of the few kind plague doctors left. She offers food, shelter, and the chance to apprentice under her, giving him the opportunity to heal the city instead of bleeding it dry.

But Michael and Melena dream of more than survival. They crave wealth, pleasure, and power, no matter the cost. And they expect Wallace to stand with them.

Now, caught between Kreila's vision of hope and his siblings' lure of indulgence, Wallace must choose between becoming a healer in a broken city or following his family into a life of ruthless ambition, where the price of luxury may cost him his soul.

Chapter 1

Year 1351 after the Cataclysm

"Grab, right alley, sewer, home. Grab, right alley, sewer, home." I whispered this under my breath like a silent prayer. Maybe I was just nervous. Maybe luck had finally run out on me. I'd stolen from this man four times already. He was old, could barely see, and the street was always crowded enough that he never spotted me coming.

"Wallace's Pickled Goods," read the peeling sign above the storefront. The building looked like it was breathing its last. The neighboring shops looked ready to collapse, too. This part of town wasn't built for adventurers or rich snobs. It was too poor, too forgotten. The guards barely patrolled here, usually too busy eyeing a girl who might justify their next divorce. The time was right. The place was perfect. No one would care, and no one would notice.

"Grab, right alley, sewer, home," I repeated it one last time.

Across the street, hidden behind a stack of boxes beside two boarded-up storefronts, I waited. I just needed the right crowd—big enough to cover my movements but not so tight that I couldn't slip through.

Minutes passed. Then, I saw it. Dinner time.

I burst through a gap in the crowd, not stopping even when I bumped into a few people. The store doubled as the old man's home. Out front were shelves lined with jars, and at the far end was a table where he sat, slowly taking payments. On the opposite side, far from his reach, was a jar of radishes near the bottom of the shelf. It was just low enough to be overlooked and just high enough for me to grab.

I closed in fast. The old man was distracted with a customer and didn't notice me until I snatched the jar and turned to run.

"You prick!" he yelled, grabbing a broom like it might actually help. But it was too late.

I had already slipped back into the crowd. No one paid attention. No one cared about a stolen jar of radishes. No guard was rushing in to be a hero. I ran to the other side of the street until I spotted the same manhole that had saved me more times than I could count.

I shoved the jar into the old sack, gritted my teeth, and heaved the manhole cover aside. The ladder dropped into heat, stench, and darkness. I climbed down fast.

The sewer hit me like a slap—humid, rank, thick with the smell of rot and old piss. Rats scattered everywhere, and a few didn't bother. It was the kind of place where you caught something awful or wound up dead for nothing. My kind of place.

I hit the floor and broke into a jog. I knew this route. There was just enough water to move the sludge along, and landmarks clear as day. You could get lost near the skeleton with a wizard hat slumped like he'd died mid-spell, or by the elvish graffiti glowing faintly, unreadable and pointless, or by the rotting tree branch.

Above, tavern music seeped through a crack in the street, and light filtered through the next manhole, which made me slow down. From the left tunnel came rushing water. From the right, shouts and scuffling. I kept straight.

The ladder was damp and slippery. I climbed fast, sack in hand. The manhole was already moved—caused by another runner, maybe. Didn't matter.

Back on the surface, the air didn't help. I still reeked like a corpse in cheap cologne. The pickle store was nearby, and it didn't look like anyone had followed me. The old man wouldn't dare anyway, not for a jar of stolen radishes.

I stuck to alleys and back routes, head down. The sign was still there: a bear and berries above a shattered window, the door leaning like it wanted to fall in. Home sweet home.

I checked behind me. No shadows. All clear.

As I walked a block toward the place, I caught the sound of people gagging. Couldn't blame them. I stank like something that had died twice. Luckily, everyone around here smelled like that. This part of Elton was home to the homeless and drunkards, folks eating what passed for food: rotting scraps and rats. The local delicacy, apparently.

Sometimes I wondered what it might be like, living somewhere with windows that weren't broken, roofs that didn't leak. Food that not only smelled but tasted great. But thoughts like that were dangerous. They made you sloppy.

I shook my head and opened the door that clung to the building by nothing but hopes and dreams, and there they were, Michael and Melena, waiting in their matching stolen sailor shirts and pants, with their long, oily black hair. The twins were the same height, wore the same clothes, and even shared the same fish-scented perfume, which paired beautifully with my signature rat aroma.

Melena was easy to tell apart, she styled her hair to match whatever caught her eye on the street. Today's look was pigtails. Michael, on the other hand, didn't care one bit. His hair was always the same: straight down to his shoulders.

We all competed for the best outfit, and while they really tried, no one could beat my black curly hair, this month's finest pillowcase—complete with grass stains—and my signature potato sack shorts that proudly reeked of mud.

They stood near the most iconic features of our home. The hole in the roof was our chandelier. The moldy, broken bar served as our dining table. And the barstools in front of it—one of which squeaked like a dying rodent were our thrones.

"Another Wallace Hit!" they both shouted in unison, our new code for 'another flawless heist at the pickled goods graveyard.'

They had decided that shouting the name of whoever I stole from was no longer just a joke, but a tradition. Wallace's shop was the easiest target in town, so his name stuck around.

"Hi, Michael! Hi, Melena!" I shouted back. Their names were borrowed from the remnants of other people's lives—a whiskey jar Michael found, and a broken bow with "Melena" scribbled on it. None of us knew our real names, so we took turns handing out nicknames.

"Radishes this time. I know you wanted carrots, but they were on the top shelf," I said.

"Looks like they were selling whatever this is in bulk," Michael replied, holding up a weird, whiskered fish.

"I pushed some lady over by accident, but it turned out to be a good distraction—no guards this time," Melena added proudly.

We climbed onto the barstools to admire today's haul. I puffed out my chest as I emptied my rucksack: a bunch of radishes, one copper piece, a metal spoon, a wooden fork, and a pair of shoes that didn't fit me.

"I think it's clear who's today's winner," I said with a smug grin.

Michael pouted as he opened his own sack, pulling out a soft purple rock, a handful of wooden buttons, and some posters with words we couldn't read—something about a horse.

But Melena had come prepared. She dumped her sack out like she was unveiling treasure, then planted her hands on her hips.

"Nope. It's me day!"

The bag spilled open to reveal five copper pieces and a broken watch—enough to buy real food, the kind rich people wasted on things like bread and that disgusting wine.

Melena flashed us her middle finger. "Ha!"

Her victory pose was short-lived. The creaky barstool beneath her finally gave up, snapping and sending her crashing to the floor. It was too old to hold her weight any longer.

Michael and I laughed so hard we couldn't breathe, tears welling in our eyes as we watched our sister flail around, trying to collect herself. She sat up and dusted off her shirt with a full-on frown.

"It's not funny. I almost died!" she huffed.

I burst out another laugh, but as I did, I zoned out a bit. I didn't like tagging our successful jobs as 'luck,' but that was what this was, and I didn't know how many more 'Wallace jobs' we could get away with before the guards started noticing. Or before someone worse than the guards did.

Chapter 2

One night after dinner, I remembered that it was around this time when I met the twins and we became a family. We don't know which god smiled down on us that day, but we were happy to have each other.

I don't remember how it all started. My memory was shaky. What I do remember is that, two years earlier, in the late fall, two adults stood above me. Their clothes were filthy—stinking, stained with beer. Their pale skin was speckled with acne. We were in an alley behind a tavern. The air reeked of rotting fruit, and it was the middle of the night. I could still hear the music and cheering from inside.

The two of them smelled like ale and spoke as if they had just hit some kind of drunken epiphany.

"Wait right here. This dumbass and I have to go get something," the familiar woman said, sarcasm lacing her voice.

The familiar man slapped her on the back of the head hard enough to make her groan. "Yeah, she forgot something at the house."

I don't even remember us owning a house.

"You need to stay right here," he said, giggling.

"Yes, stay right here. We are gonna come back and grab you!" the woman added with a smile.

I watched them walk down the alley without me, both of them laughing as they disappeared from view.

"Who were these two?" I asked myself. They seemed so familiar, and our pale white skin looked the same.

I don't remember. All I know is they took a left at the end of the alley, and I never saw them again.

I stayed there for two days, starving and reeking of liquor. The tavern people ate well. I knew this because they had little to nothing left for me to scavenge.

But I could only be a loyal kid for so long. Eventually, I left the alley and searched for the two, but I couldn't find them. I asked passersby and city guards, but no one knew who I was talking about. A pale white couple with black hair wasn't enough to set them apart in a city of tens of thousands. It didn't help that I never got their names. I don't think they ever gave them to me.

I spent the winter in the sewers, throwing rocks at rats and begging in broken Paljavish just to scrape together enough coins for food. It was cold, chaotic, and brutal. Winter is when the depraved and homeless fight to survive. The streets were blanketed in snow, but piss and sewage stained the ice. The sewers, once barren, filled up fast with dirty homeless people in tattered fur, their teeth chattering like broken bones.

"Look, I'm so sorry, little one, but there's no more room"—I heard that one a lot from orphanage staff and priests. "You can stay a night here in the shed." Or, "You can stay for one night, but you need to leave in the morning." Those two lines became the difference between staying alive and freezing to death.

"Go screw yourself!" and "Scram, you rotten kid!" were also common. But unfortunately, curses and the occasional slap didn't do much to keep me warm.

Luckily, I managed to scavenge some clothes: a large blue tunic that was way too big for me. It doubled as pants once I tore it up to fit. It wasn't winter-proof, but it helped. I also found a blanket made from the grey fur of a wolf and slippers made of sheep wool.

I hadn't eaten in almost three days and couldn't get anything, not even in the middle of the night.

That's when the dog showed up.

I remember lying in one of Elton's many alleys, being stared down by a dog with patches of fur missing. It stood there, waiting for me to ring the dinner bell. It was nearly midnight. Most of the town was asleep. The ones still awake didn't care about a mutt about to eat dinner.

The alley I lay in was mostly clean—no trash, no other people, just frozen puddles scattered across the ground. That meant I was the only thing in its line of sight.

I watched as its brown eyes came closer, the stench of rotting flesh hitting me with every limping step it took. It started growling, thick saliva dripping from its jaws. It was going to kill me.

I couldn't fight back. I was too weak to move and could barely make a sound to alert anyone on the street.

So this is how it ends? I thought. Not with a scream or a fight. Just… dinner for a dog.

Suddenly, a sharp rock came flying past me and the dog's head. Then another. Then another. The dog, blood dripping from its head, turned and fled. A little girl with a long stick shouted at it, while a boy kept hurling rocks, missing most of his shots with his terrible aim. But it was enough. The dog left me alone.

They both approached, oily black hair stuck to their pale faces. Their blue eyes met mine. Both wore brown furry tunics torn in several places. Their brown pants and oversized shoes were tied on with rope. They smelled like the sewers. Their clothes reeked of frozen dung.

They waved. "Hi!" the girl said.

I lifted my hand with what little strength I had. They tilted their heads, then glanced at the ribs poking through my skin.

The boy pulled out a whiskey bottle filled with water and handed it to me. The girl followed with two carrots. I devoured the gifts. At that point, anything would've tasted like heaven. I wanted to thank them for saving my life, but all I managed was a weak "hi."

They didn't linger. They waved again, said "bye-bye," and ran down another alley.

Two weeks passed as the temperature kept dropping. If it weren't for a blanket I found, I would've been dead. It was perfect. Too big for me, which meant I could wrap myself up in it more than once.

That day was lucky too. I came across half a bag of potatoes, some beets, and a water pitcher I'd stolen from a tavern. A feast fit for a king.

I was walking down another alley behind a marketplace one evening when I saw them again. Snow covered everything. The alley was mostly used for storage—boxes and barrels everywhere, the air thick with the smell of frozen garbage.

There they were. The twins. Curled up next to each other. Pale as bones. Skinny as skeletons. Shaking. Dying.

I jogged up to them and stole their line. "Hi!" I said.

Their blue eyes met mine, and they gave a quiet, shaky "hi" in return.

I didn't hesitate. I took off the blanket and wrapped it around all three of us. Then I pulled out the food I had saved for myself and shared it with them.

Their matching smiles made me chuckle, my breath freezing in the air. That night, we curled up together, waiting for the night to pass. Our body heat kept us alive.

And by morning, we all smelled like rotting fruit but were alive.

There we were. Three kids with the same pale skin, the same oily black hair, wrapped in one oversized blanket.

We haven't spent a single day apart since.

Chapter 3

I crept behind a box, peeking around its edge at the target. Melena crouched behind an empty barrel she had knocked over. Finally, Michael strolled past us with a book held upside down, pretending to read words he couldn't understand. All six of our eyes were locked on the target for the upcoming heist. A bakery. The smell of fresh beef pies and sweet cakes drifted out through its windows, practically begging us to take what we wanted without paying.

The location was perfect. A bakery shop with a barber to its left and an alley to its right. The wooden buildings looked like they had just been put up, the wood still had that bright tan color you only see when it's fresh. And this wasn't the ghetto. No sour stink of sewage, no heaps of trash on the sidewalks. The front windows were clean enough to see straight into the shop. We could spot the owners working behind the counter. People in this part of town dressed cleaner, too, and they were way more polite than anyone back where we came from.

The alley had cleared out just in time, and the streets were quiet. That made it easy for us to communicate without shouting.

Michael paced in front of the store, eyeing the door. A couple of strangers passed by, asking what game we were playing and where our parents were. I looked over at Melena and gave her a nod. She nodded back. Then, trying to be sneaky but failing miserably, she yelled, "Hey!" across the street to Michael. He flinched and quickly backpedaled toward our box-and-barrel outpost.

Behind us, two buildings sat on one side of the street, half-transformed from old wooden shacks into the same fresh tan houses that seemed to be popping up everywhere. That side was empty, which meant no one was watching our backs.

"The baker's a fat lady. This won't be a fast, easy heist," Michael muttered.

"Wait," I said, catching something he hadn't. I pointed at the door in front of the bakery. Hanging above it was a bronze bell attached to a hook—the kind that rings when the door opens.

"An alarm. I didn't notice!" Michael gasped.

"And worse…" Melena added. She pointed to a city guard whistling as he walked past the shop. He wore green padded armor and a metal breastplate with the country's bear crest stamped into it. A pike rested in his grip, and a brown leather cap sat low on his head.

We all shivered. This job was way more complicated than we'd expected.

We hurried back to headquarters, the abandoned tavern we'd claimed, to regroup and rework the plan.

The twins and I were brilliant for kids our age. Most 10-year-olds would be out chasing sweets. But not us. We were different. We weren't just after the pies; no, we were after the money and the pies. That way, we'd have enough to buy new autumn clothes and still afford tickets to the fancy circus outside the city. We wanted to see the red dragon flying and the red jester dancing above those crimson tents, which they showed on the posters we still couldn't read. But we didn't need to read. We knew what a dragon and a clown looked like.

And if I was honest, it wasn't just about the fun we would have doing that, it was about being kids again, even if only for a moment.

So, we gathered around the fireplace in the abandoned tavern we called home. The fire was lit with sticks, scraps of paper, and whatever old books we could find. The fireplace itself was built from faded red bricks, most of them cracked or chipped. Above it, a rusty metal rod held up a black iron pot that hadn't seen stew in a long time.

I grabbed a charcoal stub and a scrap of paper—well, paper-ish—and drew our plan. My first attempt was a mess, but I flipped the page and started over. This time, I managed a rough sketch of the bakery using an old sheet we tore from a journal we'd found. We used whatever junk we had lying around to mark where each of us would go. I was the half-broken but proud wooden toy pig. Melena was the green pincushion. Michael, the shot glass.

We'd picked our roles ourselves. I'd seen Michael fail to figure out how a slingshot worked, so I made myself the archer and the distraction. Melena would be the thief, the one who'd grab the pies and the coins. Michael, of course, would be the talker. His job was to act like a customer, or at least someone pretending to be rich enough to belong in a shop like that.

To pull it off, we needed disguises. So we scrubbed ourselves down with whatever "clean" water we could find in the river running through the city. It was brown, but not sewer brown, so we counted it as a win. We even bought new clothes to help hide our usual stink. We settled on matching brown tunics, brown pants, and brown shoes. We wanted something fancier, but the market had these colors on discount.

After two days of planning, the heist was ready to begin.

The twins had moved a barrel next to a stack of boxes beside the bakery, and Melena climbed onto Michael's shoulders to reach the window on the alley-facing side. The alley was still clean and empty— no people, no creatures. They both gave me a thumbs-up, and I knew it was my time to shine.

Across the street from the bakery, I stood on top of a box that barely held my weight. I took aim and fired. My shot was perfect. All I needed to do was knock the bell off its hook. I even had several pebbles in case I missed the first time. But unfortunately, my aim was so perfect that I hit the hook itself, ripping it off the wall completely. The bell and the hook crashed to the ground.

"Hello? Who is that?" the baker's lady groaned from inside the shop.

This wasn't part of the plan.

The bell was supposed to fall off the hook so I could grab it and use it to distract the guard. But this crash was loud, and now we were exposed. I saw a city guard at the end of the street turn toward the bakery. He raised a hand to shield his eyes from the sun. He was about thirty feet away. I panicked for a second—then heard another crash, this time in the opposite direction, the sound of breaking glass.

Whoever made that noise, thank you.

I signaled Michael to head for the door right after me to begin his part of the plan. Then I sprinted across the street, scooped up the bell and hook, and ran straight toward the guard.

"Ring! Ring! Ring!" I shouted, waving the bell above my head as I ran past.

The guard looked down at me, his tanned skin and scruffy brown beard catching the light. Up close, I noticed his uniform was torn in places. Holes in the brown padded armor, and his pants smelled like wine.

"Uh, yeah, kid, what's wrong?" he asked, squinting.

"I saw some rats down that road, fighting with sticks! One of them had a hat! Isn't that exciting?" I said, all wide-eyed and excited.

While he stared at me, I glanced over his shoulder. Michael was walking into the bakery like he owned the place. I couldn't catch everything he said, but the last thing I heard was a bold, grown-up sounding, "Well, well!"

I snapped back to the guard. My job was to keep him distracted, and I wasn't about to mess that up. So I circled around him, making sure he kept looking at me and not the bakery behind him.

"Are you a lost kid? Where's your mom?" the guard asked, sounding concerned.

This was also not part of the plan. He was supposed to be watching the rats fight.

"Um, she's watching the rats too. They're putting money on the brown one. Wanna come!?"

He blinked. This guy was different. Most guards didn't look at me twice. His face twisted with confusion. "Uh, yeah, kid, sure, let's—"

But he didn't finish.

Suddenly, several blocks away, a loud thunderclap broke the air. The sky was clear, sun blazing, so the sound didn't make any sense. Everyone around turned toward it. Shouting started coming from that same direction, far from the bakery.

Without saying another word, the guard straightened, gripped his pike, and took off running toward the noise.

I followed a few steps behind, just enough to peek around and see if anything was on fire. The road ahead opened up into a four-way intersection. Multiple guards came flying around the corner, weapons drawn—some had spears, others swords—and they all looked ready for war.

More citizens stepped out of their homes, squinting toward the disturbance.

"Make way!" one of the guards yelled.

As usual in Elton, the guards' outfits and gear were a mess. They all wore green, the country's color, but no two were dressed the same. Some had padded armor, others leather, and a few were in chain mail. Their weapons looked like they came from a pawn shop—some rusted, others shining like they'd never seen a fight. The city guard always looked broke and confused.

I hugged the wall of a nearby building to stay out of the way. Once it looked like the wave of guards had passed me, I started circling back toward the bakery to meet the twins.

Just as I stepped around the corner, something slammed into my face—hard. Another guard's thigh crashed into my nose, sending us both sprawling to the ground.

He landed right on top of me.

He was slim, not heavy enough to crush me, but enough to knock the wind clean out of my lungs.

The guy wore the usual green padded armor and brown pants, but his gear looked brand new, not a single stain on it. He also had a chain hood, and I could see his brown skin through the gaps in the metal, his hands and face uncovered.

Before he could say anything, he pushed himself up onto his knees and started coughing. The first one hit me straight in the face. He quickly turned away, still close, just a foot from me, and covered his mouth with his arm.

My nose burned. I could smell the blood before I saw it, leaking from one nostril and running down to my lip.

"Oh gods, are you okay?" the officer asked, horrified. He stood up, then reached down and helped me to my feet. The dirt on my clothes wasn't too noticeable thanks to the brown outfit I wore. He brushed himself off with his hands before patting the dust from my sleeves as well.

"Kid, you gotta be careful, okay? Here, take this."

He handed me a white handkerchief that looked like it had just been washed. It seemed old, but it was clean enough, and I grabbed it quickly to stop the bleeding from my nose.

"Go try to find your parents. And if you can't find them, come find one of us, okay?"

"Sir, yes, sir," I replied, saluting him with the now-bloody handkerchief.

He gave me a strange look before taking off toward the thunder. I headed back to the bakery.

I returned to our barrel outpost across the street.

"My mother only purchases the finest peach pies in all of Eltonia, madam. You must impress me," Michael shouted in a snobby accent.

Laughter bubbled from inside the bakery.

"He is the cutest little guy," said the elderly man.

Michael kept going, telling them this was serious business. The old couple, both pale-skinned and dressed in spotless white tunics, listened to him with amused smiles.

As he worked his charm, I spotted something moving beside the bakery. One of the side windows creaked open, letting out a wave of sweet and savory smells—fruit pies, meat pies, and the sound of that loose metal hinge swinging in the alley breeze.

Melena's head popped out the window. She waved me down.

I jogged over and helped her hold the stolen goods as she steadied herself on the wooden boxes stacked below the window. I made sure to grab the pies—this whole operation was my idea, after all.

One of them smelled like peaches. The other had the rich scent of beef.

"Where's the coin?" I whispered.

"The coins were in a bag under the desk in front. But before I could grab it, Grandpa came in, and I had to bail. But I got a silver!"

Acceptable. "Not bad," I said.

"What flavor are these?" I asked.

"I don't know. I didn't ask them."

Before we could start the taste test, we ducked back across the street to our barrel outpost. A few people walking by gave us strange looks, probably trying to figure out what kind of game we were playing.

I rang the bronze bell from across the street, aiming toward the bakery. Not long after, the door swung open.

"Well, my mother will be hearing about this place. You should expect many new orders. Bye!"

Michael came running across the street, shouting, "Did we do it!"

His arrogance earned him a double shush—me and Melena both putting our fingers to our lips.

We slipped into an alley across from the bakery. I hung back for a second to make sure no one was following us.

Looking back, I saw the chubby baker woman standing in the doorway, laughing and waving a towel in our direction. I couldn't make out what her husband was saying, but he was laughing too.

They knew. They realized they'd been played, that we'd robbed them blind.

But instead of calling for the guard, they just stood there laughing, the woman wiping tears from her face.

I turned and ran down the street to catch up with the twins, but not before wiping my nose again with the guard's handkerchief. I hadn't realized how much blood had soaked into it.

"Was it always this dirty?" I asked myself.

Chapter 4

Most of what I learned about the kingdom came from stories in taverns. Scouting around the city also helped to get an eye on who was in charge and where the best places were to make some coin. The Kingdom of Eltonia was the most significant human country on the continent, with Elton as its largest city and capital. The city was massive, home to over 300,000 men, women, and children from all walks of life. It held both the richest and poorest people in the country; all crammed into a place constantly trying—and failing—to build fast enough to fit them all. This led to hastily built housing in the ghettos, which stood out sharply. The homes there were rotting, crumbling, and patched together with whatever the residents could find.

The ghetto took up the east side of the city, where most buildings and shops looked like they were either about to collapse or had been pieced together from scraps. One part of a house might be a faded green while the other side leaned red from rust-stained repairs. The structures were mismatched, moldy, and tired. People here couldn't afford full repairs, so they either did nothing or only fixed whatever they thought mattered most.

Coughing echoed through the streets. Mud squished beneath heavy boots. The sour stench of spoiled food clung to everything. That was the east—our part of the city. And it always felt like the people here weren't eating much of anything. That hunger made folks selfish. They worked themselves to the bone just to scrape together enough for dinner, with nothing left for anything else.

On the opposite side of the city, to the west, lived the rich. They had brand-new mansions built from smooth stone, walked on paved brick roads, and had access to the best-trained city guards. Not that they needed them. Most hired their own private security anyway. If a house in that part of town even showed a hint of age or damage, it got fixed or torn down and replaced with high-end materials; Brick, Polished wood, Fancy everything. The people there walked around in pristine clothes, reeking of perfume, and not a speck of dirt on their skin.

Between the two extremes sat the middle class. Roads here were made of gravel and stone. Clothes weren't torn or filthy like in the ghettos, but they weren't elegant either. The buildings were decently maintained, especially since this was the part of town where adventurers and traders passed through. If you were looking to panhandle, this was the best bet. In the poor part of Elton, folks might just ignore you—or worse, rob you for what little you had.

The city was mostly human, and the country wasn't exactly welcoming to non-humans. Elves from the Tylvian Union and dwarves from the Paljavan Republic were technically allowed in, but only to sell their goods and get out. If they stayed, life got difficult fast. Eltonians saw elves as pointy-eared snobs, dwarves as cranky little men, and orks as brainless brutes. The rarer non-humans had it even worse. Minotaurs, fairies, lizardmen, they weren't expected to be citizens. They were expected to be slaves, servants, or background decorations. Nothing more.

One of the more appealing parts of the country—at least to those in power—was its thriving slave trade. Slavery was legal here, and it wasn't just allowed; it was built into the economy. A lot of people disapproved, sure, but the ones with money and authority called the shots. And they always chose cheap labor over ethics.

In Elton, finding shelter before nightfall was essential. If you had to be out, you stuck to the bright and noisy parts of the city. But the dark corners—the ones people ignored—were where the real horror lived. That's where you'd find what folks whispered about as "the silent auction."

Peasants, drunks, and lonely kids wandering alleys after dark might spot hooded figures on rooftops—watching, whispering, taking notes. The unlucky would turn a corner and get clubbed, disappearing without a trace.

The slavers didn't usually go after people who'd be missed. No crying wives, no desperate parents. But *usually* didn't mean always. Every now and then, they got bold. Or greedy.

I remember one night during a silent auction, a child almost got taken, if it hadn't been for a stranger who intervened, things would have ended differently. That moment stuck with me.

And the worst part? Heroes came here from all over the continent, determined to stop it. They marched in with their armor, their magic, their blades. Some even freed a few slaves, caused a stir, and rattled a few cages.

But the more they fought, the more valuable they became.

The stronger you were, the higher your price. Suddenly, you weren't just a threat—you were a prize. Something to hunt. People paid to have them taken. Didn't matter who they were. Man, woman, old, young, noble, or nobody. If someone wanted you, they'd send a small army or the deadliest mercenary money could buy.

In Elton, you didn't get to choose whether or not you were part of the auction.

The government? Technically, it was a constitutional monarchy. Royal family. Parliament. All that. But everyone knew it was a rotten lie. The whole system was owned by lords, gangs, and companies fat with coin. A member of parliament didn't serve the people—they served the highest bidder. That meant immunity from crimes, tax cuts, or laws twisted to suit one person's greed.

Anyone who tried to rise with a kind heart didn't last long. They were either dead, disappeared, or on the verge of selling out once they realized they could retire at forty if they just stopped caring.

The military wasn't much better. The guards answered to the same corrupt lords. The ranks were filled with mercenaries, thugs, and—once in a while—some poor soul who actually cared about others.

But they were rare, like everything decent in this place.

While most people were rude and selfish, that only made the good ones stand out even more. The kind-hearted lords and business owners—the ones who did care—gave almost everything they had to help the downtrodden. There weren't many orphanages or homeless shelters, but the few that existed were often run by a single person who simply wanted to help. Soup kitchens were always packed with the poor, but behind the pots, you'd find a wealthy lord stirring the broth, flanked by guards for protection.

Every now and then, a passing adventurer or mercenary would take a job without asking for payment and end up rescuing kidnapped children. Generosity in this country was rare, but when you found it, it felt like meeting an angel in disguise.

Still, Elton was hard to live in. The selfish, racist culture meant you were more likely to get punched than helped. So, you can imagine the chaos that ensued when the harvest that year turned out to be abysmal, and the winter was the coldest in a decade.

Suddenly, the soup kitchens ran out of food. The orphanages had kids sleeping on cold floors. Churches were filled with priests teetering on the edge, trying to hold on for one more prayer. The rich noticed their food wasn't as fine as it used to be. The middle class skipped meals every other day. And the rest of us? We were left with nothing.

We ate each other, not always with teeth. Sometimes with lies. With betrayal. With desperation.

Did we regret what we had to do to survive?

Even if you were lucky enough to find food, it wasn't like the cold would give you a break. I think that was the winter that finally broke my family. We fought for everything we had, knives in hand, against people trying to steal from us what we had already stolen from someone else.

That winter, we huddled together every day. If not for warmth, then for comfort. We clung to each other, crying over the things we'd done just to stay alive.

Chapter 5

Those peach and beef pies were the last good meals we'd have for the rest of that autumn. We had spent the money we'd saved for the circus on winter clothes. We couldn't read, so we didn't realize the circus had left three days earlier. All of us bought fur coats, pants, and shoes, but the fur was made from low-quality pelts. Our brown fur outfits looked more like they came from old dogs than sheep.

As the temperature dropped, the fighting among the poor worsened. Rumors spread of violent men lurking in the streets—desperate, dangerous. One night, we overheard whispers in the market about a gang attacking anyone caught alone after dark.

Michael brought each of us a knife and taught Melena and me how to use one after seeing someone else use one on a guard. The knives looked like cooking knives—iron blades with wooden handles.

Every time the twins went to the market to steal, they ran into more people with the same idea. Melena stabbed someone's toe to get away once, and Michael almost bit off a fisherman's finger while escaping with her. I wasn't as ferocious as them—probably because I didn't need to be. I was good at giving a sad face while panhandling, enough to get the occasional copper. But I always had to be ready to run from other homeless folks who saw my luck and wanted a piece of it.

In my free time, I kept trying to stop by the pickle store. But something was off about that pickle salesman. My missions were getting too easy. One day, before the temperature really dropped, I noticed a jar full of radishes, carrots, and cucumbers always sat on the bottom shelf, labeled "not for sale."

"Grab, right alley, sewer, home. Grab, right alley, sewer, home."

As I ran up to the storefront, slipping through a small crowd, I made it to that jar on the bottom shelf. It was easy to grab. But right as I tried to get away, I tripped. Somehow, I kept the jar from breaking as I tumbled. Then that old man, Wallace, came around the table and stared me down. He wore a green tunic, brown pants, and leather shoes. I stood there, frozen in fear. I'd never been to jail before and had no idea how I'd survive it.

But something weird happened.

The old man smiled, picked up his old wooden broom, and turned away with a whistle. "Must have been the wind!" he chuckled.

I stayed frozen, not realizing I was free to go. Then he turned back and said calmly, "Go on. These are on the house. Nobody wants to buy those anyway," he said with a giggle.

I made my way to the sewers again, sticking to my usual route. But more people were in the tunnels this time of year, all looking skinny and weak, with barely any winter clothes on. The stream that usually ran through the tunnel had frozen over, so I had to watch out for slick puddles scattered along the stone walkway.

The sewers still smelled like piss and faeces, but in winter, I started smelling something worse—like rotten flesh coming from certain tunnels. I never went down those. I didn't want to find out what was down there, or what might come out to find me.

"It's Wallace!" the twins shouted as I stepped into our home, but something felt off. I noticed Michael had a bruise on his cheek, and Melena's shirt had a splash of blood.

"It got pretty crazy, but I'm a master at fighting," Michael said, waving his knife around like it was a fairy wand.

I looked over their haul. It was way more than usual. Even with the bruises, we had enough to buy an extra blanket and pay a passing cleric to use some healing magic on the twins.

But as the temperature kept dropping, the spoils got thinner. We started having to take turns skipping meals. Some nights, one of us wouldn't eat at all.

Our home started attracting unexpected guests who came to sit by the bonfire. Sometimes it was stray animals. Other times, it was kids like us or homeless folks just trying to warm up for the night. Thank the gods, most of them had a conscience. They didn't ask for anything—just sat by the fire, kept quiet, and left in the morning or whenever the rain stopped.

Still, every now and then, we'd wake up to find some bread missing, so we started taking shifts on watch.

One night, the three of us had to live through the kind of nightmare we always hoped we'd avoid.

A homeless man walked into the bar where we slept. Whiskey bottle in hand, clothes reeking of sewer water. His skin was pale white, and his blonde hair was matted and filthy. His face was covered in bruises and scars. His eyes were a dull brown, with heavy bags under them, and his beard was thick and wild with clumps of mud stuck in it.

He wore a red tunic under a black dogskin jacket that had more holes than fabric. His pants were ripped in so many places you could see a tear near his crotch, exposing his underwear. His shoes looked new, but they were stained with something that looked like blood.

"Evening," he said, walking up to our bar.

The twins and I stood by the fireplace, knives in hand, watching him as he rummaged through the cabinets. He kicked over the dark wooden stools and tore cabinet doors off their hinges. He dug through drawers, searching for food or drinks.

"Stupid kids, you drank all the good stuff!" he shouted, slamming doors and flipping containers in a rage. He was looking for ale that wasn't there.

After someone stole our food one night, we made a rule—whenever anyone entered our home, we'd form a defensive perimeter around the supplies in the corner of the room.

The man let out a deep sigh and grabbed a pitcher from one of the cabinets. Then he turned toward us and saw the three of us huddled up tight around our bags and the chest where we kept what little we had.

He threw the empty pitcher against the wall. It shattered, glass spraying everywhere as he started shouting, "What do you kids got there?!"

He walked toward us, pulling out a piece of black wood with rusted nails sticking out of one end.

"I don't wanna hurt you kids. I know you're desperate. But so am I."

We knew he was. But so were we.

We hadn't eaten in almost two days. All we had left were a few scraps of bread and some cheese—not enough to make a full meal for even one of us.

He got closer, reeking of whiskey and piss.

"Go away!" Melena yelled, brandishing her knife.

"No!" I shouted right after, pulling out my slingshot.

All three of us were shaking, breathing heavy.

"Get out of the way, or I'll make you move!" the man growled, gripping his club tighter.

Then it happened.

We smelled it before anything else. Michael had pissed himself. He was shaking even harder than we were.

As the man took another step forward, Michael—trousers soaked—lunged at him with his knife.

The man screamed. Michael slashed deep into his left leg, and blood spilled everywhere.

Melena rushed in behind him, letting out a war cry as she charged.

But the man was ready. He punched her square in the face with his free hand, dropping her to the ground. She curled up, writhing in pain.

I grabbed a sharp rock I'd saved just for this moment, loaded it into my slingshot, aimed for his face, and let it fly.

It hit him—but not where I wanted. Just a graze. A shallow cut opened on his chin.

The man roared and kicked Michael in the stomach. The blow knocked the wind out of him. Michael collapsed, gasping on the floor.

The man limped toward me, blood pouring from his leg. I had one last shot.

With everything I had left, I screamed at the top of my lungs and aimed for his eyes with another sharp rock. This time, my aim was true. The rock slammed into his right eye.

He howled in pain, blood leaking through his fingers as he tried to cover the wound. "You bitch!" he screamed, raising the nailed club high above his head.

I couldn't move fast enough. I was too scared.

By the time my body responded, it was too late.

The club crashed into the side of my head. Nails tore through my scalp, stabbing into my skin. I hit the ground hard, barely conscious, barely able to keep my eyes open. Blood trickled down the side of my face. My ears were ringing so loud I could hardly hear anything around me.

Then something else took over. A banshee, wild and furious, seemed to rise up inside my sister. Melena let out a blood-curdling scream and lunged. Her knife drove deep into the man's gut.

He was still trying to fix his torn eye, too distracted to notice her blade until it was already inside him. Blood soaked his shirt, spreading fast as more of it gushed from his stomach.

He tried to backhand her, but missed. Melena rolled away just in time as the man dropped to his knees. Michael's earlier attack had done more damage than we realized.

That was his last move.

Michael followed Melena's lead, screaming so hard it must've torn something inside him. He charged. The man tried to lift his club to block, but Michael was too fast.

He drove his blade into the man's neck.

The man dropped the club, clutching at his throat with both hands. Blood sprayed out between his fingers. I could see the eye I had hit was still leaking, blood seeping fast down his face.

The man decided to haunt us before he died.

As he collapsed to the ground, blood choking his throat, he muttered something that would stick with us forever.

"Thank you," he coughed, blood bubbling from his mouth.

My breath caught. "Why would he thank us?" I wondered. Was it relief, regret, or something else entirely?

He was fading. His eyes barely open, watching the twins stare him down.

Michael and Melena shrugged as they didn't care about his last words. They lunged.

Both of them ran to him and started stabbing—again and again and again.

They didn't stop until they were sure every organ had been destroyed. Heart. Lungs. Liver. Brain.

By the end, the man wasn't even a man anymore. Just a heap of torn flesh and bone in a pool of blood, soaking most of the floor.

After a moment of silence, Melena swallowed hard, her heart pounding. "Did we have to?" she whispered, but the cold night swallowed her words.

Michael, covered in blood and piss, turned toward me. His eyes locked on mine.

"Wallace!" was the last thing I heard.

That look was the last thing I saw before I passed out.

I drifted in and out after that. Consciousness came in waves.

Sometimes I woke to one of them yelling, "Help!" or "Please help, he's gonna die!"

They worked together, trying to stop the bleeding. Pressing a towel to my head, pouring water, doing anything they could.

Melena sat with me, my head in her lap, blood staining her pants. Her face was soaked with tears.

"Please, gods. Wallace, no!" she cried.

Somehow, even through all that, I was glad our nicknames stuck. At least they'd know what to write on my tombstone.

Then Michael sprinted out of the building. He came back less than a minute later with a priest. The man stank of wine and wore a stained white cloak.

The priest took a long sip from his wine, then muttered under his breath as he saw blood, "The rich feast while the poor bleed—God's patience wears thin."

I could barely hear him through the ringing and haze.

"The hells do you want?!" the priest suddenly snapped. "I'm not a charity."

Melena rushed to our supplies, gently laying my head on the ground.

Everything was starting to fade.

The last thing I heard before going under again was the priest muttering, "Yadda yadda, goddess of light protects and what haves, yeah."

Then I felt it like a warm, tingling sensation against my skull—and slipped into sleep.

Chapter 6

I woke up to Melena's face sleeping beside me, her left eye blackened, and the worst headache I'd ever had pounding in my skull.

I sat up slowly, trying not to wake the two of them. But it was pointless. Michael saw me move and shouted, "Wallace!" loud enough to wake Melena.

"Are you okay? Are you okay!" he cried.

"Yeah," I mumbled.

I looked them both over. They didn't seem as beat up as I was.

Then they nearly killed me with love—hugging me so tight I thought I'd pass out again. Their tears ran down their faces and dripped onto mine.

I paid them back with tears of my own.

The city guards were kind enough to show up an hour after everything had gone down. They were generous enough to remove the homeless man's body, but not before we stripped him of his clothes and found three pieces of copper. Just enough to keep us from starving.

The twins and I even debated whether we should take some of his flesh to eat. But the guards showed up before we could make that call.

We had to be careful which parts of his dogskin jacket we took. We didn't want anything soaked in blood.

Once we had picked the body clean of anything useful, the guards arrived. One of them lifted the corpse onto his shoulder. The man's blood still leaked from his body, soaking into the guard's green uniform.

Another guard pulled out a large red bottle and poured its contents onto the blood pooled on the floor. The liquid began to bubble, steam rising into red gas as the blood disappeared.

The smell lingered for days.

We didn't get to relax. No time to breathe.

We rested that night. Then we got back to it.

The twins went out stealing food and anything we could sell. They always got more than I did, but I held my own panhandling.

January wasn't as bad as December.

The temperature seemed to rise. We noticed ice melting in puddles and dripping from icicles. But I started feeling slower than I had before. Headaches hit me every day, stealing what little energy I had left. Then came the coughing and sneezing, waking me up in the middle of the night.

Not that I was doing much sleeping anyway.

I dreamt of the man we killed. "Thank you" would've become a curse if I didn't know why he said it. The twins' teary faces, covered in blood as they stabbed him again and again, trying to find places they hadn't already hit—that image stayed stuck in my mind.

I saw them wake up in fear, their eyes wide and their hands shaking, during my watch shifts. When that happened, I'd hug them. Try to calm them down.

They were having nightmares, too. Probably worse ones—focused on me, nearly having my skull bashed in.

Shame the priest or the mages didn't have anything to take away the trauma. Or bad dreams.

Of course, during food runs, I kept running into the man who probably saved my family from starving more than once. The old pickle seller.

I stopped by his shop again. The shelves were only half full now. The jars were lighter than usual, and the prices hadn't dropped. The ones he left out for me looked worse—pickles with cuts in them, carrots that were smaller than before. And for the first time, there wasn't a single jar on the bottom shelf.

I was greedy. I gave him my unstoppable puppy eyes.

But this time, the old man didn't budge. He knelt and placed a hand on my head.

"Sorry, kid. I can't spare much right now. Times are tough. I'd take you in if I could, but I can barely feed my own family. Please don't be upset."

There was real pain in his voice. I wanted to argue. I wanted to tell him that I had a family too, and I was the one keeping them fed.

But something inside me said to let it go.

"Thank you," I said—the first words I'd ever spoken to him.

It was enough. His frown broke into a small smile.

"You're welcome, kid. Get out of here before it gets colder."

He waved. I nodded and made my usual way back through the sewers.

Despite the weather getting warmer, I started seeing more people in the sewers lately—hiding from the cold or from city guards. Their clothes were all over the place: some had scraps of fur stitched into their coats, while others had almost nothing at all. One bald Black man was shaking in a dirty brown tunic and pants, barefoot, teeth chattering. I saw plenty of folks with even less on, but I figured the ones walking around like that wouldn't last long. They'd be corpses before the week was out.

By now, I've figured out how to avoid thugs. Don't stop running. Don't stop and chat with people. And stay away from the worst parts of town if you can. That last one's tricky, though. Every part of town feels like the worst part when it's winter. Even trying to head to the rich areas wasn't easy. You'd still run into crowds of panhandlers tearing each other apart over half-rotten bread.

Weirdly enough, my coughing kept most folks from bothering me. Snot dripping down my chin, wheezing loud enough to scare off anyone halfway smart. But that same sick look helped when it came to begging. Made me seem extra pitiful. Some folks tossed me a few extra coppers just to get me away.

The good news? We managed to break even. Got just enough food and supplies to scrape by. And after that, the homeless man dropped dead in our shop, and fewer people tried to squat there overnight. That was the only upside to a body stiff on the floor. Even though the worst of winter looked like it was fading and the ice had started to melt, it was still brutal. Cold rain hit us like slaps on the skin. On other days, hail beat down like the sky had it out for us. Snow or not, it didn't let up.

One rainy night, we sat around talking about what we'd do someday when we were grown. Michael said he wanted to be king of the country and make food and candy free. He'd give everyone a home and make sure his castle was guarded from the worst threat of all: girls.

He said his castle would be made of ivory, guarded by dragons and bears.

Melena shot that down quickly. She wanted to be a legendary knight—killing evildoers, slaying dragons, rescuing princes or princesses trapped in towers. But both of them agreed on one thing: they needed to be rich first.

Then I gave them an answer they didn't see coming.

On my rounds through the city, I sometimes saw adults in goofy costumes, singing songs and dancing in front of crowds. They'd act out scenes with props, pretending to be monsters, heroes, even washed-up politicians. That's what I wanted. I wanted to be an actor. Dress up in ridiculous outfits, sing songs about adventure, and perform in silly shows. And with the money I made, I'd send kids into the streets with food and toys to hand out.

But I told them the food would be mostly chocolate and peppermints. Vegetables were for chumps, I figured.

The two of them laughed hard as I danced around like a clown for a few minutes, even though my coughing made it hard to keep up the act.

Lately, that cough has been getting worse. Harder to control. I'd started noticing blood in my handkerchief. The twins noticed, but all they could do was add more blankets and look away when I coughed up red.

In a rare show of cleanliness, they asked me to sleep a little further away. Said they didn't want blood or spit getting on them. I wasn't used to that. I'd grown used to one of them curled up against me for warmth. But they made up for it by piling extra blankets on my side. And at least I didn't have to deal with Melena's kicking or Michael mumbling to monsters in his sleep.

We'd all gotten sick before. Usually, it passed. Or we stumbled into some kind soul who knew how to help. Not this time. We weren't lucky enough to find a healer. So instead, we waited. They made sure I had a little extra water, extra rations, just in case. We waited for the cough to go away.

It didn't. It got worse.

My rounds got cut short. I had to slow down and take deep breaths more often. Couldn't do much besides panhandling anymore. The twins picked up the slack, doing whatever they could to take care of me.

We had to go back to strict rationing, but we scraped together just enough to see a doctor. Outside the city, there was an area where traveling salesmen and doctors set up shop. Even some non-humans were out there, claiming to sell rare luxury items from foreign lands. The whole place was crammed with carts and tents in all shapes and colors.

We wandered around, trying to find a healer who wouldn't bleed us dry. Eventually, we came across a doctor working out of the back of a cart. Not like we had many options—we couldn't afford much else.

She was loud, always singing and dancing in front of her setup. Her dark leather tunic, pants, shoes, and that weird bird mask made her look official in a strange way. On top of it all, she wore a black witch's hat with little jewel-like ornaments dangling off it. Her outfit looked clean, and her voice was warm and cheery.

The cart itself was nothing fancy. Tan-colored wood, a few boxes, a table stuffed in the back. It was hitched to two strong-looking white horses. In front of it, she had a long black table and some chairs set up. All over the cart and tables were bottles in different shapes and sizes, filled with colorful liquids. I spotted a tall beaker bubbling with purple stuff, and there wasn't even a fire under it.

"Going bald? This one will bring your hair back! Wanna get strong and fight off bandits? This one'll let you lift a horse with one hand!"

She had a dozen lines like that. Things we didn't even know were possible.

The three of us stepped closer. That got her attention.

The doctor leaned down with a grin. "Now, how can I help you, three gumdrops?" Then she reached out and pinched Melena's cheek.

"Hello, ma'am. I can't stop coughing," I told her.

The twins nodded and spoke in unison. "He coughs in his sleep, too!"

"Well, you came to the right place! I, Doctor Professor Stanton of House Stanton, am here to serve!"

With a dramatic flourish of her leather cloak, she pulled out a tiny chair from behind the table and motioned for me to sit. She really knew how to put on a show.

As I sat down, she grabbed a doctor's bag packed with odd tools. She rummaged through it and pulled out something that looked like the magnifying glasses the rich kids used. She told me to open my mouth and peered inside.

"Yep. I've seen this before," she said.

Then she pulled out a small metal plate hanging from a string around her neck. She pressed it gently to my throat, then my back, then my chest. It felt cold, but I didn't flinch.

"Yep, it's cancer!" she said in a joyful tone.

The twins and I just stared. None of us knew what that even meant.

The doctor's eyes lit up behind her mask. "Don't worry, kiddos, I've got just the thing! I'll whip up something fresh just for you!"

She sprinted to the back of the cart and climbed up to a small table she had set up on top. It was hard to see, but we watched her mix a variety of bottles—bright colors, thick liquids—into one big jar. Then she tossed in what looked like a glowing cube and a green flower that was puffing out smoke. She shook the bottle hard, poured it into another one, then another, like she was making a magic trick out of it. Finally, she poured the mix into a tall, fancy rectangular bottle. The kind you'd see holding expensive whiskey.

With a loud "Tada!" and a burst of confetti, she hopped down from the cart, holding the glowing jar like it was a treasure. She twisted the lid open, and steam rolled out. The liquid inside was bright green but clear enough to see through. It smelled like lemons—real lemons— and that flower inside made the scent even stronger. She was good. Real good.

The three of us looked at her, wide-eyed.

"That'll be one silver!" she said, beaming.

We froze.

That was everything we had. Weeks of begging, rationing, hustling. Gone in one go.

We glanced at each other, then at our coin pouch.

"I'd say he's only got a few weeks to live," she said, voice suddenly quiet, leaning down low. "You guys wanna save him, right?"

The twins nodded slowly. Without saying a word, they handed her all the money we had.

She passed me the jar. "Drink up, bud. You'll be good in a day or so!"

I drank every drop. Not a drop left behind. It tasted sweet. Real sweet. Sharp lemon with something herbal underneath.

Even though we knew we'd be skipping dinner that night, and probably tomorrow too, we still said it together:

"Thank you, Doctor Professor Stanton!"

She bowed and waved us off.

I don't remember if she said it... or if it was someone else. A stranger, maybe. But someone whispered, "Give it a day."

Chapter 7

It wasn't a day. It wasn't anything. So that night, when I coughed, I figured by tomorrow it'd be gone.

It wasn't.

The next day, I was still coughing and still wheezing. Blood in my throat. Could barely walk. Maybe I heard her wrong. Maybe she meant two days.

Some days, I would go outside just so I wasn't choked up inside, but whispers from the street about the doctor always made me shiver.

"The doctor leaves when the money dries up," one ragged boy muttered as I walked back past.

He shook his head at me pitifully as he added, "That's what happened last winter, too."

A week passed.

It got worse.

I waited. I waited and waited, and I didn't get better. So I stopped waiting. Hope turned sour in my mouth like spoiled broth. I think even the twins stopped believing, though they never said it out loud.

We didn't have the silver for another healer. So the three of us went back to find her. She was bright. She knew what to do. She had to still be there.

Imagine our shock when we found out her cart was gone. The whole tent, horses, table, everything vanished overnight like she'd never been there.

She was gone.

And it started to snow.

Days later, the twins were getting nervous. They started trying to steal more coins, hoping to afford medicine. But we didn't have the means anymore. Even with strict rationing, we barely had enough food to get by.

I could hardly move. At most, I could walk a block, sit and panhandle, then crawl back home to rest. My lungs were shot. A trip that used to take minutes now felt impossible. And the snow made everything worse.

The man we killed had enough cloth on him to piece together a coat for me, but it was ragged and torn. Anyone walking by would've thought I looked like a dying, hairy dog.

I spent most of the day curled up in the corner of our shelter while Melena and Michael argued about what to do. Something was spreading through the city. More people were getting sick. That meant fewer meds and higher prices. The supply dried up while demand kept climbing.

The twins tried to find a priest. But the ones they found had other priorities—like drinking or sleeping with women.

Then they tried stealing supplies from nearby hospitals. The problem was that we didn't know what we were looking for, and even if we found something, we didn't know how to use it.

Once, they tried walking me to a care house. It was packed.

"Please help my brother! He's sick!" Michael shouted.

"I got wealthy men I can't even get to. We're too full. Come back another day or with more coins," a nurse told us. Her apron was smeared with dark brown stains.

We tried another care house.

The nurses there didn't bother pretending to care.

"Where are your parents? Get them," one snapped, already turning away.

Days passed with the three of us trying everything we could to get help.

Then the twins decided to do something desperate.

They were going to break into a care house and steal as many potions as they could carry. We all knew how dangerous that was. Care houses didn't just hand out potions, they had armed guards and too many eyes watching. Stealing a pie was one thing. Dozens of expensive bottles? That was another story.

"I'll be okay. We can wait for an opening," I said, barely getting the words out through my breath.

The twins shook their heads.

"We need something now. I won't let you die!" Melena's voice cracked when she said it.

"I'm working on a good plan. Don't worry, Wallace. Just rest, please."

They decided they'd scout the place in the morning and pull off the heist that same day. That night, we ate together. Michael had managed to get me some soup, and we cooked it in a dented pot over the fire pit.

There we were. A bunch of ten-year-olds, planning a heist to save my life.

We giggled while drawing out the plan on scraps of paper. Michael sketched a rough map of the building, and Melena pointed out where the windows were. They were planning everything—without including my broken pig toy, which they usually treated like a good-luck charm.

The plan was messy. Cause a major distraction. Set a fire to pull the guards away. Then, in the chaos, they'd sneak through a side window, grab whatever potions they could, and bite or stab anyone who got in the way.

I told them how scary it was.

They told me they'd been practicing their knife work.

I said they could die.

Melena promised she wouldn't.

Michael told me I worried too much.

Then they hugged me.

"You're worth the risk," Melena said.

"I love you two," I whispered. My lungs didn't have much left in them.

"We love you too," Melena said.

"I was gonna say that too!" Michael added.

The fire pit faded to black. They lay down beside me and drifted off to sleep.

I couldn't sleep. "Don't you dare," I kept whispering to myself. I was preparing a script, my last attempt to talk the two of them out of the plan. I had to keep my own secrets, too. I couldn't tell them that it was getting so hard to keep my eyes open, that even breathing and talking felt like a full-body task. I knew I was dying. And I knew I might not even be alive to see the two come back tomorrow night. If they didn't return tomorrow night, I'd wish I was already dead.

They told me I was worth the risk. But I decided I had to try something reckless to save myself. I might get hurt, maybe even die doing it, but they were worth the risk, too. It was snowing outside, but it was a trip I needed to take.

I saw what I thought was a herbalist's shop. It smelled like mint tea. It was a two-story wooden house painted white, and the front door had carvings of a teacup and a syringe. We knocked on the door once, but no one answered. We tried again another day, but an elderly neighbor told us the woman was out of town.

I figured she must've had something. And if she was out of town, even better. I tried earlier to convince the twins to hit the place, but they argued hard against it. Said they had tried stealing from someone around there before, and the neighborhood acted like a cult. Alert one person, and the whole block shows up. Attack one, and you're dealing with everybody.

What made it worse? A few of them were retired guards and army types—people we couldn't beat in a fight.

Was it a dumb idea? Yes. But I couldn't live with the idea of my brother and sister out there risking themselves for me. So I waited until I heard their soft breathing, waited until I was sure they were out cold. I grabbed my winter coat and a few rocks, and I marched.

I felt like death. Every step felt like a dozen, and walking a single block felt like running a marathon. The gravel roads weren't slick enough to make me fall, but frozen puddles waited around every corner.

For better or worse, the streets were nearly empty that night. House lights were out. Not a single city guard in sight. The snow and the silent auction probably made the trip not worth it for most folks.

The herbalist's store was only a mile away. Back before I got sick, I could jog there without even thinking. Now, just walking toward it felt like dragging myself across death's doorstep. The wind howled. I was numb everywhere, but my lungs, and they burned like fire. But I had to keep going.

Every now and then, I saw a dark shape on a rooftop, but none of them seemed to care about a limping boy in a tattered coat.

Melena was caring and cunning. Michael was funny and clever. My life was so much better with them in it. I had to keep marching until I found the shop.

A small circle of shops clung to a crooked lamppost, like moths around a dead lantern. I leaned against it, blinking through the snow, until I saw the mark—

A teacup. A syringe.

I'd found it.

The apothecary looked too clean for someone like me. A white wooden house, tucked between older stone buildings, with windows that still gleamed despite the frost. It reminded me of the temples we used to pass in the rich part of town—quiet, perfect, untouched.

I scanned the front, no guards. No citizens. Just snowflakes and silence.

I peeked through the window at the front of the shop. It was completely dark, no sign of life. I saw what looked like a large wooden desk with a staircase on its left. Behind the desk stood a bookshelf stacked with dozens of bottles and dried plants.

The house looked solid from the outside, and the inside seemed well- kept, no stains, no damage, nothing out of place. I scanned the front of the store one last time before heading around back.

The backyard was a small garden, boxed in by a white wooden fence with a gate protecting a neat patch of blue and white flowers. There was a back door and a window to the left of it. I peeked through the back window and saw what looked like a kitchen or maybe an alchemy station.

In the center of the room stood a fireplace with a big black cauldron sitting underneath. Beside it were a few long metal tools, probably used to stoke the fire. To the left were more shelves and cabinets filled with glass bottles, syringes, and herbs. It was hard to make out many details. The place was dark, and my eyelids were getting heavier by the second.

I scanned the yard and found a smooth rock, big enough to help break a window. I waited for a moment when the wind picked up, howling loud enough to drown out my thoughts. That's when I did it.

With the rock in hand, I shattered one of the windowpanes. I did my best to avoid the shards as I reached in to unlatch the lock. I pushed the window up and climbed through, but I was so exhausted I collapsed straight onto the floor with a loud thud.

My vision blurred as I looked down. When I finally came to, I realized I'd landed on the broken glass. My hand was warm, and I saw blood dripping from it.

I moved like a snail, slow and quiet. My body was too drained to move fast, which probably helped me stay quiet. Looking around the room, I was sure now it was some kind of lab or kitchen. Plants, medical tools, and glass bottles covered the tables.

The plants were all different—some bright orange flowers, others strange purple mushrooms. The medical tools looked complicated. I had no idea what most of them were for.

And unlike the plague doctor's stash from before, the glass bottles here were simpler. Just straight glass cylinders sealed with cork tops.

All I had to do was steal a few potions. Drink whatever looked like it might help.

The day room was dark, but that was fine. I didn't want to be seen. I'd been doing this long enough to be used to it.

The glass bottles on the counter all looked empty, so I kept searching. I opened the largest cabinet I could find, but it was full of books. The next one held more empty bottles. Another was filled with medical tools I didn't recognize.

I tried to keep quiet, but the coughing made it hard.

"No," I whimpered in frustration.

It was okay. They must've been in another room.

Then a voice called from one of the hallways. Warm, but stern.

"Hello? Who is that?"

Maybe I was hallucinating again. Another dream stirred up by fever and desperation.

To my right, I saw the soft light of a candle being lit from down the hall.

I froze. Too scared and too tired to move.

"No, no, no," I whispered under my breath.

My breathing sped up. My heart was pounding. My thoughts were racing, and I didn't know what to do. I pulled out my dagger, barely able to grip it through the blood and the shaking in my hands.

I hadn't pulled a blade on anyone before. I didn't even know if I could. But I kept my hand near my coat pocket, just in case.

I was here to steal. I'd already broken in. What would I do if someone came down those stairs? Beg? Run? Die?

It hit me all at once—how bad an idea this was, that I could be killed. Or arrested. All while just trying to survive. And worse, the twins would never know what happened to me.

Then she appeared.

A tall woman stepped into the room, wearing a nightgown. She held a lantern in one hand and a syringe in the other. Her skin was pale, her hair gray, and the bright blue of her gown stood out like firelight in the dark.

She was clearly old—gray hair, sagging skin, deep bags under her eyes.

In her hand was a slim syringe with a glass center, glowing with a bright green liquid. Her blue eyes landed on me, full of shock and confusion.

"What are you doing here, young one?" she asked, her voice soft but firm, almost like an angel who didn't have time for nonsense.

I stood there, trying to decide whether to scream and run or lunge at her with the dagger.

But I didn't get the chance to choose.

My lungs and heart caught up with me. Breathing became impossible. My chest felt like someone was driving a blade into it.

Before I knew it, my legs gave out. My eyelids sank.

And I collapsed to the floor.

"Oh gods!" was the last thing I heard before everything went black.

Chapter 8

My eyes opened to the sight of a cup of tea at my bedside. The cup was pale white with a handle, and it carried the warm aroma of honey and ginger.

I looked around to see where I had woken up. I was in a room with two beds. The bedframes were made of dark black wood, and the mattresses looked stuffed with hay wrapped in white sheets. Over me was a red-dyed cotton blanket, and behind my head, a red feather pillow.

Morning sunlight lit the room through a nearby window. Like the other rooms I'd seen, this one was painted white. A second bed sat a few feet to my left, with a wooden chair at its foot. Between that bed and mine stood a drawer with a cup of tea, a glass of water, and an extinguished lantern on top.

On the far wall, I spotted a cabinet filled with books, herbs, and tools on its shelves.

My breathing grew heavy. I was scared. I didn't know where I was.

I looked toward the door, left slightly ajar, and tried to get up. But my body ached so badly it felt like just thinking about moving caused pain. Every limb was sore, every joint stiff.

Then I noticed something—my breathing had eased. My chest felt lighter. My throat no longer burned. But even with that, the groans I made while trying to escape must have reached the other room.

"Don't be in a hurry, kiddo. You're going to hurt yourself. Here I come."

Her voice was soothing. Joyful, even.

I heard her footsteps as she slowly approached and pushed the door open.

There she was.

Tall, old, and slim, with gray hair down to her shoulders. She wore a dress that looked homemade, maybe even older than she was. It was blue and white, with little elk stitched around the waist. The pattern continued down the long sleeves toward her hands.

She was carrying a jar filled with flowers and mushrooms. She walked in and sat down on the bed beside me.

"Customers usually come through the front door during working hours! You're gonna have to pay for that window back there!" she said with a giggle and a kind of pride in her voice.

"You were minutes from dying, you know. Black winter lung is a slow one to treat, and by the time the coughing starts, it's almost too late. But unfortunately for the reaper, I'm the best healer in the city. Your guardian angel must be strong!"

She chuckled again.

"Hello," I said, my voice barely above a whisper.

"Oh gods, where are my manners? Good morning, young man. What's your name?"

"Wallace. My name is Wallace."

She extended her hand.

"Pleasure to meet you, Wallace. My name is Abigail Kreila, but everyone calls me Granny Kreila. I'm afraid that 'old hag' or 'that witch' are no longer acceptable nicknames," she said, laughing at herself.

Her laugh was scratchy and proud, but somehow comforting too.

I sat up and brought the tea to my lips, taking a sip. I could taste the ginger and honey working together to soothe my senses, followed by a wave of warm peppermint. It was delicious. As the tea moved down my throat, I could feel my body start to relax.

"I'm sorry," I whimpered. "I thought I was gonna die."

I told her everything—that I was desperate, that I didn't want my siblings to get hurt looking for medicine. I told her they were planning a heist.

Then I froze.

"Oh gods," I muttered under my breath, realizing something awful.

The twins must be out there, looking for me.

I tried to get up again, but while my breathing had improved, my body still refused to move.

"Calm down, kiddo. What's wrong?"

"My brother and sister, Michael and Melena, don't know I'm here. They might be out looking for me!" I said, panic rising in my voice.

"Don't worry. I can go find them and bring them to you."

I was stunned by how calm and confident she sounded. She stood up, and in a blink, a dark purple syringe slipped from her sleeve into her hand. I had no idea how she did that.

She squeezed the bottom of the syringe, and thick black ooze dripped from its tip. She let the syringe fall to the floor, and the ooze began to bloat and stretch, then slowly shrink again.

The sound it made was wet and pulsing, like slime rearranging itself. It twitched and shuddered, then stilled. What stood there now looked like a large dog.

Its fur was ebony black, and its eyes glowed purple. Its skin drooped around its face and ears like melting wax.

Kreila walked over to the cabinet and pulled out a red collar and a matching bow tie.

"This is Bobby, the bloodhound. Bobby, please go fetch his siblings."

She turned to me, smiling gently.

"Wallace, dearie, can you tell me what they look like?"

I gave her their descriptions—brown tunics, pale white skin, thin and fragile from barely eating, and bright blue eyes.

The dog walked over and sniffed me from head to toe as I lay there, too weak to move.

Then he rested his head on the mattress beside my hand.

"He wants you to pet him," Kreila said, excited.

I did what she said. His tail wagged long and slow in approval.

Then he left the room, and a moment later, I heard a door open and close.

Kreila walked over to the cabinet and pulled out what looked like the same bird mask the other doctor had worn. I flinched when I saw it.

She noticed.

"What's wrong? Don't like the mask? I can find a different one if you'd like."

This one was different from the others I'd seen. Hers was white, with blue jewels scattered across the top.

I looked away, avoiding her eyes.

"Doctor Professor Stanton had that too," I said, barely louder than a whisper.

The old lady burst into laughter.

"Who is that?!"

I explained everything to her about the doctor's visit, what she told us, and what she did. She listened with a mix of amazement and disappointment, her face changing after every other sentence.

"Oh no, dearie, that wasn't a real doctor. That was a con artist. A thief who steals by making things look and sound interesting. Imagine selling salt and calling it sugar—that's what they do."

I looked down, ashamed.

"Why on earth would you go to a charlatan like that? I've only been gone a month on a little getaway. There are other doctors in town."

I explained the twins' situation where we lived, what we ate, and why I tried breaking in.

She sat beside me and sighed.

"I'm so sorry you're going through that. I didn't know the churches and orphanages would be full this year. But you and your siblings must be pretty smart and tough to get through all that!"

She gave a soft laugh.

Then she stood up again, resting her hands on her hips.

"All right. Let me try to explain this in a way your child's mind can understand. You caught a nasty cough from someone, and it wore your lungs out. You coughed so hard your throat got torn up and started bleeding. That drained the rest of your strength. The sickness isn't that contagious, which is a miracle, so your siblings haven't caught it."

I listened to every word like I was in a trance.

"You almost died, young man. So I gave you medicine that healed your lungs. But your body's still running on empty, so you can only move around a little. I want you to rest."

She went back to the cabinet, pulled out gloves from her pocket, and grabbed an empty syringe. She turned toward me as I clutched my blanket, ready to use it as a shield.

"Oh, you can relax. All I need is a drop of blood, and I can make sure you don't have anything else to worry about."

"No, no needles!" I shouted, panic lacing my voice.

She tilted her head, set the syringe down on the nightstand, and chuckled.

"Oh, I've been playing this part of the game for sixty years. I know what to do."

Then she pulled out another syringe. This one didn't look normal; it was white, with several colors swirling inside the glass tube in the middle. She tossed it at the ceiling with barely any effort. It stuck.

"Watch this. Have you ever seen fireworks before?"

Before I could answer, the syringe fell and broke apart midair. What followed was a soft explosion of confetti. The tiny pieces floated down, then began popping gently, showering us in color.

I was mesmerized. The smell hit next—sweet, like fruity candy. The pops were barely louder than whispers.

I'd rarely seen magic used. It was so beautiful I didn't even notice the quick tingle of pain in my left arm.

I paused, then turned to Kreila. She was grinning, holding a syringe filled with dark red fluid.

"The oldest trick in the book!" she laughed.

She stood as the light show fizzled out.

"Give Bobby some time. Elton is a big city. I can have others look for them if needed. For now, get some rest. Can I get you a book to read or toys to play with?"

I shook my head. "I can't read."

Her joyful look twisted into one of disdain.

"Gods above and below, what has this city come to! I'll be right back."

She bounced to her feet and stomped out. When she returned minutes later, she was holding a book with farm animals holding hands under a rainbow.

"That will not do at all. I will teach you to read as quickly as possible."

She spent the next hour showing me pictures of animals and the letters they matched with. I told her I wanted to hug the lovable ork representing the letter "O."

She said that wouldn't be wise.

Before long, we heard barking from the front door. Then the quick scuttling of feet and paws came our way.

The twins followed the dog into my room, and they didn't let me say a word before pouncing on top of me, tears in their eyes, sweat dripping from their heads.

Kreila smiled at me, fully aware that my aching body now had to deal with the weight of two ten-year-olds.

They were both gasping, smelling like they'd run a mile.

"Why did you leave?" Michael shouted, smacking my face with a hit that had no force behind it.

"We thought you died!" Melena cried.

"He almost did," the hag said with a chuckle.

Kreila dropped another syringe onto the floor, though I couldn't see what she was trying to do. But then I noticed the door creak open behind her.

The twins and I were too wrapped up in tears and hugging to pay it much mind. Two more white wooden chairs floated in, followed by a blue tea set, all carried in by an invisible force.

"I'm sorry. I'm so sorry. I thought you'd get hurt if you tried to steal from the clinic. I didn't want to see you hurt," I said, my voice heavy with guilt.

"So you hurt yourself?!" Melena snapped, mimicking Michael with another soft backhand to my face. Their technique and timing were both terrible.

"Now, now, slapping him won't help. Please, calm down and sit," Kreila said.

The twins were still crying, too hard to understand her.

"Please now, children, sit down," she said again, this time softer, more patient.

When that didn't work, Bobby the bloodhound let out a bark so loud it could've cracked a window. It shook all three of us.

"Have a seat, kids, please," Kreila said with just a hint of irritation.

The twins, surprisingly obedient, sat on the two chairs that had been set out for them.

"You must be Michael and Melena. It's nice to meet you two. I'm Abigail Kreila, but you can call me Granny Kreila. Everyone does."

She poured water from a blue teapot into two cups and handed them each one.

"Your brother here is still very sick. He'll need to stay with me for a few more days so I can keep an eye on him."

She walked over and kneeled down beside them.

"You two were brave and kind for helping him. But now it's my turn to help. I'll give you both a place to sleep. I'll make sure you all get some food, too."

I didn't know how, but I could already smell broth cooking from another room—even though she hadn't left ours.

"Where are your parents? Where are you three from?" Kreila asked.

I explained that we lived in an abandoned tavern and had been on the streets for years. She gasped, covering her mouth with one hand.

"Gods, no wonder you were so skinny. Gods, the three of you look terrible."

She stood. "Here's what we'll do. You three stay in this room for now. I'll bring some old toys I have and get food ready in a few. Bobby, please get the captain."

Bobby gave a confident bark and trotted off.

The toys she brought weren't broken or covered in mold—just dusty. That alone made them better than anything we'd ever had.

The twins and I talked about the night's events, stuffed animals in our hands. Not long after, Kreila came back into the room with two bowls of soup in her arms, and one floating quietly behind her.

"Whoa," I mumbled.

The soup smelled warm and rich. Inside the brown broth were carrots, peas, and chunks of potato. It tasted just as good. We tore through it, manners forgotten, leaving Kreila visibly disgusted—not that it stopped her. She came back with biscuits in both hands.

Those vanished, too.

"If that captain is coming, I can't have you three smelling like the sewers. I'll have a bath prepared for you soon."

"Thank you!" we all said at once.

She let us bathe in an old wooden tub, one after the other. She gave us flowery soap and a sponge. She left us to it, probably because we reeked. It wasn't our first "bath," but jumping into lakes wasn't the same.

After we were done, she told us clothes would have to wait— nothing in the house would fit us.

By evening, after some more rest, I could finally stand and walk a bit, though every movement still felt harder than it should have.

After she gave the twins a quick physical, an old man and another guard entered the shop. A bell jingled above the door to announce their arrival.

The old man was dark-skinned, missing one eye, and leaned on a cane. The guard behind him wore a steel helmet and the green-and-white banner of the Kingdom of Eltonia. The old man's uniform was faded, patched in places.

The younger guard removed his helmet.

I froze. It was the same one who'd fallen on me earlier.

"Your dam—" the old man started, then stopped himself when he realized kids were in the room. "Your dog is very loud and persistent, Abigail."

His voice was deep and tired.

The younger guard knelt to meet my gaze.

"I remember you. I bumped into you a few months back," he said with a grin.

He seemed kind, a rare thing in Elton's guards.

"You're in good hands. Granny here helped me when I was sick some time ago, too!"

He rubbed my head, which luckily didn't stink anymore.

We were brought to a dining room that doubled as a lab. The long table looked magically stretched.

This woman must've been the most powerful mage ever.

"I'm Captain Towsin. Retired Captain Taylor Towsin. I led the city guard for a short time—likely long before you three were born," the captain said.

He pointed to the guard standing beside him. "This is my son, Private Howard Towsin. He's been in the guard for about two years, but he's got his eye on becoming captain someday."

Granny Kreila then explained everything, how we'd lived on the streets for years, how I stumbled in during the snowstorm.

"God of light," the captain muttered, shaking his head. "The Kingdom of Eltonia's rulers and gangs would rather stuff their pockets with gold than help starving kids. They focus on the elite and ignore everyone else. It was rough back when I was in charge, but it's only gotten worse since I left."

He looked down, frowning.

"I got injured five years into my service. Never got the chance to make the changes I wanted."

Kreila cut in.

"You saved a whole building of people and fought off a mad mage and a cultist by yourself. The people you led loved you. The people you saved would build you a statue if they had the means. You're a hero. Don't talk like you didn't change the city."

"Ha! If that's true, then tell the city to raise my retirement payments. Maybe then I can afford to build the statue myself," he said with a laugh.

"We've got to try to help them," the private said, concern heavy in his voice. "They won't survive another winter like this."

Kreila sighed.

"I've only got one room upstairs, and it's packed with boxes. I've got three beds down here, but those are for patients who need to stay overnight for treatment. Taking in all three kids means I'd either have to send someone home or cram them together with the others— which could be a death sentence if someone sick shows up."

The captain spoke up.

"I'll try to pull some strings, maybe get them placed somewhere in a few days. For now, I say keep them here. Howard can help move the boxes and clear space for one of them. The other two can stay in the overnight beds. If the plague shows up, I'll shove them in my attic."

"Please, please, please, please!" the twins shouted in unison, joyfully knowing they would be out of the snow.

Matching their energy, I joined in. "Yes, yes, yes, yes!"

"Ha!" the guard captain chuckled. "Living in those streets makes an attic look like a palace!"

Kreila slapped his shoulder. "Don't say something like that!"

"I'll see if I can grab them some clothes tomorrow. Shouldn't be too hard," the private said. He glanced down at our outfits—layers of rags and furs, thrown together on what looked like pillowcases.

"Lucky you found us in this part of town. Everyone around here's a retired guard or soldier. Gangs don't show their faces, and guards still stop by for advice. We can take care of you three. But honestly, how in god's name have you survived this long?"

We told them.

Stories of theft, strict rationing, and keeping ourselves safe from the homeless wanderer. The more we spoke, the more the adults' faces changed—shock, horror, guilt.

"Gods, I'm so sorry," Kreila whispered.

"You didn't deserve any of that," the captain said, shaking his head. "I wish I'd known sooner."

He let out a sigh.

"I'd be tempted to march to the royal palace myself if it'd help. But they're just as corrupt as the gangs. With corruption comes money for fighters. That's why none of the people I endorsed were chosen as captain. They couldn't be bribed or threatened."

Just then, several wooden cups floated into the room, and a steaming teapot poured tea into each one. The scent of peppermint filled the air, the steam clouding the room in its warm smell.

We froze.

"How did you do that?!" Michael shouted.

"Well, I'm so powerful that all my furniture has a will of its own. You can talk to them, too!" Kreila said, laughing.

"Hello," Melena said to the teapot.

The teapot gave what we guessed was a nod, then finished filling the cups and drifted back to the kitchen.

The adults laughed, but to us, it felt like a noble gesture from an invisible servant.

The guard captain told us he would try to pull together some funds from the neighbors and his own savings to help find us a place to live. He promised he'd be back in a few days with somewhere for us to stay, even if it meant squeezing us into an attic.

"Don't worry, kids. It's still my job to help out. Thanks again, Abigail, for helping. You're an angel in the city of demons." The captain said.

"A strange but kind way to put it," she replied.

"Rest while you can." He said to us with uncertainty in his eyes before heading out.

We wanted to play more, but she told us it was time for bed. She laid out a bedroll in the storage room. After that peppermint tea, our bodies betrayed us. Sleep pulled at us fast.

Michael and Melena played rock-paper-scissors for the good bed. Michael won.

Kreila gave me more potions, this time hidden in tea to make them easier to drink. For better or worse, she told me peppermint was the only flavor she could make right now.

"I think you just need another day or so of rest, and you'll be good to go outside again. But for now, get some rest," she said.

I nodded with a little smile.

"Good night, Michael," she said, before realizing he was already fast asleep. She chuckled and looked past me before closing the door.

"Good night, Wallace. Sleep well."

"You too, Granny. Thank you so much."

She smiled—really smiled—then stepped out and gently shut the door behind her.

As I lay there, I turned to my right and saw Michael asleep, the moonlight faint through the window.

I spent the night thinking about how kind the people here were.

The priest we met on the streets used to say the gods were kind, but I was never sure if that was true.

Maybe they were real. Maybe they sent us an angel—an angel with gray hair, white skin, and a warming smile.

I wasn't even sure if I believed in angels or gods before. But if I did, this is what their work might look like.

Chapter 9

The following day, after breakfast, the twins were told to play outside with Bobby. They had just broken a glass jar of basil on the floor and were running wild around the shop. The housing area we stayed in always had a guard passing by every few minutes. With the houses so close together and all the neighbors being guards or their families, this was probably one of the safest places in the city.

I wanted to play too, but I still felt kind of tired after running just a little. Kreila told me playing like that would only slow down my healing. So, to keep me company, she stayed inside and read to me, teaching me letters and the animals that went with them. She said she planned to teach the twins, too, but first needed Bobby to wear them out.

The rest of the day moved more slowly, wrapped in the comfort of books and hot tea. A few hours passed, then we both heard the bell at the front door. She stood up and walked over to answer it. I got up and crept behind the wall where I could peek out with a clear view of the door and the front desk.

A tall man stood there. His skin was tanned, his hair a mix of brown and gray, and he wore what looked like hunting clothes trimmed with black fur and red scales. He smelled of whiskey—but not the kind I'd catch whiffs of near the tavern. This one carried something deeper, smokier. Apple tree wood, maybe. It was way better than normal.

The man glanced at me for a moment. His red eyes struck me with fear. I started to step back, trying to get away from that awful stare, but then he smiled and looked back at the desk.

Something about him made me nervous. That smile… like he was already ten steps ahead in a game no one else knew they were playing. Like he was smiling at a joke only he understood.

"I see you're running an orphanage now, Abigail. That one there and the two out front... or are they ingredients for a new potion?" he said with a chuckle. His voice was deep and made my skin crawl, but the laugh that followed was oddly... smooth like velvet over glass.

"Oh no, Barron," Kreila said calmly. "The guards and I just want to find them a safe place to stay, out of the snow."

She turned toward me. "You can watch, dearie, but don't interrupt, okay?"

I nodded.

"I will be going on a hunting trip soon with some of my benefactors. I need the usual poison," he said.

"Of course I can. What's your target this time, Mr. Blackwood?"

"Just a pack of Werebears. Nothing I haven't hunted before. Just two bottles should do," he said with confidence.

"It'll just be a moment."

She pulled a mask from the side of her hip and slipped it on, then walked into the laboratory, putting on gloves as she reached her station. She glanced over her shoulder and saw me staring at all the plants and bottles lining the shelves.

"You're going to need something to protect yourself if you're going to be in here," she said, pulling out a syringe dripping with black ooze.

I stepped back in fear.

"Don't worry. This doesn't go into you. It goes by your feet. It'll give you some clothes to wear while I work."

She walked over and dropped the syringe on the tip of my shoe, somehow missing my toes entirely. The ooze poured out and began wrapping around my body. I froze, startled, but Kreila calmly insisted I stay still. The black ooze hardened into sleek black leather, forming a full plague doctor's outfit—complete with gloves, a belt, and sturdy shoes.

I looked up at Kreila. The ooze was wrapping her body too, but hers turned into flowing white silk adorned with bird feathers and small jewels across the shoulders. Her mask looked like the one I'd seen earlier, a bird's beak style, but this one had delicate gems running along the beak.

She held a blob of ooze in her hand, stretching and reshaping it like clay. Before I realized what she was doing, it had solidified into a child-sized bird mask with a strap on the side.

She handed the mask to me. "This is one of our most important tools as a doctor. It keeps out sickness and helps us not smell the bad things we might run into on the job."

She helped me put it on, then gave me a warm smile.

"It looks great on you." She chuckled. "I have a mirror upstairs. I can show you once we're done."

"For now, please just sit over there. I'm just having you watch, okay? I don't want you getting sick again."

I found a stool in the corner and sat down. She started pulling plants from the cabinets—some stored in jars, others not. I couldn't see everything from where I was, but I caught glimpses of her grinding green-colored plants into a powder using a mortar and pestle.

When she was done, she brought out some odd-looking glass bottles mounted on metal stands. A few were connected to each other with tubes. She lit a candle beneath one of the bottles and poured in what looked like water. Then she added the light green powder, stirring it until the color shifted throughout the mixture.

She went over to another cabinet, this one marked with a red skull and secured with a lock. She pulled out a key and opened it. Inside were strange-looking plants and mushrooms.

"Some animals are really tough, so we have to use poison to help weaken them. It helps keep people safe from monsters."

She pulled out what looked like a black flower with an orange stem.

"Some plants can make people or monsters feel sick. So we have to be really careful with them."

I started to stand up for a better look, but the moment my foot touched the ground, she snapped her head toward me.

"Ah! Stay there. I don't want you to get hurt, okay?!" she said, making me jump.

I sat back down on the stool, just like she said.

She dropped the flower into the boiling jar and stirred the now dark green mixture. Then she put out the flame, and the liquid cooled from a boil to room temperature. She grabbed two smaller bottles with tape on them, pulled out a quill and ink, and wrote something on each label. She poured the dark green mixture into the bottles. As soon as she was done, the original jar suddenly evaporated into dust.

"That was amazing!" I shouted at the top of my lungs.

She flinched—her whole body tensed—and I heard deep laughter echoing from the other room.

"You've got a fan now, it seems!" Barron chuckled.

Kreila knelt down, still holding the two bottles. "Yes, a fan that I'd rather not scream at me while I've got poison in my hand!" she shouted back.

"Sorry," I whimpered.

She returned to the front desk. I peeked out from my usual hiding spot and watched her.

"That'll be ten gold, Mr. Blackwood."

"Damn, winter makes everything cost more," he sighed.

"You're rich. Don't you gawk at me," Kreila laughed.

"So will you be, charging this much?" he shot back, handing her several gold coins.

The man looked over at me. "You and your friends out there with the dog—stay safe," he said, heading for the door.

"Thanks for your time, Mrs. Kreila."

"Be safe, Mr. Blackwood. See you again soon," she said.

"Bye-bye!" I called, waving at him from behind the wall.

He left through the front door. A second later, I heard the sound of the twins chasing after the dog. I peeked out the window and saw them playing tug-of-war with Bobby using a brown rope. It looked like an even match.

Suddenly, I felt tired again, so I went back to bed.

By afternoon, I heard the front door creak open again, followed by a stranger's voice shouting inside. I went back to my usual hiding spot—a corner beside the doorway near the front desk—where I could see Kreila and the newcomer without being noticed.

The blonde woman was bleeding from the right side of her neck. Blood dripped from her hand onto her orange dress as she tried to cover the wound. She was panicking, tears in her eyes, breathing fast and shallow. Kreila stood behind the desk, calm and still, with that same strange, stoic look on her face.

"Help! Someone stabbed me with a piece of glass!" the woman yelled.

Out the window, I could see the twins and Bobby peeking in.

"Now, miss, take—" Kreila started.

"Oh gods, am I gonna die? You have to fix this!" the woman cut her off, hysterical.

"Sit down and let—"

"Gods, I'm gonna pass—"

This time, the woman didn't finish. A glowing yellow syringe shot into her right shoulder. Kreila had moved faster than I could follow—her hands flashed from her sleeves like lightning.

The woman froze. Her blue eyes went wide as she stumbled back. Then, suddenly, she collapsed—but stopped about a foot above the floor.

"Excellent catch," Kreila said.

The woman floated there, suspended by something invisible, slowly moving through the air toward the patient room where I'd been staying. Kreila glanced at me and motioned for me to move aside. I stepped back as the floating woman passed, carried by that unseen force.

Kreila lay on one of the extra beds. The invisible force sat her upright. Kreila walked into the room after her, but not before noticing me following close behind.

"This may be hard to watch, Wallace. I think it's best if you play with your siblings for a moment, dearie," she said gently.

I realized I was still in my plague doctor outfit.

"I'm all dressed up to help, see!" I said, eyes bright, trying to convince her.

Kreila rolled her eyes. "Okay. I'll let you know when you can come take a look, but not right now. Just stay out in the lab or go outside, please."

Before I could reply, the door closed.

I stood there anyway, trying to listen through the door.

"Wallace, I wasn't born yesterday. I didn't hear your feet move."

"Sorry," I muttered, then ran off to join Bobby and the twins outside.

Bobby made sure Melena didn't go sneaking in. He tugged her shirt, pulling her back and keeping her away from the shop's entrance.

"What happened? Did you see?!" Michael shouted.

"Yeah! Granny just threw a needle at the crazy lady, and then she calmed down and started floating," I said.

The twins' jaws dropped.

"She's a witch!" Melena yelled.

"But it was so incredible!" I said, still buzzing with excitement.

The twins didn't share my amazement

"She's weird. Nice, but weird," Michael muttered.

His attempt to talk me out of being impressed didn't work.

They both looked down at my leather plague doctor outfit.

"You look like that one lady with the mask from the market. The one who gave us that juice," Melena said. "Are you gonna steal from Granny this time?"

I shook my head and told them about Kreila's work with poison—and how that other plague doctor had been a total con artist.

Before they could ask more questions, the bell above the front door jingled.

The stranger walked out. Her eyes looked calm now, like whatever panic she'd had was gone. She held a potion in one hand.

"You saved my life, Doctor Kreila. You're a lifesaver."

Kreila followed her out, smiling.

"While that potion and treatment were on the house, I'll charge you if you come back with the same injury!" she said with a little laugh.

The woman passed us, glanced down at the twins, and gave us a warm smile.

The twins and I headed back into the shop, with Bobby trotting along behind us.

"What did you stab that lady with?" I asked Kreila.

"Oh, she was just scared, so I gave her something to help her calm down. Then I used my invisible servant to walk her over to the room."

"Someone stabbed her?" Michael asked.

"Sometimes people have too much to drink and start fighting with fists instead of words. Nothing I haven't seen before."

Kreila leaned down and pinched the twins' cheeks with both hands.

"So I'd better not see any of you three there anytime soon?"

"Yes, ma'am," we all said in unison.

"Good. Now, continue with your games. Wallace, you can sit outside for a bit, but please don't run or push yourself. Or you'll end up stuck in bed longer."

The twins decided they needed a new way to beat Bobby at his games, so they slipped out the front door.

Before joining them, I stepped back into the clinic bedroom to take off my mask. That's when I noticed the sheets on the bed were bunched up into a tight ball. The bundle hovered past me, then floated into the fire pit and instantly burst into flames as it hit the embers.

"You saved that lady's life. How did you do that?" I asked, wide-eyed.

"Oh, it's a complicated answer," she said with a soft smile. "But I used magic to quickly heal her wound."

She knelt down in front of me and held out her hand.

"Magic starts from the chest—or soul, and then travels through the fingertips, or wherever the spell comes out."

As she spoke, a few sparkles flickered from her shaky fingers. It wasn't as flashy as the stuff I'd seen earlier, but it still looked amazing to me.

"Some people can't do this well, so they use a shortcut."

She pulled out a clear glass syringe and held it near her heart. Slowly, the syringe began to fill with a sparkling, glittery substance.

"I use an old syringe technique. Think of it like a shortcut from my soul to the syringe."

She gave it a light squeeze. This time, sparkles burst out from the needle—way more dramatic than what had come from her fingers.

"It's a lot of work and learning," she said. "But once you get it down, it's pretty easy."

"How long have you been doing that?" I asked.

"Well, I would tell you, but that might give away how old I am, and I can't have that," she chuckled.

"Eighty-eight?" I guessed.

She looked at me with a smile that somehow managed to hide a murderous intent.

"Wallace, it's best not to ask a lady her age. Just know I've been healing people for quite some time."

"Was I close?" I pressed.

She didn't answer. She simply turned around.

I took that as a sign to drop it and walked outside to join the twins, ready to be the deciding player in finally beating Bobby.

Later that cold evening, after a dinner of warm bread and a pot of flavorful vegetable soup, the captain returned with a smile on his face.

"Well, I've got some good news," he said as he sat down at the table with the four of us.

"There's an orphanage called Elton's Bird Nest, it's a bit of a walk, out toward the west side of the city. They've got beds open. Problem is, there are only two right now."

He sighed, rubbing his beard.

"Well, it's better than nothing. I can send some extra coins to help them stay afloat, too," Kreila offered.

I thought to myself that Kreila was too kind for this world, or at least for Eltonia.

"We can either wait for another bed to open up," the captain continued, "or try to find a different orphanage that has three spots open at once. But I wouldn't hold my breath. Not many folks adopt in the winter, and Eltonians don't adopt often."

"Can you take all three of us?" Michael asked.

The captain shook his head. "Unfortunately, I don't have the resources or space to take in three kids. The room I mentioned before was only meant to be temporary. I'm too old to raise children, and my son is always busy."

A somber look fell over all of us. Then, some of Kreila's kindness took root in my mind.

"You two can take the beds. I can keep waiting," I said confidently.

"No!" the twins shouted.

"We need to stay together," Michael added.

The captain looked down, his face heavy with guilt.

"I know it's hard," he said. "But all we have to do is have Wallace stay with one of us until another bed opens over there. We can send some extra coins to help out. And it's not like he won't still be in the city. Hells, you three could still meet and play together every day."

"Is it a good place for them?" Kreila asked.

"The best we'll get: three meals, beds, and teachers. Cheap, but I think it'll do."

The twins looked crushed by the news.

"We don't wanna leave you again," Michael whimpered.

I slid off my seat and walked over to them

"We're still gonna play every day. I'll bring Bobby," I whispered.

"You better," Melena whispered back.

We didn't like this. We had made it through all these years by staying as close as we could. But we knew this might be our best shot, at least for now.

The captain offered to take the twins to the orphanage the next morning.

"Oh, this isn't a funeral. You'll see each other probably every day," Kreila said.

We finished our dinner, and the captain said his goodbyes before heading out.

"Can they stay with me tonight?" I asked.

She nodded and summoned her servant by dropping a clear syringe to the floor. The servant prepared the beds in the patient room—laid them with clean sheets and pillows, even though it wasn't necessary.

Despite the extra space, the three of us chose to sleep together in the same bed. That was what we were used to. We'd been doing it for years. It was uncomfortable, but comforting. Normal.

We stayed up late, whispering plans about stealing pies and how being in two different places might help us plan our escapes even better.

When morning came, the cold slipped in early. Kreila made scrambled eggs and toast for breakfast, and made sure we all bathed before the day began. By the time the captain arrived, we smelled like peppermint.

We were dressed in our matching orange tunics and brown pants. The captain wore his worn green military coat, and his son—clad in rusted steel armor—carried a wooden chest filled with colorful new clothes for the twins.

"Are you three okay?" the captain asked.

We gave slow, hesitant nods.

"Alright, lads. Let's get you both over there."

The twins walked up to me, arms open, and hugged me tight.

"We love you," Melena said.

"I love you more," Michael added.

"I love one of you more," I replied.

We all chuckled.

Even though we knew this wasn't goodbye forever, we hugged like it was.

"I'll be there tomorrow to say hi," I said. "Or we can meet at headquarters."

"What headquarters?" Kreila asked.

We just laughed and didn't answer.

The twins had decided that the cold, abandoned tavern had too much history to give up. It felt like a good middle ground between the orphanage and Kreila's shop.

I looked back once from the street—bundled and brave, and I waved until my hand went numb.

As the guards led them out into the howling cold, we all agreed to compete over who could shout goodbye the loudest.

Melena won.

Chapter 10

My body had fully recovered, my chest felt free, and my breath came smoothly, so I spent most of the day playing with Bobby and the toys inside the store. Sometime during the evening, I walked over to Kreila, who was standing behind the store counter. Candles lit the room, and her eyes were locked on a dark green book.

"What are you reading?" I asked.

"Oh, this is my old diary from when I was an adventurer. I figured it was time to decide what to do with it."

"Can I see, please?" I said, giving her my classic puppy dog eyes

"How did you learn manners?" she asked, smiling.

"Begging," I answered.

"Oh. Yeah, that'll do it," she laughed. "I'll read you one entry, but you have to go to bed after, okay?"

I looked toward the window and saw the moonlight shining over the city.

"Okay!"

She sat me down on the clinic bed and poured warm vanilla tea using her invisible servant.

She told me a story about traveling with a coven of witches who once ran into a group of elves. The night was warm, and everyone gathered around a campfire surrounded by trees. The tall blonde elves believed they could make a better-tasting potion than Kreila and the other witches. A young Kreila felt insulted and accepted the challenge. Little did the elves know, she had just bought a new, great-tasting white wine from some gnomes.

While the elves were focused on making their fancy concoction, she quietly poured some of the wine into the bottles she used for her potions. The catch? Kreila forgot that this gnome wine was way more potent than the stuff back home in the Kingdom of Eltonia.

The competition was brutal. Everyone got drunk. Eventually, it turned into a wild exchange of hats between the elves and the coven. The coven's brown hats were short and pointy but kind of sad-looking—deflated, almost. Still, they decorated them with colorful jewels and glitter. The elven hats were small too, but bright green and pointed straight toward the sky.

Once the elves realized they'd been played, they decided to end the challenge with a drinking contest. Kreila was the best drinker in the coven—known for never having hangovers. She agreed to go head-to-head with their leader and held her own, especially considering she was secretly using a syringe to drain the wine from her mug. She hid the thing under her long sleeves and managed to convince the elves she was some kind of drinking machine.

Their leader fell backward into the grass. The elves conceded.

Kreila, victorious, decided to claim her prize. She closed the book and smiled at me. Then she walked upstairs and came back down with a bright green witch hat, trimmed with several white feathers that made it look like it had wings.

She was a fantastic storyteller, and I laughed at her solid attempts at humor.

"You're the best witch ever!" I said to her.

"Oh, thank you, sweetie. But don't go shouting that, or mages across the city will come looking for a duel," she replied.

"I wanna be a plague witch, too!" I said with enthusiasm.

Her smile dimmed a little.

"Oh, Wallace, that work is tough. Other jobs are easier and pay more."

"But I wanna be like you," I whimpered.

She frowned.

"Wallace, we can talk more in the morning. Get some sleep."

"But I wanna talk now," I pouted.

"Please rest, Wallace," she sighed.

I crossed my arms and pouted harder.

"I'm not sleepy. Tell me more stories."

She shook her head, gasped with a jolt of energy, and pointed at the ceiling.

"Oh gods, is that the bat!" she shouted.

I looked up. The bat was either invisible or moving so fast I couldn't see it. But I didn't have time to wonder. I felt a quick jab in my shoulder.

I turned toward Kreila. She had a smug smile on her face.

"Sweet dreams."

I didn't get to respond. My eyes got heavy, and everything went dark.

I dreamt of a tavern full of people. The walls were dark brown wood, and the ceiling matched. It was a warm evening, and lanterns hung along the walls. The people wore brown and black leather garb, some with silver armor strapped to their arms and legs. They danced fast to songs about broken hearts, ale in hand. The whole room smelled like every kind of liquor I could think of, swirling together in one loud, dizzy mess.

I turned my head toward the main bar. A man played a lute on top of it while a woman danced beside him with ale in both hands. Both of them wore tight black leather armor and had silver knives strapped to their hips. Their outfits looked freshly made, maybe by a leatherworker who took pride in detail. Rings covered their fingers—some gold, some silver—and they had matching blue eyes and skin pale as candlelight. They were tall, elegant, and moved with confidence. I told myself they looked like the twins.

Michaell was the one on the lute, singing about an unfortunate breakup. Two women in orange dresses backed him up, one playing a drum, the other on a pan flute.

In a blink, Melena stopped dancing and whipped a knife across the tavern. It landed dead center on a target board, even though it flew past at least three people on the way. Nobody flinched. It was like they trusted her, or maybe they were too drunk to care.

Everyone was having so much fun. But something felt off.

I didn't recognize the place. I didn't see anyone who looked like adult me. Even worse, I noticed I couldn't move. My body just wouldn't respond. And no one seemed to know I was there. People looked in my direction sometimes, but their eyes never stayed. Others passed right by me like I was made of smoke.

No one was looking at me. Not really. They looked through me like I was already gone.

Then Michael raised his voice. He stood tall on the bar, and the whole tavern went quiet.

His voice was smooth and warm, almost too perfect, like he'd stolen the voice of an angel.

He lifted his wine glass to the sky. The drink inside glowed purple.

"Ever since that crying idiot left, the money has been rolling in! No stupid rules. No piece-of-shit doctor trying to play hero!" Michael laughed, loud and cruel.

Melena found another table to stand on.

"It's been three years since he's been gone, and we've doubled our size in that time!"

Michael pointed at Melena.

"But I still miss that fool. The only thing that'll bring him back now is some burned lass!"

The bar chuckled, but I couldn't laugh or move.

"So I want to give this toast to our little brother. Our favorite tail-chasing con artist with a heart—Wallace. Maybe he'll be back once he's gone broke being nice! Cheers!" Michael shouted.

The whole bar raised its glasses and echoed the cheer. Music picked back up. The dancing started again.

But for better or worse, they couldn't hear me. I shouted their names from the corner, asked for help, begged them to see me. Told them I was still here with them. Still alive. Still me.

I woke up with a tear in my eye. Looked around. I was still in the clinic. It was quiet, still dark outside, just before sunrise.

But there was candlelight glowing from the other room, the lab.

I stood and walked slowly to the door.

There was Kreila, slumped over a desk. Eyes closed. Still breathing. She was asleep, and it looked like she'd passed out mid-thought. The gray quill in her hand had dried ink at the tip.

I tried to step back and return to my room, but the floor betrayed me. A plank creaked under my foot.

She stirred. Slowly raised her head, groaning like every bone in her body ached.

"What are you doing up this late at night?" she asked, her voice thick with exhaustion.

I decided to forgive her for drugging me earlier. If staying awake made me look like her, then maybe it was worth it.

"It's just before sunrise, ma'am. Are you okay?"

"I'm fine, dearie. I was just writing a book."

"What kind of book?" I asked.

"It's about me and my work. Wanna make sure I record my thoughts. I figured it would be good to keep me busy," she yawned.

"Can I help? I can't write, but I still want to help," I said eagerly

"You keep wanting to watch what I do and help. What are you after?" She grinned.

"I want to be like you one day. You cure people and make them smile. I wanna do that, but with the whole city someday."

"Oh, Wallace, that's sweet of you to say. It's hard to do that in Elton. So many hurt people," she sighed.

"So why do you keep helping them if it's hard?" I asked.

She stumbled to her feet, rising from her chair, but held her composure.

"Because it's the right thing to do, Wallace. Sometimes you don't get rewards, but it's still the right thing to do. Because someone has to."

The words came out soft, but heavy, like each syllable had weight. Her shoulders drooped. Her eyes looked far away, as if searching for a part of herself she'd forgotten. For a second, she looked tired in a way that sleep couldn't fix.

I looked down at the floor for a second, then walked over to her side and looked into her eyes. I brought out my puppy eyes for this critical moment.

"You didn't have to help me or the twins, but you did. I really wanna be like you."

I saw her eyes begin to tear up, and she let out a soft sigh.

"We need more kids like you, Wallace. People who wanna help."

"Then teach me how to," I said.

She chuckled and rubbed her eyes. The laugh was quiet, like it took effort to lift her face into a smile. Then she gave a long sigh—one that seemed to take the last of her energy.

"We aren't doing anything until you learn to read and write."

I smiled at her, and she smiled back.

Wallace, age 10

August 10th, 1354

Dear Granny,

I'm sure you're wondering where my last notes from yesterday's training went. I want you to know that I saw Bobby the bloodhound conjure himself from your syringe. He then went into my room and started shredding them.

I was lucky he only went after yesterday's notes.

I was going to ask for your help, but I didn't want to make you repeat yourself. Plus, the twins and I had to find the guards to report Bobby's crime. There is absolutely no reason to punish me. I have already apprehended Bobby and will make sure he is punished for his actions.

Thank you for your endless support. Please don't be upset.

From an upstanding citizen,

Wallace

Wallace, age 10

August 11th, 1354

Dearest Granny,

I would like to apologize for my misdoings. You did not have to take me to court like that in front of the Captain and his son.

Melena was not a good lawyer for me, and Michael's support for Bobby was completely uncalled for.

I'm disappointed that a judge like yourself couldn't see the guilt in Bobby's eyes. But I'll have you know—I'm going to keep a close eye on him from now on.

Sorry about the notes.

Thanks,

Your loyal student,

Wallace

Chapter 11

"I'm putting it in now, Grandma," I said, placing the blue mushroom—long stem, bone-dry cap, and cold to the touch into the flask. We both stood in front of a large flask resting on a dark stone, the surface radiating intense heat that boiled the blue substance inside the glass. With my mask on, I couldn't smell a thing, but Kreila had already warned me that was for the best.

It was a warm spring afternoon as Kreila and I worked on a new order. We were both suited up in our plague doctor attire. Mine was the standard: leather robes, gloves, shoes, and the usual bird-like leather mask. Kreila, of course, was still rocking her signature blue and white get-up, with white feathers covering the upper half of her body. She always said she wanted to be the best-looking plague doctor in the city, so her outfit was never basic, it had sparkling jewels or shining feathers stitched in somewhere.

Kreila noticed me place the mushroom and reached to mix it with the blue substance, but then she gasped.

"Wallace, dear, that's not a purple tylvian mushroom; that's the snowball mushroom! I looked away at the birds for five seconds." She turned to face me, stepping away from the flask. "Why didn't you tell me you were color blind, Wallace? Purple and blue are completely different."

"I'm sorry," I whimpered.

Then the mixture started smelling like burning wood. The liquid shifted from blue to a dark, ominous purple.

"Well, that's okay. It just means we'll smell like burnt wood when it explodes!" she chirped.

"Wait, what do you mean when it explodes?!" I said, panicked.

"I've always loved you, Wallace."

A syringe slid from her sleeve and was swiftly thrown, jabbing into my shoulder. Before I could get another word out, the mixture foamed over the rim of the glass. A sudden blast of purple dust and shards erupted, covering the laboratory in a thick cloud.

Our uniforms were instantly coated. The air reeked of a strange blend—burnt flowers mixed with scorched wood. My mask and upper body were blanketed in the dust, while Kreila, who had turned just before the blast, had most of it clinging to her back.

Without missing a beat, she walked to one of the wooden cabinets and opened it. Inside were rows of jars filled with plants and mushrooms in every shade and shape imaginable. She pulled out two jars—each held a mushroom with a tall stem and a dry cap, but one was deep purple and the other a bright blue.

Turning to me, she held up both jars.

"You see, son, this is purple, and this is blue," she said calmly. "Tylvian purple mushrooms help calm the tonic. But the snowball mushroom?" She shook the jar slightly. "It excites it. That's what makes it explode."

"I'm sorry," I repeated.

"It's okay. But you'll be on cleaning duty with the servant. Then I want you to stand back and watch me make the tonic again. You'll get it someday," she said, trying to comfort me.

"Why was that syringe in me?" I asked, pulling it from my arm. I hadn't even felt the prick going in or coming out.

"That was in case the explosion was worse. If any glass or debris had pierced your uniform, it wouldn't have hurt you. But it looks like you're fine."

Before I could respond, the front door creaked open. Heavy boots thudded against the wood floor.

Kreila and I turned as Barron stepped into view, brushing ash from his dark coat like it was a daily nuisance.

"I'm sure you'll make a fine doctor someday, Wallace," he said with a knowing chuckle, voice warm despite the chaos.

Barron had placed another order for a smoke screen for his upcoming hunting trip and must have been waiting patiently at the front of the store, likely having heard the explosion but wise enough not to interrupt Kreila mid-lesson.

He leaned in the doorway now, arms folded, amusement etched across his weathered face.

Kreila sighed through her nose. "You've got perfect timing as always."

"I try," Barron replied. "Besides, it's not a proper visit unless something nearly explodes."

Kreila dropped two syringes onto the floor. I could sense the servant had been summoned, as a brown towel floated into the air and began wiping down the tools. One of the syringes looked strange, it had a horn instead of a needle at its end. Then it flipped upright, the horn pointing toward the ceiling.

With a sound like a sudden storm, the syringe began pulling the purple powder into itself, forming a small tornado above it. The dust lifted from our clothes, the desk, and nearly every surface in the room. Though not perfect, most of the powder was sucked into the syringe, packing its glass center with a thick swirl of purple.

Kreila stepped forward and picked up the syringe, gripping it firmly. It began to dissolve in her hand, both the syringe and its contents vanishing into a thin black mist.

The rest of the powder and broken glass were left to me and the unseen servant. Together, we cleaned it up with a brush, a towel, and a bucket of water.

Barron, dressed in his black and green hunting gear, stepped into the lab. Around his neck hung a necklace with a ruby rose at its center. His jacket was cut from fine black leather, his pants shimmered like green silk, and his boots were made from polished black leather.

He leaned casually against the wall, his heavy steps causing the floor to creak.

"Be proud, young man. I remember when you started two years ago, you'd scream at the smallest mishap. Now it's just anxiety, yeah, it seems." He pointed at me with a steaming cup of tea in hand.

"Your posture, try not to bend your knees when you're in front of important people."

I hadn't even noticed, but as Barron entered the laboratory, my legs started shaking with fear. He was a kind man, but his booming voice and muscled arms were intimidating. He bent down to meet my eyes.

"Healers, herbalists, and potion makers have a tough road ahead of them, you know. Handling all those ingredients, the medical treatments, it can be scary."

He placed his hand on my shoulder, even though my leather garbs were still coated in purple dust. His grip was firm.

"That also means they end up doing most of the work, most of the time. Which means they'll mess up a lot. But once they get it right, they become well-known. So don't rush it, son."

He gave my shoulder a couple of reassuring pats. His voice was slow and deep, but his smile softened everything he said. It made his words easier to carry

Then he stood and looked at his hand, now covered in purple dust. He brushed it off on his green pants, leaving a bright stain.

"Well, good thing all my meetings are over. Straight home after this," he chuckled.

Kreila walked in behind me, holding a small box filled with four jars—potions and poisons. The box had two rope straps on the sides, making it easy to carry with one hand.

"Do I need to remind you what they do, Barron?" she scoffed.

"I've been coming here for over a decade, Abigail. I'd like to think I know by now," he replied. "I'd argue you're the best healer in the city. I'd be crazy to go anywhere else."

"Well," she said with a smirk, "either you love my work, or you've lost your mind from drinking those potions for so long."

Barron smiled. "Thanks again, you two. Take care."

He exited through the front door and closed it behind him.

"You still have a job to do, Wallace," Kreila said sarcastically from behind me.

"Yes, ma'am," I groaned and picked up the towel to keep cleaning.

"If I may ask," I said as I wiped down some of her tools, "did you make a lot of mistakes when you were learning?"

"Wallace, you're always learning new things. Which means you'll keep making mistakes—doesn't matter how old you are," she said. "A few years back, I added the wrong flowers to a man's potion. Cured his stomachache, sure, but he had to run to the outhouse every few minutes for days."

"Who taught you how to be a witch doctor?" I asked.

"Started with my mother, she was an herbalist," she said, wiping her hands on a cloth. "Then I studied medicine, traveled around, and picked up more along the way."

She gave a small shrug. "Made plenty of messes in the process. Still do, sometimes."

Kreila always had a way of comforting me when I messed up. She'd laugh it off and say something nice, but I wished her sarcasm didn't sting as much. I knew she didn't mean to hurt me, but sometimes her words felt sharper than they needed to be, like they were pointing at every part of me that still didn't measure up. I wanted to impress her, not feel like a walking joke.

Chapter 12

The past two years as Kreila's apprentice have been rough, but she says I've made decent progress. After teaching me how to read and write, she started handing me books. She figured that giving me a pair of round glasses would help keep my vision clear after hours of reading, given that is all I would be doing for the next few years. First, it was about herbs, and later on, it was about physiology. She was kind enough to find books that were simple enough for a kid, slowly guiding me to more complicated ones. I didn't think I'd care about things like how muscles work or how different roots affect the body, but somewhere along the line, I started enjoying it.

Some books, though, were straight painful to get through. I mean, nobody needs to memorize a hundred kinds of beakers and burners when every potion maker uses the same two. After having to read so often, I began wearing the glasses even when I wasn't reading, though I never really needed them.

Kreila would test me on what I'd read and punish me if I failed or acted up. Her idea of punishment was either chores or what I'd call soft torture, like making me collect plants without gloves or any protective gear. I'd come back itching all over and looking like I lost a fight with a forest.

One of the first things I learned was basic first aid. The second was to keep quiet when people showed up, because saying "eww" doesn't count as medical talk. Kreila also made it clear that staring at patients is rude, especially when it's a woman who needs a physical examination.

Mostly, my job was to clean her tools and keep the shop tidy. I also helped move jars around and check on patients who had to stay overnight. Whenever she worked on a patient or brewed potions, I could watch. She only recently started letting me help, and the results have been all over the place.

A few months passed, and Kreila was getting ready for another one of her business trips. She would be gone for a few weeks to handle some classified work. She made it clear that I wasn't allowed to know what these meetings were about and warned that if I tried to come or follow her, my apprenticeship would be over. I asked a few questions anyway, but her tone changed, and it wasn't anger. It was worry, like she was trying to shield me from something bigger than either of us or someone.

She told me the shop would stay closed until she could trust me enough to run it on my own. Kreila understood that I had survived on the streets for years and knew I could handle being by myself. Just to be safe, she let Captain Townsin and the neighbors know she'd be away. They were asked to check in every now and then, just to make sure the shop wasn't turned to ash in her absence.

Before leaving, Kreila left me some bookwork to study. She said she'd be testing me once she got back. That wasn't a bluff. Last time I flunked one of her tests, she made me taste her latest fruit-flavored potions. I'm convinced she never ate fruit before in her life, or her taste buds were permanently wrecked. Grape-flavored healing potions tasted like bitter grapes that despised the idea of sugar. The apple ones? They tasted like rotting apples that dreamed of being sweet but never made it.

To top it off, she handed me a lavender skin ointment. At first, it smelled alright, almost calming. A few minutes later, it turned sour and started to reek like burnt hair. That was her idea of punishment.

While she was away on her trips, neighbors would check in on me, but the ones who showed up the most were the Captain and Barron. Captain Townsin would stop by to make sure everything was in order and drop off extra food. Barron, on the other hand, would occasionally swing through just to share stories about his hunting trips. He often mentioned how proud he was of the progress I'd made. One time, he even said I should take over the store when Kreila retired.

That hit me harder than I expected. I didn't know how to feel about that. The idea felt too big. I caught myself staring at the shop walls after he left, wondering if I really belonged here. But Barron liked the thought of still being able to buy his supplies from the shop. Since he couldn't work directly with Kreila, he figured having her apprentice in charge was the next best thing. Sometimes, he even slipped me a few extra copper or silver coins so I could get myself something I actually wanted.

Even with Kreila gone, I found comfort in the company of the twins, who still made time to meet me at the tavern every day. The orphanage they lived in had decent food and beds, but the staff didn't always seem happy to be there. They made sure the kids knew how to read and write, but the twins told me there were days when the children got yelled at or spanked.

The orphanage received funding from a generous benefactor, which allowed the twins to go on apprenticeship trips. These trips helped them figure out what kind of work they might want to do before leaving the orphanage for good.

Despite all that, we still lived like kids. We didn't steal as much as we used to since food wasn't a problem anymore. But we still had our eyes on things we couldn't afford. Now that we were no longer in the slums, we wanted jewelry and artifacts to call our own. We no longer wanted the cheapest clothes. We wanted real silk and bearskin.

Michael would often attend plays and meet with actors to learn how to deliver speeches and engage with people. He was always showing off his tunics, and they did look new. But he could rip a hole in one just by pulling on it the wrong way.. In his free time, he used what he had picked up to stir up trouble with the girls and boys at the orphanage or nearby schools. He liked to joke that over the past two years, he had several boyfriends and girlfriends at the same time, then acted all innocent whenever he got caught.

Melena, on the other hand, wanted to learn how to fight. She spent time watching the city guards train at a barracks in town. She told the caretakers and the officers that she wanted to become a guard herself, but that wasn't the truth. Melena didn't just want to fight. She wanted to understand how the guards operated and how they moved around the city. That way, she could steal or brawl in places where they wouldn't be.

She loved the rush of fighting. What she really enjoyed was figuring out how to beat someone, even if it meant cheating. But one night, she admitted something to Michael and me. Part of the reason she was so eager to fight was that she wanted to protect us. It was one of the few times she let herself be vulnerable, and it stuck with me. We told her she didn't have to worry about that. We would protect her, too, with Michael's smooth talking and my potions.

The twins said they would try their best to stay out of the Bird's Nest whenever they could help it. The place called itself the best orphanage around, bragging about its polished wooden walls, three full meals a day, and cozy rooms. They took me to see it once. It had warm brown wood across the front and a bright blue bird painted right on the door. They told me it gave them chances they had never had before.

The headmistress and her assistant taught the kids how to read and even helped them find local apprenticeships. That was how Michael ended up going to Bard's College, and how Melena got into the city watch buildings.

It was a shame that all the clean walls and friendly smiles were just for show. The whole thing was a publicity stunt. The owner, Lady Carylon, was a wealthy noblewoman who used her money to climb the social ladder through her bank. She used the Bird's Nest as a marketing tool. To impress investors, she performed, acting as if she genuinely cared about the needy. She showed up only three times a year and never came without her guards and a line of bankers behind her.

Lady Carylon would shake the hands of a few kids and then leave without saying another word. The food, clothes, books, beds, and assistants were all brand new, but only in the most technical sense. Everything was the cheapest version money could buy.

When I first visited, the beds looked fine, but sitting on one told the truth. The beds, made of dark pine wood, were either so stiff they hurt your back or so weak they collapsed within a few weeks. The three meals a day the twins got were better than the scraps they found on the street, but they still had to deal with a disgusting kitchen filled with fruits and vegetables that were nearly moldy.

Still, even with all that, the three of us knew that it was better than sleeping in that dark, freezing tavern, eating rats for dinner. Sometimes

I wake up in the middle of the night and think about that time. It doesn't even feel like it happened to me. I look at the shelves I've organized, the potions I can now brew, and wonder, am I still the same boy who once stole bread and ran from guards? Or am I becoming something else?

Despite the tavern's rotting walls and crumbling floor, the three of us had decided that it was our home away from home. We still met there almost every day. We talked about what had happened that day, helped each other with school assignments, and, as always, used the place as our headquarters for plotting.

With some extra copper and silver we managed to scrounge up, we put together enough to buy a cheap set of chairs and a table. After a few years of working and saving, we got rid of all the rotten furniture and broken glass. We even had the entire roof replaced with new wood.

Between the money I earned from Kreila's shop and the coins the twins collected from their pickpocketing runs, we had a bit of extra coin to throw around. But we knew we wanted more. We dreamed of seeing the tavern fixed up properly, with solid new floors, clean walls, and real windows that didn't rattle when the wind hit them.

As we got older, our ideas for making money became riskier. Stealing pies was behind us. We had already agreed to meet up one night soon to talk about what we were going to do next.

Chapter 13

I pushed the door open at the tavern. It was noon. Kreila was out on another trip, and I had already finished my studying for the day. I walked through the tavern, taking in the dark, rotting walls and the floor creaking under my steps. Above me hung a broken iron chandelier, its candles still clinging to the edges. The rope holding it up sagged, barely doing its job.

"I should replace that," I muttered, not because anyone told me to, but because I saw the danger and knew better now. Funny how I was once the danger.

I glanced over at our usual table and chairs near the furnace, my hand brushing the edge of the oak tabletop. It wasn't much, but I appreciated the place for what it was. The three of us had spent a lot of time in taverns like this across the city, taking notes on what we could do to improve our own spot. The barkeeps never bothered us, as long as we didn't cause trouble or try to buy ale.

Unfortunately for Kreila and the Bird's Nest, these taverns also taught us how to insult each other like we thought grown folks did. Or at least how we imagined they did.

Even with Kreila gone, I found comfort in the company of the twins, who still made time to meet me here every day. We didn't say it aloud, but this place had become something close to home.

Suddenly, I looked down at my stomach and saw two pale arms wrapped tight around me. Before I could even react, my feet left the floor. My view whipped from the fireplace to the ceiling, then to the wall behind me, until my head smacked the ground with a loud thud.

"Too easy!" Melena shouted, letting go of my waist.

Her grappling and stealth skills had paid off; my head throbbed with pain. I rolled onto my side and saw the twins in their dark tunics, grinning smugly above me.

Deciding not to wear my glasses when around the two turned out to be a wise decision; otherwise, they would find a way to break or steal them.

"Wallace was a good man. It was a shame he fell to the floor and died that day," Michael said, solemn and sarcastic.

"Shame they never caught the devilish rogue who killed him," Melena whispered, deadpan.

I climbed to my feet, rubbing the back of my head and trying to laugh off the hit, while they cracked up. Worst of all, those two were outgrowing me fast, I had to tilt my head up just to look them in the eye.

"Your work's still sloppy. You get caught too easily, you." I shouted, but they just kept snickering, strolling over to the table by the fireplace.

A flicker of old irritation stirred in my chest. They were better, faster, stronger, and they knew it. I'd been playing catch-up ever since Kreila took me in.

Right then, I pulled a syringe from my pouch and held it close to my chest. I took a deep breath and pictured oil—slick and chaotic, slipping, tumbling. The syringe grew heavy in my palm, and I hurled it at the floor in front of Melena.

It moved too fast for them to catch. The needle hit the floor and started leaking a light brown oil from its tip. Melena heard it strike the wood, but before she could take another step, her foot slid out from under her. She crashed down with a loud slam.

Michael watched her hit the floor and decided to sing her an obituary.

"Here lies Melena, a sister above them all. Though a second was all it took to hear the angels call."

The two of us burst out laughing as Melena struggled to stand up.

"You could've torn my shirt, asshole," she mumbled.

"You bruised my skull first, so I call that even," I smirked. But inside, I relished that win. Just once, I'd landed the surprise. Just once, I wasn't the last to react.

"Come on, let's get our meeting started, you two," Michael said, walking toward the fireplace. A few pieces of the old wooden furniture were still piled nearby. He reached behind them and pulled out a small bronze lute with a polished brown wood body—fancy-looking and way too expensive for the dump we were in.

Michael plucked a few strings and hummed a tune. Instantly, flames roared to life in the fireplace, casting a warm glow over the room.

We all sat down at the table, facing each other.

"Any good news?" I asked.

"Well, we've got the start of a plan. Gonna take some time to set it up, though. Gotta get on their good side first," Michael said, scoffing.

"Captain Lyons of the city guard has a daughter. She shows up at the base a lot. About our age. Her name's Penelope."

"So, what are you thinking?" I asked.

"I had a tour of the north side of town a while back. Marble walls, gold everywhere—real upper crust stuff. Captain lives out there."

"Wait. Are you trying to rob the captain's daughter? Does this plan come with a will and testament?" I said.

"No, we're not suicidal, moron. But what if I talked to the girl for a while—got on her good side?" Michael smirked. "When I stopped by to grab a knife from Melena, I passed her and gave her my ever-so-charming wink. She smiled. Blushed a little, too," he added proudly.

I didn't say it, but I hated how easily things came to him. I couldn't lie, I was a little envious of the twins. Their bloodline had been kind to them. Both taller than most kids our age, and better looking, too.

"Michael gets on her good side and gets her out of the house. I spy on the folks and figure out when the captain and his wife aren't home. Then we sneak in when no one's watching and grab what we can," Melena said.

"Makes sense. But the captain probably has guards all over the place," I sighed.

"That's where you come in," Michael said. "You distract the guards. Melena gets inside. I keep the girl busy."

"What's our backup plan if this goes sideways?" I asked.

"I'll have a change of clothes and a fresh haircut when the job's done," Melena said. "Worst case, we run to the sewers. No guard's gonna chase us in there."

"I'll propose to the lass if I have to," Michael added.

"And what if she says yes?" I laughed.

"Then I'll ask the captain for her hand. A teenage wedding, full of wine and women!" Michael chuckled.

Even as I laughed with them, a knot sat in my gut. This plan was bold, even for us. And for the first time, I felt something I hadn't felt in a while: hesitation. Were we just getting too good at this? Or too reckless?

"We'll need gear for Melena and clothes for you, Michael," I said.

They both looked confused.

"I'm sure we've got all we need—knife, rope, bags," Melena replied.

"No. We need something better. A way you can grab a bunch of stuff without dragging around a huge sack," I said, thinking for a moment. "One of those bags that can hold way more than it looks like it should. Almost bottomless."

Melena grinned, but Michael gave me a hard look.

"Magic stuff's expensive. Where the hell are you gonna find that?" he asked.

"I don't know yet. I'll figure something out before the time comes. But we also need to get you some new clothes," I told him. "If she's gonna believe you're some charming heartbreaker from Midtown, you've got to look the part, and smell like it too."

"We'll have to do some more pocketing for that, even more than we already do," Melena muttered.

Robbing will take time. And we were already toeing a line.

"For now, just do what you gotta do," I said, glancing at the two of them.

And as they nodded, I looked into the fire and saw a different boy reflected, a boy who used to steal bread just to survive, now planning to rob a captain's estate. And for the first time, I wasn't sure if I liked him.

We'd been picking pockets for a few years now—getting better with each pass. When we did get caught, the sewers always scared folks off. Mostly the old or fat ones. We stuck to people who looked like they wouldn't miss a few copper coins.

Life on the streets was hell for the three of us. We didn't want to drag anyone else into this mess, force them to pick between rats and squirrels for dinner. Still, we talked often about giving some of the extra coin back to the Bird's Nest; help them get real books, supplies, something better than scraps..

There were even a few old beggars who'd been on those streets longer than we'd been alive. We figured they deserved something too.

After swapping stories about botched potions and schoolyard schemes, the three of us rose from our seats. Melena jogged to the door, then suddenly stopped and turned, eyes locked onto mine.

"Oh no, I've got business with you."

"Me? What did I do?" I asked, raising my hands defensively.

"I flipped you, and you flipped me. I don't like draws!" Melena snapped.

We faced each other from opposite ends of the tavern. Michael stood off to the side, clearly amused.

"Uh oh, you've hurt her pride, Wallace," Michael said with a scoff.

I turned toward Melena, flashing a sarcastic grin.

"I don't know what you're talking about. I just saw you slip on some old oil. That wasn't me," I said, laughing.

Melena pulled an iron dagger from her belt and pointed it at me.

"I challenge you to a duel. A duel to the death!" she shouted.

Michael raised an eyebrow at us both.

"Yeah, yeah, you know the rules. Nothing that'll hurt too badly. Just tap or pin," he sighed, pulling out a small lute from his back.

"Funny thing is, I'm stronger than the two of you right now."

"Shut it!" I snapped at him.

"You wouldn't be able to beat me without your stupid needles. Fight me with honor, you wretch," Michael shot back.

"Honor? You mention cheating every time you fight," Melena cut in, glaring at me like she meant to bury that dagger.

"I accept your challenge, witch. Brace yourself," I said proudly.

Michael lifted his hands.

"I'll tell you when to start."

I looked into Melena's icy blue eyes. She stood with one knee forward, knife low by her waist. My palms were sweating, but I knew what I had to do. She was stronger. She was faster. So I had to be smarter. Going hand-to-hand would be a foolish mistake.

"Look around," I muttered, my eyes scanning the bar for something—anything-I—I could use.

"Go!" Michael shouted.

Like feral wolves, Melena and I sprinted toward each other. But just before we closed the distance, I glanced up at the ceiling—at the chandelier.

With only seconds to act, I hurled a syringe toward it, just missing the rope that held it barely in place. The second it left my hand, both twins went pale.

We all knew that chandelier was hanging by a thread—old, rusted, ready to drop with a sneeze. They looked at me like I was ready to kill her.

I charged forward. Melena, distracted by the syringe, didn't react in time. I grabbed her knife hand and shoved it away from her body. Her eyes snapped to me, and I felt her strength kick in, trying to force the blade toward my chest.

But she wasn't quick enough.

With my free hand, I pulled out another empty syringe and pressed it close to her neck, just a hair from breaking skin.

"Dead!" Michael and I shouted in unison.

I let go of her arms and pulled the syringe back.

Melena's face twisted from panic to pure fury.

"You scared me to death, you jerk!" she yelled. "I thought you were going to crush me with that thing!"

"You've been defeated, vile witch. Go back to the hell from which you came," I said, grinning.

Before I could step away, she grabbed my shirt collar and yanked me back toward her. Her grin was wide, wild—eyes locked deep into mine.

"One of these days I'm going to gut you and…"

Just then, a few soft notes plucked from a lute filled the air.

Melena's eyes went blank. She let go of me and stumbled backward.

"Screw you," she mumbled, before dropping face-first to the floor.

Her snoring filled the room, loud enough to assure us she was down for the count.

"I love that spell. I'm doing it anytime she looks like she's about to throw a tantrum," Michael said.

"When did you even learn that?" I asked.

"I've got my secrets. And you should be thanking me," he replied.

"I could've handled it myself," I muttered. "Just let her yell a bit. She would've gotten over it."

Michael looked at me, let his shoulders drop, and sighed.

"I'm afraid, Wallace... I have terrible news. Because I love you both so much, I must ensure that all my gifts are shared equally."

Before I could say a word or take a step back, he strummed two strings on his lute.

The spell hit me like a boulder. My body turned to lead. My knees buckled. My head spun.

The last thing I saw was his smug, self-satisfied grin as the world dissolved around me.

"You're both dead. I win, as always," he chuckled.

And then everything went black.

Chapter 14

As the months dragged on, my room filled up with notes and books. It was small, just enough space for a drawer, a desk, and a bed, but not much else. Kreila at least gave me the courtesy of a decent cotton chair, knowing I'd be buried in books for the rest of my life.

With a few extra copper, I was able to buy another pair of glasses, just in case I threw them across the wall after reading more books about test tubes and mage burners. That, or if twins broke them, which they often did.

One spring morning, I woke up to the rich, dark aroma of black coffee.

"Oh Gods," I mumbled.

Kreila didn't drink coffee often. She said it made her jittery. According to her, the only time she touches the stuff is when something big is going down, like an important day or a test.

I rolled out of bed and threw on my plague uniform. Same black leather I've been wearing for years. Then I jogged downstairs and found Kreila standing near the front desk, dressed in a blue and white dress. She had that familiar grin on her face, the kind that made you think she knew something you didn't.

I walked up and looked up at her towering figure.

"What's going on?" I asked.

"Well, you're supposed to start the day with a good morning," she replied with her usual sarcasm.

"Good morning," I muttered.

"Today is a test day, Wallace. I want to see how well you've remembered everything we've talked about."

"But you didn't give me time to study, ma'am."

"No, I didn't. And that's how it goes!" She chuckled.

I glanced outside. A bunch of the neighbors were gathered in the square, laughing and clearly gossiping about something.

"Okay, ma'am. What do I need to do?"

"Today, Wallace, I'm a ghost," she said with that devilish grin of hers. "I want you to run the shop this morning. I'll be right here, reading a book and listening in on how you handle things."

She paused, then added, "Don't be scared, Wallace. I'll help you if you need it."

My face went pale, and my hands started to shake. I'd never been given a test like this before. Sure, I had been studying like Kreila asked, but I wasn't ready to take one this soon, especially not on actual patients.

What if I messed up? What if I forgot the wrong herb or used the wrong dose? What if someone actually needed help, and I couldn't do it?

"Okay," I mumbled.

She leaned in and patted my head.

"You can do it. I believe in you."

"Gods," I whispered under my breath.

Before I could say anything else, she walked to the front door and shut it behind her.

I glanced out the window and watched her stroll over to the elderly crowd of neighbors. Kreila started laughing, tossing her head back as she joined their gossip. After a few more laughs, she turned and made her way back to the shop. When she came inside, she slid into a chair by the desk and pulled out one of her romance novels.

I could never tell what she was reading. All I knew was that she loved romance, and I wasn't old enough to touch her collection.

"Um," I murmured, but her eyes were locked on the pages.

I turned back to the window and spotted one of the neighbors walking toward the shop. The whole elderly crowd stared at him as he approached, laughter following him like a trail.

"Oh gods. I get it now," I said aloud.

The door slammed open, and a gust of wind blew in behind him. His gut strained against his tunic, and his matted brown beard stuck out like it hadn't seen a comb in days. He waved a handkerchief in the air and pointed straight at me.

"Oi, doctor! I need your help!"

It was Allen, one of the neighbors' sons. He worked at the bakery down the road, but you'd think he ate everything he baked. He'd once told me he had a background in acting, and I was starting to believe it as he hacked dramatically into his handkerchief.

I looked over at Kreila. She was still reading her book, smiling like this was her favorite chapter.

Allen pointed again, louder this time. "You're the doctor, right?!"

"Uh, um," I stuttered.

"I don't see anyone else here, you fool!" he barked.

Kreila's smile widened.

A flicker of irritation flashed through me. I didn't have time to play clown for this whole village. I reached for my dark syringe and summoned a small pool of ooze into my hand, shaping it into a bird mask. Ducking under the desk, I grabbed some lavender and stuffed it into the mask. Then I grabbed a chair and stepped around the corner.

"Have a seat, sir," I said, my lavender-scented mask in place.

The wooden chair creaked under him, groaning along with the floorboards. His shirt looked more like a rag soaked in spit than clothing. Sweat poured down his face, and his nose dripped like a broken tap—though underneath all that, his flushed skin gave him away.

"What's your name, sir?" I asked.

"Uh, Thomas… yeah, Thomas!"

I grinned. Fake names were apparently part of this performance, and Allen was all in.

"What's going on, sir?"

"Can't you see I'm covered in snot and spit?! Do something, you—" He cut himself off and lowered his voice. "Young man," he added, suddenly polite.

I hesitated, the glass vial in my fingers trembling just slightly. Was it cold in here, or was I nervous? I pulled a small syringe from my belt. The glass vial was marked with colored indicators for different illnesses. As I walked toward him, he grimaced.

"You trying to stab me with that thing?!" he shouted.

I needed to triage him fast, and distraction was my best shot. My eyes darted to the window beside us, which faced the neighborhood square.

"Oh, I didn't know it was their birthday. Where did they get the cake?" I muttered.

Just like I hoped, he turned his head, squinting out the window at food that didn't exist.

With his attention elsewhere, I gave his right arm a quick, light poke and drew a drop of blood.

"Mother f—!" he yelled, catching himself before he cursed again in front of a child.

I shook the vial and waited for the liquid and blood to mix. Within seconds, the mixture turned a bright lime green.

"Which one is this?" I mumbled.

I walked away from the man and jogged behind the desk. Pulling open Kreila's medical book, I felt the weight of its old leather cover, worn smooth from decades of use. Inside, the first page displayed a rainbow of colors, each tied to a diagnosis and reference page.

"A basic cold," I muttered.

"What in God's name are you doing over there?! Come fix me!" the man shouted, followed by a loud, wet sneeze.

"I just have to ask a few questions before I can make your medicine, sir!"

I returned to him, book in hand, flipping through its pages for the right cure.

"When did this start, sir?"

"Uhm," he stalled.

I glanced over my shoulder. Kreila, still buried in her book, held up two fingers without looking up.

"Yeah—two days," the man said quickly.

"Does anyone else you know have this too?"

"Nope. I just got done mining ice minerals."

"Okay, I'll be back to make your potion. Just wait here!"

I jogged off toward the laboratory, eager to get started. Behind me, I heard the deliberate steps of Kreila's tall frame. She leaned against the doorway, still reading, eyes never leaving the page.

"Okay, cold, it's a cold. It's simple," I mumbled.

I turned to the book for guidance. Just ginger root, mint, and chamomile, all mixed into the standard tonic base used for most potions.

I gathered the ingredients quickly, Kreila's eyes trailing me as I moved around the room. I dropped the plants into the black pestle and started crushing them into a fine powder. The smell was exactly what you'd expect, but the chamomile was strong. Too strong.

I glanced back and caught Kreila smirking with quiet amusement.

"Did I do it right?" I asked.

She said nothing, just returned her gaze to her book.

I poured the powder into a beaker with the tonic. The mixture turned a pale orange. Carefully, I set it on a stand above a red stone placed on an iron plate. Taking a deep breath, I leaned in and exhaled onto the stone. At once, it glowed bright orange and began to radiate heat from its core. A flame sparked to life, licking the bottom of the beaker.

After only a few moments, I grabbed the beaker with iron tongs and slowly poured the potion into a glass bottle. The mixture needed just a touch of heat to be complete. I sealed the bottle and walked it over to the customer.

"About time!" he groaned, snatching it from my hand.

"Please drink it."

Before I could finish, the man downed the whole bottle in one go. He let out a thunderous burp that echoed through the room, then sighed deeply.

"Give it a few hours to kick in. For now, you need to get some rest," I said gently.

After a few moments, I looked over at the man. His eyes were starting to close, slowly and heavily. He tried to stand, but his body sagged, and his voice dropped to a sluggish mumble.

"Did he mess up?" he muttered, like he'd just downed a dozen beers.

"What's wrong, sir?" I whimpered.

"What the hell did you put in this, lad? I feel like I'm going past."

My mind snapped into focus. I hurled a syringe to the floor, summoning an invisible servant—just in time. The man swayed forward and began to fall, but the servant caught him inches above the ground.

"Oh gods!" I yelled.

I turned to Kreila. She inhaled deeply—then burst into laughter that echoed through the entire shop.

"What did I do?!" I shouted.

Still laughing, Kreila walked over and dropped another syringe to the floor. Within seconds, Allen began hovering toward the inpatient room, slowly drifting as if carried by a breeze.

"He's a heavy one. He'll need two," she said with a chuckle.

Then she leaned down toward me with a smirk.

"Where to begin, I wonder... Oh! Let's start with the obvious. You needed the potion to be mostly mint and ginger, with just a pinch of chamomile. But what do you make? That was mint and ginger running for their lives from a tidal wave of chamomile," she said, grinning widely.

"You also should've let the potion simmer a little longer before serving it. And most importantly—never let a patient snatch a potion from you. They're supposed to sip it, not chug it like a drunk at a festival night."

I looked down, embarrassed.

"But," she added, her tone softening, "you technically passed. You cured his cold, triaged him properly, and caught your mistake before it turned into a real problem. I'll give you a 'B.' It's a start!"

I gave a light chuckle as a smile crept across my face.

"Thanks, professor!" I shouted.

"Don't thank me yet. That was part one of the exam. Part two is where things get interesting!"

"Wait, what do you mean?" I asked.

She stood up and walked to the door. As she opened it, she glanced toward the center of the neighborhood and shouted, "Guards!"

I turned to the front window and froze.

Captain Towsin was being carried by his son, Private Howard. Both of them were drenched in what looked like pig's blood, or maybe soup, stumbling toward the shop in full panic. Kreila calmly returned to her seat by the counter as I stood at the window, stunned by what looked like a battlefield rescue.

Then came the dreadful kick of reality.

"Help! My dad got bitten by a red dragon!" Howard shouted.

The claim was ridiculous. A red dragon that size wouldn't bite the captain, it'd eat him whole. If he only lost an arm, that'd be a miracle.

I dropped a syringe and summoned my servant.

"Bring him in! This way!" I barked.

"Is the dragon still out there?" I shouted, trying to break the illusion and maybe escape the test.

"Uh, no! I killed it myself!" Howard said, his voice a mess of panic and pride.

I glanced at the captain's face just in time to see a subtle grin. He was in on it.

As I led them to the clinic bed, Kreila followed behind us, still buried in her book, though I could hear her snickering. She kept the book held high, shielding her smile.

I helped the captain onto the bed and began triaging him. He wore his standard white-and-green captain's armor, steel plating and all— but his left sleeve was rolled up to the elbow. The rest of the arm and hand were soaked in red stains that reeked of fruit.

"He got his arm torn off! We need to stop the bleeding!" Howard stammered.

I rushed to the other side of the room, flinging open the medical cabinet in search of a belt to use as a tourniquet.

Behind me, I heard Kreila giggle.

"Oh no, it's gone! Looks like you'll have to make one," she chuckled.

I paused, scanning the room for a cloth to turn into a tourniquet. Then I remembered—I was wearing a belt.

Without wasting a second, I yanked it off and rushed to the captain's bedside.

A groan echoed from across the room. My other patient was starting to wake up.

"What's going on?" Allen muttered.

"Shut up, I'm working!" I snapped.

Suddenly, the captain turned his head away from me, his shoulders trembling. His son did the same, both trying and failing to keep straight faces. The captain let out a loud, uncontrollable laugh, his whole body shaking on the bed.

I glanced over at Kreila. She had turned away, too, clearly trying to stifle her laughter.

"Sorry, doctor," Allen mumbled behind me.

"Ow, ow, ow—my arm!" the captain groaned, finally regaining his composure.

I got back to work, wrapping my belt around his upper arm, just above where I figured the injury would've been. I pulled hard to tighten it—earning a grunt from the captain that quickly turned into more muffled laughter.

Then I grabbed one of my syringes and jabbed it into his arm. It was a wound-healing shot, meant to stop bleeding fast. But I knew if no real wound was present, it wouldn't do much.

I paused, thinking through my next move. Then I remembered, I needed to ask questions. Look for details. Observe.

I began patting the captain down, adjusting and lifting parts of his armor to check for any other fruit-stained wounds.

"Was he hit anywhere else? Burns, bites, anything?"

"No, just had the arm slashed off by the red dragon's claws!"

"Was it a bite or a claw?" I asked.

"Uh… I think it was the bite!"

"You're a lucky one," I told the captain.

I kept checking him over, but didn't find any injuries beyond the fake arm wound. Assuming the bleeding had stopped, I gave him another healing syringe and wrapped his arm in fresh bandages.

I raised my hands above my head. "And now we let him get bed rest and make sure he doesn't die."

"Fair enough. The scene is complete," Kreila said, snapping her book shut.

The captain sat up immediately. "Not bad, Wallace. I didn't die, I don't think!"

"Thank you, sir. Please don't fight any more dragons."

"I sure hope not," he said with a laugh.

The captain and his son both patted me on the back. Allen stood up too, stretching his arms with a groan.

"Better nap than I usually get, I suppose."

Kreila pulled out a small copper hand and extended it toward the performers.

"Nonsense, that was fun, Kreila," the captain said, handing her my belt. His son nodded in agreement.

Allen walked over too.

"I'm not a charity. I asked for two copper."

Kreila reached into her pouch and placed the coins in his hand. He rolled them around between his fingers, then turned to me.

He handed me one of the coins. "Use it to make better-tasting drinks!" he said with a wink.

The three of them walked out the front door, and I turned back to Kreila, who was already buried in her book again.

"I'd give that a B," she said. "You handled it pretty well. Just remember to find ways to comfort both patients. You also need to numb the pain before the panic sets in. Numbing the pain was a step you missed."

I nodded, fully focused, so focused that I didn't realize my pants had dropped to the floor.

Kreila turned around, saw me, and burst into laughter.

"Taking your belt off was clever. I didn't think you'd actually do that!"

Embarrassed, I yanked my pants back up and fastened them with the belt. Kreila leaned down and gently patted my head.

"You did great, Wallace. I'm proud of you."

"Thanks, ma'am. You taught me well. I'll be like you in no time!"

"Oh, please. If you want to be like me, you'll need more charisma, better fashion sense, and enough sarcasm to fill a fortress." She giggled.

"I'll get there sooner than you think. Who's to say I don't already have it nailed?"

She gasped. "Gods, that sounds exactly like me. Go to your room." I refuse to look into a mirror with legs.

"Who's to say you aren't already looking into a mirror, ma'am?"

"Wallace!" she shouted.

Chapter 15

The day after my acting exam, Kreila decided to take me to the market with her. The town square was filled with colorful tents and wagons offering everything from wine to exotic pets. The people there were usually kind, as long as you were willing to buy something. Since I never had any money, they typically left me alone. Kreila, on the other hand, was well known. Every few feet, someone would wave or greet her warmly.

The market wasn't crowded. Kreila only visited shops that weren't too busy; she didn't like large crowds. As we walked, she told me to stay close and keep a hand on my waist in case of pickpockets. I found this amusing, she didn't know what the twins and I used to do for fun. She seemed innocent, but I knew better. Kreila could drop a gang of thieves without breaking a sweat.

A young elf stepped out from the side of a wooden building and approached us, taking Kreila's hand.

"Hello, Mrs. Kreila! How have you been?" he asked.

"Oh, I'm doing well, young man, but who are you?!" she chuckled, clearly confused.

The elf turned from Kreila and looked directly at me.

His eyes were a bright teal that caught me off guard. It felt like he was staring straight through my soul, as if he were searching for someone he knew. There was something comforting about the way elves smiled and spoke. Their voices had a natural elegance. His brown skin and black curly hair contrasted beautifully with his green hood and brown tunic.

"Walter, right?" he asked.

Kreila stepped between us.

"Can you please tell me who you are before asking any more questions? I'm only here for herbs and nothing else."

As she positioned herself between me and the elf, I noticed her long sleeves shift. Her fingers curled inward, and just barely, I caught sight of the tip of a syringe.

"Oh, Mrs. Kreila, I do apologize. I forgot to introduce myself!" He stepped back slightly.

I glanced toward the alley behind him. It was empty except for a lone drunkard at the far end, who seemed completely absorbed with a piece of bread.

"It's me, Mrs. Kreila, Thomas! Don't you remember me?"

"Um, no, I'm afraid I don't. If you don't mind, we'll be on our way. Please take care."

She began to pull me away, but we didn't get far.

"I heard you killed a poacher for taking out a family of bear cubs. Don't you remember?"

In an instant, he was beside Kreila, whispering something into her ear.

Kreila froze. Her eyes widened and her jaw dropped. But just as quickly, her expression changed. A warm smile appeared on her face.

"Oh, Thomas, I remember now! I nearly forgot it was you," she laughed, though her laughter softened quickly into concern. "Where are your parents, Thomas? They'll be worried sick about you," she murmured.

"We were in the area, and I wanted to meet Walter! I heard you took in an apprentice," he said, circling around her to look me in the face.

I knew elves lived longer than humans, but this boy seemed about my age, just a bit taller.

"Hi, Walter. I'm Thomas," he said, extending his hand.

I shook it. "It's Wallace, but nice to meet you, Timothy!"

Thomas grinned. "I'm not good with names either!"

He pulled me toward him. For a moment, I thought he was reaching for a syringe, but instead, he embraced me in a hug.

"Your mom is the greatest!" he laughed.

"Mom?" I gasped. The word hit harder than I expected.

Just then, the drunkard at the end of the alley started coughing loudly. I looked over. He wore a green hood and had a white beard. His skin looked dark, but the shadows hid most of his face.

"Oh, I've got to go now," Thomas said. "But my dad would love to see you two someday. No need to hide in that shop for too long, Grandma!" he added with a chuckle.

Kreila leaned down and embraced him.

"You run along and tell your father I said hello."

She turned to the alley, facing the hooded man, and waved. The man waved back.

Thomas ran down the alleyway toward him, waving goodbye to me as he went.

Kreila and I turned back toward the market.

"Who was that?" I asked.

"I have an old family friend whose father knew my husband and me. I don't see him often, but when I do, I appreciate the time we spend together. They're good people. I just wish I could see them in better shape."

"What do you mean by that?"

She hesitated. "His family has been struggling with...money and getting their house fixed."

Her tone lingered on "money," like it wasn't the whole story.

"Oh wow, that's rough. But they seemed nice. I'd love to learn more about him."

She smiled as we turned a corner. "I'll tell you some stories when we get home."

But I could tell she was already choosing which ones not to tell.

We spent the rest of the day buying bottles and supplies for the store. Most of it was boring, but walking through the herbalist shops was a blessing. The air was a clash of fruit and flower aromas, each scent battling for control of our senses. It was incredible. Kreila picked herbs that could recreate that same clash in a warm, soothing tea.

We returned to the shop before sundown, and I helped her organize the herbs in the pantry.

As night approached, I helped her cook, chopping carrots and onions for the stew. Kreila loved making stew. She always said it wasn't hard to make, and once you learned to do it well, you could do it well every time. When the pot was finally left to boil, she sat me down at the table so we could watch it together.

"Glad you grew up in Elton today and not years ago. This city used to be hell, just alleys and broken roads."

"It's always seemed like that to me," I replied, with the same sarcasm I inherited from her.

"Did you read the books about the Bear Wars, Wallace? I might've misplaced it around here somewhere."

I had it in my room, buried under Burners, Beakers, Bottles, and elven herbology.

"I do wish I had a more entertaining book for you to read, but those two are the easiest of them all, I'm afraid."

The books Kreila had me read as her apprentice ranged from fascinating to sleep-inducing. They weren't all bad, but most were just mediocre. Still, I'd take reading Elvish potion-making over begging for coins any day.

Kreila never explained why I needed to know so much history. Maybe it had something to do with the people she met on her trips; nobles, merchants, sometimes even cloaked figures who whispered in languages I didn't recognize. Whatever the reason, she insisted I memorize timelines and rituals, as if my future would one day depend on them.

Kreila taught me the basic history of the continent. The dozens of old gods who ruled the world from above and below. They waged war on each other across the four realms for centuries until an unknown being called the Cataclysm nearly killed them all. The survivors united and destroyed the Cataclysm together. Ever since then, only two true-blooded gods remained: Ezella, goddess of nature, and Urus, god of death.

The new gods were created from whatever organs, blood, and limbs were left by Ezella and Urus. Now the realms live in peace, each balancing the other. Everyone on the continent marks history by the years before or after the Cataclysm.

Her question about the Bear Wars must have triggered something.

Sometimes I wondered if that story was a warning more than a lesson.

The books told me about the history of the Kingdom of Eltonia, how the Eltons, descendants of their demigod ancestor, came to be. He was a powerful druid on his mother's side. The goddess of nature had cursed the family after being insulted by one of their own. As punishment, she impregnated their bloodline and marked them with a sigil resembling a bear. From that point on, every member of the Elton family was born with a bear-shaped birthmark.

They ruled the kingdom for centuries, though not all were noble. Some were mediocre, others cruel or outright deplorable.

Over two hundred years ago, the neighboring Paljavan Empire tried to reclaim its lost territory by opening a vortex to hell. Their goal was to control the demons and use them in war, but the project failed. Instead, an uncontrollable army of demons spilled out and tore the continent apart.

The kingdom wasn't prepared. Desperate, they hired warlords to help defend the country.

It was a bloody struggle. Eventually, the Church of Light led a crusade with an army of heroes to close the vortex. Though they failed to seal it completely, they weakened it enough to stop many demons from crossing over. This gave the Kingdom of Eltonia and the surrounding nations a chance to fight back. They launched counteroffensives and reclaimed their land.

But victory came at a cost. The kingdom was bankrupt. They couldn't afford to pay their army, let alone the thousands of mercenaries who wanted nothing more than coin to return home and rebuild their lives.

That's when Lord Darius, armed with immortality, a power sword, and an army of loyal mercenaries, decided to overthrow the kingdom and wipe out the Eltons. Many warlords joined his cause, and in less than two months, the kingdom fell. Nearly all of the Eltons were slaughtered, with only a few escaping to the elven kingdom on the kingdom's border.

Darius then crowned himself king and married Verona, who was also immortal, though for reasons no one truly understood. The newly crowned King Darius claimed his immortality came from a genie—a powerful wish-granting demon, but he never confirmed whether Verona's gift came from the same source.

He ruled for over a hundred years, until sixty-two years ago, when Kendrick Elton returned with a new army and rose against him. Kendrick's return to power only became possible after a massive tsunami wiped out most of Darius's forces, including his descendants.

Legends say Darius had somehow angered the ocean goddess. Once Darius and Kendrick met on the battlefield, Kendrick quickly overpowered him and dragged his unconscious body to a river. Witnesses claimed Darius was swallowed whole by a sea monster—what scholars now believe to be the largest beast ever recorded.

He has never been seen again.

Victorious, the new King Kendrick reclaimed his throne and tried to reassemble parliament to help govern the kingdom. But Verona still lived, and so did the corrupt lords and power gangs who had practically run the country for over a century. For the past sixty-two years, almost every law, every funded project, every idea the king has proposed has been shut down by parliament.

One of those ideas was ending slavery. The practice had only been legalized during the demonic war, yet Darius kept it in place long after the demons vanished. The slave lords and corrupt businesses adored him for it. Even worse, Kendrick's family became targets. Assassinations happened left and right, and his only son was murdered, leaving his wife and remaining family devastated. These days, the king and his family hide in their marble palace, rarely making public appearances anymore.

"Thomas and his family used to work for the king as rat catchers and cleaners," Kreila said. "But they were let go after the king grew paranoid. He started firing anyone he couldn't trust completely. I can't blame him. He's lost almost everything."

She sat up to stir the pot, then placed two teacups on the table. From her sleeves, she pulled two syringes and squeezed them above the cups, filling them with warm water.

"Can I do lemon?"

"Of course you can."

She pulled out two teabags and placed them into the cups. The earthy scent of lemon blended beautifully with the smell of fresh vegetables.

"I used to be an adventurer," she said, "traveled all across Eltonia to the far west in Reylan. I've been everywhere. Lucky for me, I started my journey after that warp closed."

Her voice softened when she mentioned Reylan. There was something more in those memories.

The Paljavan Empire eventually became the Paljavan Republic and rebuilt its country. Here in the Kingdom of Eltonia, we had the sea to the west and two neighbors to the east: the Paljavan Republic, ruled by its angelic monarch and her army of clockwork men, and the Tylvan Union, home to bickering elves, dwarves, and fey.

The only country Kreila ever seemed interested in was the Panard Republic. The Panards were a nation of mages, ruled by mages. She told me the wisest people she'd ever met lived in their massive universities and churches.

After dinner, we walked upstairs to our rooms. Mine was across the hall from hers. Her room was filled with plants, robes, and a large bed. Mine had a small bed, a desk, and a modest bookcase. The shelves held books about epic dwarves, along with some dry tomes on herbology and vampire science. It wasn't much, but it was still a palace compared to the streets.

We got ready for bed.

"Did you hear Thomas call you my mom? I don't look anything like you."

"You're about thirteen, Wallace. I would've had to give birth to you at…" She paused. "I almost revealed my age. Never mind. Get some rest, Wallace."

"Yes, Mom," I groaned, putting as much sass into it as I could.

"Call me that again and you'll be cleaning the house—alone."

"Gods, you sound like my mother," I muttered.

But something about hearing Thomas say it had stuck with me.

Just then, I heard a thump against the wall. I turned to see a dull syringe nailed into the wood, just an inch from the back of my head.

"Sorry!"

Chapter 16

The twins and I were still planning our heist with the Guard Captain's daughter. Michael had secured a few outings with her and even claimed he got a kiss on the cheek. Meanwhile, Melena had managed to snag a layout of the captain's patrol routes and noted an upcoming ceremony at the castle that both the captain and his wife were set to attend. If we timed our heist during that event—while Michael was out on his date—the house would be completely empty.

The only thing left was a mage bag. It's a magical pouch that can carry heavy items without changing size. Twenty gold bricks would raise suspicion if we carried them in a regular bag or box. But in a mage bag?

They'd look like nothing more than a basic coin purse. And more importantly, we could be in and out before anyone knew we were there. Optional or not, Michael had also thrown in some extra requests: fancy gifts like roses and cologne. I'd been thinking about how I'd get those. They weren't hard to find, but considering we were targeting rich folks, we had to smell like them too.

Still, the weight of what we were doing wasn't lost on me. One mistake, and we'd all be locked up or worse.

I headed down to the old man's pickle store for a quick bite. After stealing from old man Wallace for so long, I'd somehow grown a craving for his vegetables. The best part? I actually had a bit of coin this time—no need to swipe anything. Not that I couldn't; I was still quick and slick enough to pull it off if I felt like it.

Same soggy storefront as always: faded, dark wood, a steady crowd passing by. The market air was thick with spice and smoke, with vendors shouting over one another to grab a sale. Baskets of fruit, bolts of dyed cloth, fish laid out on stone; everything felt chaotic but alive.

But this time, the old man wasn't at the counter. Instead, it was a teenager named Hannah. I'd seen her around before, helping out, but never working the place solo. For a second, I got worried about old man Wallace. As much as the idiot annoyed me, I'd hate to see him down bad. I walked up to the table with a smile.

"Hi, Hannah, how's it going?" I asked.

"Hey, Wallace. All's good over here," she said with a yawn. She looked tired.

Her ginger hair and freckles were hard to miss. You could tell her family had been struggling for a while. She always wore the same three outfits: a brown dress, a tan apron, and sandals. I thought about helping them out more than once. But truth be told, I wasn't that far from where they were. Kreila's shop barely broke even most months, and when it did turn a profit, it wasn't much. That's when Blackwood would step in—buying in bulk and tipping Kreila real generous.

"How's old man Wallace?" I asked.

"He's okay. Just hurt his leg recently. He's on bed rest for a bit until it heals," she replied.

Finally, something I could actually help with.

"I never mentioned this, but I'm working with Kreila, the witch doctor over on the east side of town. If you'd like, I could take a look at him," I said, a little more excited than I meant to sound.

"I don't see why not. He's inside—not far from the door. I'll let him know you're coming."

She turned around and hollered loud enough to wake the dead.

"Gramps! Wallace the kid is coming in!"

"Who the hell is Wallace?!" he shouted back.

"You'll know him when you see him!"

She waved me toward the entrance. I walked past the table and followed her to the house. The place reminded me of the old tavern— rotting walls, a small hole in the corner, and tables cluttered with jars and vegetables. There was a faint, damp smell, like mildew mixed with vinegar. I felt bad for them. The old man deserved better.

"Oh, hello, Wallace number two!" the old man said joyfully.

"Hello, Wallace number one!" I shot back with a grin.

I glanced down at his leg. His pale skin was red and swollen.

"I'm here to help. Let me take a look," I said, full of confidence.

I knelt down and pulled out a syringe to administer the cure.

"Oh no, I don't like those stupid needles, young man!" he snapped.

I knew this game—Kreila taught me the trick.

"Gods! That's a huge rat!" I shouted, pointing to a corner of the room.

He spun around so fast you'd think he planned on eating the thing.

"Ow!" the old man yelped as I jabbed the syringe into his leg and injected the medicine.

"See? That wasn't so bad, Wallace number one!" I said with a grin.

"You crazy doctors and your stupid—"

Before he could finish the sentence, his leg started deflating a bit, and the angry red turned to a soft pink.

"Well then... you mages aren't all that bad. It's feeling better. Not perfect—but better. You're the one exception on the garbage list I have for mages."

"I'll bring some oil you can rub on it to help the swelling go down. But once I do, you've gotta add Kreila to your exception list. She's the one who taught me everything."

"Sounds like a deal. How much do I owe you?"

I knew I needed the money, but then I thought back to all the times I'd stolen from him. Even when he gave me stuff for free, it was a loss on his end.

"Put me and Mrs. Kreila on the exception list, and that's payment enough, sir," I said with a chuckle.

"Thanks, son. I appreciate it. Tell Hannah to give you a jar, I insist."

I didn't want the jar for free, but I could already tell he wasn't going to drop it. The old man was stubborn like that.

"You don't need to do that, but sure—I'll take one."

I waved him goodbye and made my way back to the table with Hannah. I scanned the jars and picked out one filled with pickled radishes.

"Three copper, Wallace," Hannah said.

"Here, take this." I handed her a silver coin.

"Wallace, that's three times the price," she whispered, careful not to draw attention.

"Your old man was gonna bug me until I took one. I didn't want him paying for the legwork, so consider this a tip—and a middle finger to his idea of paying me. He's a good man. Good people get treated at a discount or free."

She walked around the table and gave me a hug.

"Thanks, Wallace. We appreciate it," Hannah said.

As I stepped away, a familiar scent of roasted nuts wafted in from a nearby vendor. The memory hit me, years ago, when I had nothing. I used to watch that same man close up shop and sneak leftovers into alley shadows for strays.

I'd been one of those strays. Now I was buying pickles and healing old men. The contrast made my head spin.

I waved her goodbye and headed back to the store.

The street narrowed near Kreila's, the air a little cooler in the shade of the taller buildings. A kid zipped by with a kite, and the wind carried bits of laughter behind him. For a moment, it all felt... normal. Like this, life might actually be mine.

It was midday, and I could already hear Barron's booming voice echoing from inside. When I stepped through the door, there he was—tall and imposing in his usual black and white robes. His presence hit me like a wall. It always did. Made me feel like he could crush me without blinking... or like I was safe for the first time in my life.

But there was always a flicker of something else too, a weird knot in my chest. Did he think of me like a son... or just a stray Kreila picked up? And what did it mean that he cared so much? Was it love or a leash?

He turned toward me, and behind the desk stood Kreila.

"Well, isn't it just the man I was hoping to see!" Barron chuckled.

He leaned down and patted me on the head.

"Kreila tells me you've been doing well in your studies. Said something about all B's."

I nodded, proud.

He turned back to her with a smirk.

"You gotta reward the boy for his work, Abigail. What've you given him?"

"Good food and a room—that's all a boy needs," Kreila laughed, laced with sarcasm.

"I'm a grandfather, Kreila. Three sons, five grandkids. I know how to raise and teach kids," Barron said. "And Wallace deserves a reward for his accomplishments. That kind of recognition makes a kid want to do more. You've been teaching him for two years—if I'd known that sooner, I would've been bringing him gifts since day one."

He looked over at me with a grin. "Guess I'll have to make up for lost time!"

"Barron, you don't need to spend the money. I can get—" Kreila started.

"Abigail, please," he cut in. "I could buy this whole block several times over—you know that. And besides, I'm investing in Wallace's future. It'd be my honor."

I wanted to laugh and fist-pump and yell, but part of me just stood there, unsure. Why me? Why now? Could I really be worth all this? Or was he just making me into something he needed me to be?

However, I couldn't stop smiling. My cheeks were ready to split.

"Really? Where are we going?" I asked.

"How about I take you all shopping at the market? And if the theater's open, we'll catch a show after," Barron offered.

"That would be amazing! Kreila, please, can we go?!" I said, buzzing with excitement.

"That sounds fine, Barron. When do you want to go?" Kreila asked.

"Right now. I'm just as excited as the boy. You've gotta spoil kids, Abigail," he said, handing her a gold coin. "Close up shop for the day—let's head out. Sound like a plan?"

"Very well. I'm ready when you are. No one's come in today besides you anyway," she said, slipping the coin into her pouch.

The joy in my face shot straight to my legs as I jumped and pumped my fist in the air.

"Hell yeah!" I shouted.

A loud slam hit the desk.

"Language, Wallace!" Kreila snapped.

"Sorry," I muttered, shrinking back as Barron cracked up behind me.

Chapter 17

The day was fantastic. We strolled through the city's colorful markets, crowded with tents and carts of every kind. Since Barron is a mage, he took us to some nearby magic schools and shops to grab a few gifts. I picked up a new bird's mask that repels liquid better, a pair of leather gloves enchanted to give me steady hands, new reading glasses, and some shoes that let me hover a little off the ground. Those boots came in clutch because Barron's big surprise was a steel broomstick. I could sit on it and fly. It was fast, easy to handle, and the boots gave me a bit of insurance in case I slipped off.

Kreila wasn't too sure about it at first. She frowned when Barron unveiled it, her arms folded tight, like she wasn't sure if it was a gift or a leash, but Barron said he would teach me how to use it if I needed help. Fortunately, she agreed to teach me instead.

We kept walking through the wild mix of market stalls. Elves sold herbs, dwarves dealt armor, and orcs showed off weapons. Voices rose in languages that weren't Paljavish, and that made some city folks uneasy. The Paljavan Empire once ruled the entire continent hundreds of years ago. When they held power, they forced everyone to speak Paljavish to tighten their control. Even with the Empire mostly destroyed, their language remains the most common across the continent.

This part of the day felt like a blur; colors, smells, people, and Barron, always knowing exactly where to go. This was also the best time of day to pick up tea supplies for Kreila. But the highlight? A halfling vendor selling magic goods had the exact thing the twins and I had been looking for: a mage bag.

Barron didn't even blink at the price. The vendor smiled like he'd won the lottery, and Barron paid in full without a word. He bought it on the spot, then handed me some extra cash to spend. Perfect for grabbing that cologne and flowers Michael could use.

Barron owns the Blackwood Caravan Company. He dealt in a wide range of goods traded from Eltonia to other countries. Whether it was liquor, lost animals, or weapons, Blackwood agreed to ship it—and even offered security if needed. He hired several mercenaries to guard both his cargo and his palace.

Barron was one of the wealthiest individuals in the country. That kind of money should have made him a target, but he always claimed he didn't need any escorts. That terrified me. I knew the Silent Auction would come after him in a heartbeat if they thought they had a chance. So if he was walking around alone, that meant he was stronger than he let on.

He'd told stories of fighting off bears and bandits with nothing but his trident and his bare hands. And I'd be a fool to think he was lying.

Later, Barron took us to watch some traveling performers in one of the city squares. Two halfling jugglers were dancing, their movements sharp and hypnotic. A half-elf stood behind them, somehow playing a lute and a flute at the same time. The flute was attached to his hat with thin wooden rods that bobbed as he moved.

Barron tipped the performers generously and then walked the three of us back to Kreila's shop.

Before leaving, he leaned down and patted me on the head.

"I look forward to seeing you grow and become a plague doctor like Kreila here. Maybe you'll even work for me someday. How does that sound?"

I nodded with glee. "I'd love that!"

Out of the corner of my eye, I saw Kreila's smile tighten, not her usual smirk, but the kind you give when your stomach's twisting and you don't want to show it. She didn't say anything, but her silence spoke louder than a dozen warnings.

He waved us goodbye and went on his way. As the door clicked shut, the room felt quieter, heavier. The echo of his presence seemed to linger like perfume that wouldn't wash off.

Kreila and I sat down for dinner, but I noticed a somber look on her face.

"What's wrong, Kreila?" I asked.

"Barron's a nice man, but he worries me sometimes. He's supposed to be as old as me, but he looks like he's barely in his fifties. The only way you can look like that is through expensive magic."

"So what? He's got the money for it, I'm sure," I replied.

"That's true, Wallace. But that kind of magic is often tied to darker things. I've healed him before, and with all the scars he has on his body, it's a miracle he's still standing."

"Well, he seems nice to me," I said.

"But there's another thing. He's been asking me to work for him on and off for the past fifteen years. A few times, he got irritated when I said no. One time, he even raised his voice, told me I was wasting my time here, and that he could make me rich working for him."

She looked down at her plate of potatoes and chicken. Her fork barely moved, like it weighed more than she could lift.

"When Steven died, Barron didn't wait long before trying to flirt with me. He bought me gifts, took me into town, and tried to charm me. I only ever saw him as a friend, but he wanted more. Not even a year had passed since Steven's death when he started trying to woo me. I told him over and over that I wasn't interested in romance. It felt disrespectful—to Steven, to me, to everything we had."

She didn't cry, but I could feel it in the air, that kind of sadness that presses down on your shoulders.

Whenever she brought up Steven, her whole mood shifted. Her tone got quieter. Her eyes, heavier.

Steven had been Kreila's husband for almost forty-five years. She told me stories about how they met, how he was a woodsman who once asked her to kill a bear that had been terrorizing the loggers.

Kreila, back then, was in her prime. She could have taken down a dozen bears without breaking a sweat. Killing one was a joke to her. But Steven didn't care. He insisted on showing her the way, cracking jokes, shielding her from hogs, and coming up with some ridiculous plan to take down the bear together.

Kreila had asked Steven why he was doing all of this. He told her he didn't want to see her get hurt.

When the mission ended, she turned down the payment, cracking a snide joke while laughing. "I'm Abigail Kreila, the kind," she said.

Steven grinned and shot back, "You're more like Abigail Kreila, the cute one."

She used to stop by his town—about two days from Elton—during her travels. Eventually, she started visiting just to see him. Then one day, Steven told her he loved her. He said he had been working overtime to buy her an expensive necklace.

Kreila was overjoyed and frustrated at the same time. She loved him too, and she was grateful for the gift. But it irritated her that he'd nearly worked himself into the ground to afford it, especially when she was far richer than he was.

A year later, he proposed. What followed was a joyful marriage that lasted forty-five years.

He insisted she keep her maiden name because she was famous. Even though she was fine with being called Abigail Anderson, he pushed back, and so she stayed Abigail Kreila.

I felt bad for her. I told her I wished I could've met him. But he had died five years ago—before the day I crashed through her window.

"I'm sorry to hear he did that," I said with a frown.

Kreila waved her hand. "Not to worry. He stopped eventually, and we became good friends. It's nice to see he cares about you, but there's a part of me that thinks he's slipping back into his old habits."

Something about the way she said it; quiet, cautious, sent a chill through me. I didn't know what scared her more, Barron's persistence or how hard he was to say no to.

Something inside me trembled. A deep sadness settled in my chest, heavy and quiet. What happened next wasn't even a thought—it was instinct.

I stood up from the table, walked around to her, and gave her the biggest hug I could.

"Hey now, I'm okay. You don't need to do that, boy," she said, giggling softly. There was sadness in her voice, but warmth too.

"I know. But it's the right thing to do. Just like you always told me."

I held her tighter, and in that moment, I wasn't just her apprentice, I was her family. And somehow, that meant more than anything Barron could ever give me.

She smiled and hugged me back, tight.

Chapter 18

The twins were set to begin the big heist tomorrow. I was anxious, and so were they. We knew this was going to be our biggest mission, but some details were still missing. Equipment? Information? I wasn't sure. A walk might clear my head.

I got dressed and made my way down the stairs, where Kreila sat behind her desk, scribbling notes.

"Good morning, Mrs. Kreila," I said, cheerful but still half-asleep.

"Good morning, Wallace. Breakfast is ready by the fireplace. I'll need your help with something once you're done."

"What do you need from me?"

"I'm worried about one of the neighbors, Allen. You remember him? The baker a few houses down. He's come down with something bad. I need you to gather supplies for me in the market," Kreila said with a sigh.

"What's going on with him?" I asked.

"He baked pies for his son's birthday. He made several attempts to get the perfect one. I think one of the pies he taste-tested was off or had spoiled fruit. His wife came early this morning, saying he could barely move. From what I can tell, there's something wrong with his kidney, and it looks severe."

I never realized Allen had a family. He wasn't around much, and when I saw him, he was always busy in his shop, too wrapped up in his work to talk. Still, his hands always smelled like cinnamon, and his apron was always dusted in flour. Lucky for him, that busyness meant he had plenty of customers coming back for more. Still, being around all that food could expose you to harmful stuff.

"What do you need from me?" I asked.

"Two things. First, go to the market and pick up a blaze flower. It's red and orange, looks like a flame. We've got one in the cabinets, but you should know it by now since we've used it before. Second, be ready at a moment's notice. I'm not sure when, but I may have to perform urgent care on him. I'm doing everything I can to avoid that, but I'm worried his family came to me too late." Kreila shook her head.

She looked tired. Not her usual kind of tired, but the kind that curled behind the eyes and clung to the shoulders.

"Because of his symptoms, I need you to stay close these next few days. I might need your help soon."

Kreila had me assist her during surgery plenty of times. Usually, I'd help her brew a potion fast or hold down a panicked patient. Most times it ended fine. Kreila rarely lost anyone in the shop. When someone did pass away—which was still rare—I was told to stay in my room and send a letter to the church to collect the remains.

"I'll eat and head to the market as soon as I can," I said, straightening up like a soldier on duty.

"Good. I'll manage things while you're gone. Just don't take too long, and stick to the main streets."

I nodded and walked to the kitchen. While I ate, the thought hit me—the heist was tomorrow. Kreila wanted me home for the next few days. The heist wasn't supposed to take long, and Kreila was skilled enough to manage herself, but the knot in my gut stayed where it was, tight and twisting. The twins and I had waited months for the captain and his family to all be out of the house. If Kreila needed me here, maybe things were worse than I thought.

I put on my plague garbs and made my way to the market outside the city wall. There, herbalists and traders sold ingredients, most of whom were travelers passing through.

I approached a trading area filled with dozens of tents. Each one held weapons, armor, charms, and carts selling drinks or medicine. I walked through the busy scene, careful not to bump into the traveling non-humans. Most of them knew this city wasn't friendly to outsiders, which made them jumpy and quick to react.

While moving through the crowd, something caught my eye. A carriage stood out, its dark, moldy wooden walls marked with a potion bottle painted on both sides. A plague doctor sat there, her head lowered, a cigar dangling from her hand. The smoke curled lazily in the air like it didn't care who saw it. Curious, I walked toward her.

"Hello?" I said as I approached. She jerked her head up and rose to her feet. Bells jingled from her attire as she moved. Her plague doctor gear looked worn, riddled with small holes and stained leather. The mask was tattered, and part of the beak was tearing away.

"Wait," I muttered under my breath.

"Hello, sir. Welcome to Doctor Professor Calem's traveling shop. You look like a young doctor who needs something to keep you sharp with all those books you're reading. I've got something for that, and something to clear your memory so you can treat patients better!"

She started juggling several vials of colorful liquids between her hands. One slipped, cutting her performance short.

"Have we met before?" I asked, recognizing the voice and the way she carried herself. It was Doctor Stanton, the con artist from years ago.

Of course, it was her.

"Nope, first time in town. I came from far out west looking to trade and help new folks!" Stanton said, clapping her hands together with her torn gloves.

"Can I ask you something about what you do? I'm trying to learn from doctors across the country, hoping to get advice for the future." I pointed to the wooden stools by her carriage. Both looked rotten.

"Oh, why of course, young one! Though my lessons are not free. Any good doctor can live on kindness alone, after all!" Stanton tilted her body slightly toward me, her voice dripping with the same charm I remembered.

"Here are two coppers. We can add to it if we talk long, but if you're honest, I'll give you five extra." I dug into my pocket and handed her two copper coins. She snatched them quickly from my hand.

"It's always a privilege. Yes, come have a seat and ask your questions." She settled onto one of the stools, hands resting on her knees, looking almost excited to talk.

I sat down behind her and drew a deep breath. All these years, I'd carried the thought of revenge. I wondered how many others she'd fooled with her fake potions. Once, I thought of giving her poison. Another time, I imagined stabbing her through the hand and watching her squirm. But age dulled those urges, and I figured I'd never see her again. Now, with her right here, the urge came crawling back. I fought it off, even as I pictured throwing acid on her carriage and watching it burn behind her. Still, I had questions.

"What made you want to become a doctor?" I asked quietly.

"That's an easy one. Helping people in need, traveling the continent for adventure, and reaching more folks to help!" she said, her voice lighting up with excitement.

"But who are you helping?"

"The people, of course, from the goodness of my heart." She said it like she was trying to convince herself more than me.

My hands clenched. I wanted to punch her, but I stopped. One more glance at her carriage and her ragged clothes told me she was already struggling. When I first met her years back, she was cheerful, her gear spotless and new. Now it looked like one decent kick could splinter her whole setup.

"You look like you're in a tough spot, doctor. What happened to your carriage and clothes?"

"Oh well, sometimes bandits come after me, and I teach them manners! I run into a lot of bandits, too many. I guess plenty of them keep an eye out for a woman traveling alone with a cart." Her voice dipped, carrying something close to sadness.

"It's hard being a doctor. It's hard just to study for it. So if you're not making much, why keep doing it?" I asked.

She stretched out her hand. "Speaking of money, another copper, please!" I slid another coin into her palm.

"Well, no matter where you go, people need a doctor. You'll always find someone who needs something from you. And you need to make a living somehow in this crazy world, after all."

I stared at my hands, then lifted my eyes to meet hers.

"I remember a doctor from a few years back. Her name was Doctor Professor Stanton. I came to her needing help. I had black winter lungs, getting weaker by the day." As I spoke, she straightened up, fixing her posture.

"She told me it was cancer and gave me a drink she claimed would cure me. But I only got worse. I was just another homeless kid on the street, coughing my lungs out, barely able to move. I was either going to die of starvation or black lung. I went back to find her, to get more treatment, but she was gone. I never saw her again."

Her tone dropped, regret creeping in as her hands tightened.

"All I wanted was help. That's all I ever wanted. But in the end, she was just another con artist who'd rather sell fruit drinks than save a poor bastard like herself."

"But you survived! It must have meant the potion worked in the end?!" she blurted, stumbling over her words.

"I was rescued by a witch. She healed me. Told me I had minutes left to live. If I hadn't found her in time, I wouldn't be standing here talking to you, Doctor Stanton."

She froze, staring at me with nothing to say.

"I wanted to see you again, to tell you what happened. To tell you, I'll be a better doctor than you'll ever be. I'll help people. I'll live in a real house, with real clothes, and I'll pull others off the streets with the money I make." I stood in front of her.

"I hope you rot." I turned away, but she started to chuckle.

"Wait, young doctor in training, I haven't given you my advice yet! You're going to need it if you want to become the doctor you dream about!" She waved her hands, gesturing for me to sit. I stayed standing in front of her, syringe ready to throw.

Stanton drew a breath and pulled off her mask. Her brown hair was ragged, her pale skin scarred, and her mouth nearly toothless.

"Sit. No, I'm not going to rob you. If anything, I'm going to save your life—with honesty this time." She grinned.

I didn't move, just leaned against the carriage, arms crossed, waiting for whatever nonsense she had to spill.

"You're right. I'm not a doctor. My dad worked in stables under a gang leader. He used to brag about taking organs and selling them to whatever sick monsters wanted them. He'd talk about infections he found in the organs, and how to treat them. At the time, I was just a barmaid. I copied what he said and left that dumb town, pretending to be a doctor." She relit her cigar and puffed slowly.

"What's your real name?" I asked.

"Ha, you want to know the fun part? I don't have one. My dad didn't care. Said I'd be dead before I hit my teens. I make up a new name every other week. Today it's Calem. I think I heard it somewhere, but I don't even remember where."

I shook my head.

"Go on, Doctor Calem. What else do you think I should know?" My patience was running thin.

"Now I want to ask you something, kid. What do you want to do? What's your aim?"

"Get people off the streets, fix the ghetto, heal with medicine and magic—not horse piss in a jar." She laughed.

"Thing is, kid, you're naive. You want to make a change in the city as a doctor? Fine, be a doctor. No one's going to stop you. But if you're trying to be the angel you think you can be, you're not going to get there as a doctor. You won't make enough money. Look at any potion seller, herbalist, or doctor. You ever see them living in a palace? A castle? No. Those who make big changes and climb to the top do whatever it takes to get there. So tell me—would you rather fix the streets, build houses, feed the homeless, or just be a doctor?"

"I'll do both!" I snapped.

"No, you won't, at least not in a way that matters. If you want to be a doctor, go ahead. Thanks for your service. But if you want to be rich and a doctor, you'll either turn corrupt, selling organs, or work for some rich thug in the city."

I froze. She wasn't wrong. Kreila never made much money, and I sure as hell wasn't going to waste my future arguing with a washed-up con artist who'd never amount to anything.

"I'm done talking to you."

"Wait!" She stubbed out her cigar, stood up, and walked toward me.

"If you're going to walk off angry at me, I just want you to know something. When you told me what happened to you, I knew the gods were cruel. I did what I had to because I owed people money. If I didn't pay, they would take an eye, then keep going until there was nothing left or they got what they wanted. If I'd known you were that sick…" She shook her head. "No. There was nothing I could have done without killing myself. Now go. This city will teach you, one way or another."

She slipped her mask back on and disappeared into the back of her carriage. The stench of mushrooms hit so strong it could make someone faint. The door slammed shut.

I walked away, heading toward the other side of the market. After finding a vendor selling the flowers I needed, I gathered them and started back toward the shop, her words still echoing in my mind.

Desperation makes people mad. I knew that. But I didn't expect someone to warn me like that. Beneath her lies, she was drowning and trying to keep me from sinking too.

But I wouldn't be like her. I wouldn't let survival make me cruel. I wouldn't put my life above a child's. That's the difference.

I finally made it back to the shop and found Kreila still buried in her book. I set the flowers down beside her.

"Thank you, Wallace. I just need to stay on guard now." Kreila let out a sigh and closed the book.

"Hey, you've been reading that thing all day. What is it?"

She turned the cover toward me. It read 1352 Shop Income.

"Just going through our sales for the year, making sure we're breaking even." Her eyes looked tired.

"Looks like Barron saved us from another loss this month."

Chapter 19

We had everything we needed for the heist. After a month of prep, we were ready to rob that captain blind. I did some digging on my own, and Captain Towsin turned out to be a saint playing a game he could never win. But Captain Lyons? Different story. I found out through Towsin and his son that Lyons was chosen because he was a yes-man. A captain of the guard couldn't afford to live on the east side of the city unless he had side money, and Lyons had plenty of that. Dirty money. Under-the-table deals.

Melena had scoped him out hard. She had tabs on his routes, clients, and every move. She even found out which of those rich east-side wretches he was doing favors for. A couple of them had assault charges dropped in exchange for donations. That kind of bribery made my skin crawl. Meanwhile, someone like Towsin was barely getting by, just scraping enough to avoid starving in retirement. That made me sad.

Knowing someone like Lyons was walking around free and getting rich off shady deals made it easy to justify robbing him. I felt joyful. The twins and I still had our rules. We never stole from good people. But scumbags with deep pockets? Fair game. We had to be careful, though. Couldn't take too much. If he noticed, it would all blow up. We just needed enough to disappear into comfort while he kept living his little lie.

Still, part of me wondered where the line really was. If someone like Lyons could hurt people with impunity, what did that say about us, using deception to survive? And what about the people around him, the ones caught in the blast radius of his wealth and our theft? Did our rule mean anything if innocent people got hurt anyway?

Michael's usual charm worked like a spell on Lyons' daughter, Penelope. She was all over him, kissing, holding hands, whispering sweet words in his ear. They were secret lovers, of course. The captain didn't know a thing. I felt bad for her. Penelope seemed nice, but I hated knowing she was just another girl in Michael's rotation. And since she was the main, that meant someone else had been demoted. Still, you had to hand it to him; the man knew how to charm.

He knew exactly how to talk to get someone excited and how to use his body language to seem enticing. Plus, Michael was handsome. Hell, both he and Melena were lookers by the time we hit our teens. Flocks of love letters would show up for the two of them, mostly for Michael, of course. Melena had no time for dating. She'd become more intimidating as she got older. Her tall stature and oily black hair gave people the impression she was some kind of undead or skeleton-like monster.

I knew how to be charming, too, but I didn't spend much time around kids our age. The closest I got was when patients my age stopped by the store. I'd wave and be kind whenever I could, but flirting? That scared the soul out of me. I practiced once or twice with Hannah, outside the store. She said I was cute, but nothing really came of it.

I told her I loved the color orange. The plan was to follow that up by saying her ginger hair matched whatever she had on. But I got cold feet, and now she just thinks orange is my favorite color. We agreed to stay friends. She told me she planned to do farming most of the year as she got older, so if we ever spent time together, it would be short-lived. I liked her plucky attitude and slim figure, but I was too terrified to look at her for too long.

It didn't help that if Kreila caught me staring at a woman's legs or chest for more than a second—whether in public or at the store—I was in trouble. She'd hit me in the back of the head or make me clean the whole house without the unseen servants' help. Because of that, I felt like I could only look a woman in the eyes or face the wrath of an elderly woman throwing syringes at me.

Even now, I couldn't figure out if flirting with Hannah was harder because of Kreila's voice in my head or because some part of me just didn't want to lie to her.

My lack of charisma always landed me in the same part of the job— distraction and lookout. The plan was simple. Captain Lyons would take his wife to the ceremony at the king's palace, and while they were gone, Michael would show up and invite Penelope for a walk. Just a few blocks to watch some street performers and maybe buy her flowers.

While that was happening, Melena would lock-pick one of the side windows of the house. I'd be on lookout duty, keeping an eye out for any guards. If someone got too close or started loitering, I'd try to lead them away from Lyons' place while Melena grabbed what she could. With the mage bag, she could carry everything out without raising suspicion. After that, she'd head for the sewers and make her way back to the tavern. I'd stay behind, making rounds around the block to make sure Michael could leave the scene without trouble. Once the job was done, we'd all meet back at the tavern.

It was a warm summer evening. Sundown was approaching fast, so we had to move quickly to avoid overlapping with the silent auction crowd. We made our way to the eastern side of the city. As always, the roads were clean and paved. The people looked like royalty, and the buildings were spotless, polished, and maintained. You wouldn't find a single bum or homeless person out here.

We had cleaned ourselves up and worn the best clothes we could afford. We didn't exactly look like we belonged in that part of town, but we passed for street sweepers or mailmen well enough to avoid suspicion.

The captain's house was a large wooden structure, two stories tall, with a thick stone chimney. Its windows gleamed, and the wood looked solid and freshly sealed. The street was just busy enough to give us cover, with a steady flow of passersby to blend into.

Right on schedule, Captain Lyons and his wife left the house. But something caught my eye. As they turned to wave goodbye to Penelope at the door, I noticed a short woman standing behind her. She wore a dress and an apron.

"They've got a maid," I whispered to the others. "But I've got something for this."

We were smart enough to plan for surprises. I had prepped a few potions we could use if things went sideways. A small acid vial, a tranquilizer syringe, a smoke screen, and one that made a loud bang when it shattered—just enough to draw a guard's attention. We had lock-picking tools too, and Melena spent her nights at the orphanage practicing on every chest and door she could find.

I handed Melena the vials and syringes, just in case. All three of us had bandanas if things got messy, and we carried a map of the sewer system in case we needed to make a run for it.

"If you have to use the syringe, you can hit her anywhere, just avoid the face and heart. Hit her there, and she might not wake up from that nap," I whispered.

"Yeah, yeah. If you distract her, I won't need to use it," Melena whispered back.

I caught one last look at the maid. She looked tired, not just physically, but something in her eyes made me pause. A kind of wariness. Like she already knew something bad might happen tonight. I shrugged it off, told myself I was imagining it, and that she'd be fine. But part of me knew better.

The three of us nodded. "We've stolen from houses before. We can do this one, too. Just keep an eye out, and we'll walk away with enough money to buy a whole bakery," I chuckled, glancing at the two of them.

"You two better start taking notes, especially you, Wallace," Michael whispered as he sprayed himself with another dose of lavender cologne. Then he strolled off with that usual confidence in his stride, heading for the front door of the captain's house.

Melena and I watched from the alley, keeping our eyes peeled for guards. Only one was nearby, about two hundred feet away, standing in well-kept padded armor with a spear in hand. He was looking in the opposite direction, away from the captain's house.

Michael knocked on the door. A moment later, Penelope and her maid answered.

"Oh, I'm sorry, I must have the wrong house. I didn't realize two angels would be here today," Michael said with a chuckle.

Penelope stepped out of the doorway. Her brown skin and black hair were perfectly complemented by a purple dress—the color of wealth. Her maid, on the other hand, looked far too old to still be in service. Her tan skin sagged from her face, like it was slowly melting.

I heard both women giggle.

"Margaret, I'm going around the corner to see those lizard men juggling. I'll only be out for a bit," Penelope said, her voice full of excitement.

"Okay, dearie, but remember your father said that if you go out, you need to—" Margaret started, but Penelope cut her off.

"Stay within a few blocks and have a guard in sight. I know, Margaret," she said in a sing-song tone like a child repeating a rule.

"This is my friend Michael. He's just a friend, and I trust him."

Margaret gave her a look of concern. "Please stay safe, dearie. Don't forget your dagger and horn."

Penelope moved her dress slightly, revealing a dagger tucked into her belt and a horn that looked loud enough to alert the entire country if something went wrong.

They both waved goodbye to the maid and walked away from the house. Once they were a safe distance and saw the door close behind them, the two quickly embraced and shared a long kiss.

"I think wearing purple makes you a better kisser. You should wear it more, princess," Michael said.

Penelope's face flushed with a warm blush.

"You smell great, too, by the way. That cologne smells expensive. Did your dad give it to you?" she asked.

"No, just something an actor from Bard College let me borrow. They told me not to wear it because it'd be too powerful and make you want to hold my hands," he said.

"It worked!" Penelope replied with glee as the two of them held hands and walked away from the house.

As Michael passed us, he gave a wink and flashed that cocky grin of his. Bastard was a showoff. Always had been. I looked over at Melena, gave a quick nod, and the two of us stepped out of the alley.

"Hate that idiot," I mumbled.

"Jealous? I'm sure that Hannah girl would be all over him if he tried," Melena chuckled.

"Hate you too," I whispered.

"You go to the window, watch the alley for people. I'll distract the maid."

I pulled the black syringe from my side, squeezing it near my face. In an instant, a black tendril wrapped around my head and formed into a standard plague doctor mask.

"Don't die," I whispered.

Melena flipped me off and crept around the alley. We checked both directions on the street. No one seemed to be paying attention—everyone already distracted with their own lives.

I walked up to the captain's house. I had practiced the lines, the hand movements.

"Sell her potions with a twist," I murmured to myself.

As I prepared my speech, I thought about the con artist again. I told myself that I was better than her, but here I am pretending to sell potions. I shook my head and reminded myself that I'll be better than her. I'll give the potion for free, and whatever money we make will help the people in the ghetto.

I knocked on the door and waited. A moment later, it creaked open, and Margrett, the maid, peered out with a curious expression.

"Hello? I'm sorry, the owners aren't home right now. Are you here to deliver something?" she asked.

I cleared my throat and put on the best accent I could manage. "Hello, young lady. My name is Dr. Miricale, from Malteria University out east. I was hoping to see if you might have a moment to browse some of my wares."

I opened a small box of potions I had made. They were all genuine, but I'd packed them in the fanciest, most unusual bottles I could find. The space between each was padded with fake jewels for extra flair.

"Oh my. Aren't you a little short for a doctor? And you sound rather young," she said, raising an eyebrow.

"Ah, ma'am, I've cured hundreds of people. But I'm afraid the one thing I couldn't cure was my slow growth. My mother was a human with the height of a dwarf, and my father wasn't much taller."

We stood face-to-face. I realized we were about the same height—five foot two, give or take.

"Well, isn't that sad? I'm sorry, doctor, but the owners aren't home, and I don't have much to spend. The neighbors might be more in need of your services," she said politely.

Suddenly, I heard something behind her—the thud of feet landing and stumbling in another room. The maid started to turn around.

I had to act fast.

"Ma'am, what seems to be wrong?" I asked.

"I thought I heard something fall. Thanks for coming—"

"Ma'am, you must've been gorgeous in your younger days. Your voice still sounds wonderful, too!" I interrupted, raising my voice just enough to catch her full attention.

She turned back toward me with a blush forming on her cheek. "Oh, thank you, dearie."

"Ma'am, I hate to say this, but I have some of the best ears in the country, and right now I can't hear anything besides your breath and heartbeat. But what if I told you I could bring your looks and hearing back to their prime?"

She tilted her head and glanced at the box in my hands. "What do you mean?"

I began holding up several colorful potions, one at a time, letting the fake jewels fall off and scatter dramatically.

"This one will make you twenty years younger. This one will give you a nice rear that'll make men swoon. These two will give you the strength of two giants. And this one—the speed of dragons."

I started juggling the potions in my hands. I nearly dropped one, but recovered quickly and kept going like it was part of the act.

The maid's face lit up with curiosity and wonder. Her eyes followed every movement, fully locked in. I kept her hooked like that for about three minutes.

"How much for the younger one?" she asked.

"You know what? Since I think you're pretty, I'll give you this one on the house," I said with a wink.

I knew the potion was technically a farce. It did make you look twenty years younger, but the effect only lasted about five minutes. Still, that was more than enough to keep her distracted.

"Just drink it before you get home to your husband. It'll make him excited to see you and give you the kind of energy you had on your honeymoon. In all the right ways," I added, lacing the words with sarcasm.

Behind me, I heard coughing from across the street. Melena was walking by, casual as ever.

I handed the green potion bottle to the maid and gave her a little bow. "If you ever need my services, I'll be traveling around. Just ask for Dr. Miricale if you need anything. Thank you for your time, Margrett the Marvelous."

She giggled and clapped her hands. "Thank you so much, young man. Please take care."

I waited for her to close the door, then stepped back slowly with the rest of the potions in hand. Once I was out of sight, I picked up the pace and crossed the street toward Melena. She had slowed down so I could catch up.

"How's it going?" I asked.

"We're rich, Wallace. I could barely count it all. The man was loaded. That captain could probably buy a palace," she whispered with a grin.

I walked with her to the storm drain and helped her descend the ladder. At the bottom, she looked up, and I gave her a quick salute before closing the drain behind her.

I walked around the neighborhood for a few more minutes before spotting Michael heading back toward the house. He had flowers in one hand and a red kiss stain on his cheek. He noticed me circling the block, and I gave him a subtle nod before making my way slowly toward the storm drain.

I looked back and caught sight of Michael giving Penelope one last, passionate kiss before waving her goodbye. Then he turned and walked toward me.

"How's it going?" Michael asked.

"We're rich," I said with a grin. "Also, turns out I'm pretty good at flirting with the elderly."

We both laughed as we climbed down the ladder and made our way through the sewers, back toward the tavern.

When we returned, Melena's eyes were lit up with joy. She held up a sheet of paper where she had scribbled the count. Two hundred gold, thirty silver, and fifty copper coins.

Two hundred gold.

A peasant or farmer could go their whole life and be lucky just to see a single gold coin. And there we were—three nobodies—with two hundred gold, thirty silver, and fifty copper coins.

"We're rich!" Michael shouted before Melena and I could hush him.

That didn't stop us from hugging tight and dancing a little.

"So, do we get one palace or three smaller palaces?" I laughed with the two of them.

"Michael doesn't need one. He can stay in the bird's nest. He didn't do any work. I did the most, so I should get the palace." Melena stood with her hands on her hips, grinning widely.

"I'm far more humble than both of you. I'm going to buy a nice house in the best part of town, right between a tavern and a bakery. So that—" I stopped, muttering under my breath, "Wait." The smile slid off my face.

Gods, Kreila was expecting me back by now. Thinking about a bakery reminded me of Allen. I needed to get back as soon as I could.

"Kreila is expecting me. Just keep the haul hidden. I have to go!" I stood up and bolted for the door, knocking over a stool as I moved. The twins staring at me in confusion. Without another word, I ran to the shop as fast as my legs would take me.

Chapter 20

I didn't stop to catch my breath. I just focused on getting to the shop as quickly as possible. I bumped into several passersby, but I didn't have time to stop and apologize. All I could throw out was a quick, "Sorry!"

I kept running. Faster. One turn, then another. My chest burned. Kreila would be fine, I told myself. She always was. But something in me twisted. Something was wrong.

When I finally turned the corner and saw the shop, my stomach lurched not just from the running but from what I saw. Neighbors crowded around the housing block, holding each other, some crying. A mother stood with her two kids in front of the store, speaking to Kreila, who was covered in blood. Behind her, two knights in all-black armor walked out carrying a wooden casket. Behind them, a woman dressed in a dark dress approached Kreila and the mother.

The Death Church. They came to collect the dead, bury them, and try to calm the grieving family. Their priest could be attacked in moments like this, so they always had security with them. Still, everyone across the continent knew one thing—when they showed up in numbers, it only ever meant tragedy.

Their priestess wore a veil that covered her eyes, and she whispered something inaudible to the grieving woman. One of the knights held a censer, smoke curling from it like a serpent, thick with the smell of ash and sage. The air felt colder near them.

The priestess then bowed to the mother and Kreila, then gently led the woman and her children away from the shop. The mother howled in grief, her two children clinging to her as if holding her together. Some of the onlookers looked crossed themselves; others turned away. While this unfolded, I caught Kreila turning toward me. Her mask stayed on, but I didn't need to see her face to know what was behind it. Pure disappointment. She walked back into the shop, and I followed her, my steps heavy and slow.

I fought to keep myself from breaking down. A part of me wanted to spin around and run, anything to escape the punishment or the tearful storm that was waiting for me. But deep down, I knew I had messed up. The least I could do was face it and apologize.

Inside, the servant was mopping up blood near the inpatient room. The table in the center was soaked crimson, a grim witness to what had just happened. Kreila stood at the fireplace, tossing her gloves, mask, and outfit into the flames. The fire consumed them, leaving her in a white dress that somehow stayed untouched by the blood.

With a flick of her fingers, a small orb of water formed and dropped into a bowl on the counter. She began washing her hands with slow, deliberate movements. After a deep breath, she turned her gaze on me. Before speaking, a syringe slipped from her sleeve. Without hesitation, she injected herself. I couldn't tell what spell or tonic it was, and I wasn't sure I wanted to know.

"Come, Wallace. We need to talk." Her voice was calm, but it cut like a blade. She gestured toward the dining table. I followed, my hands clenched tight, and pulled off my mask, exposing the tears streaking my face and the grinding of my teeth.

"I'll let you explain yourself before I say anything. So go on. Where were you?" Kreila's tone stayed level, but her eyes burned with exhaustion and fury.

"I was with the twins. We were playing, and we went farther than I meant to. I lost track of time…" The words tasted like ash. Lying to Kreila was its own kind of torture.

"What were you doing that was so important that you disobeyed my orders not to go far?"

"We… we wanted to find something that could help the twins and me…"

"And how exactly did you plan to do that, Wallace? Did you go steal something?"

I didn't have the strength to drag this out and torture myself any further.

"Yes…" I mumbled.

"Why?" Her voice stayed calm, almost too calm.

"We wanted to get the twins some better clothes. The birds' nest isn't giving them good books, bedding, or anything else. I wanted to help them get what they needed. Not just them, but the others at the orphanage and the ones out on the streets. I swear, we just wanted to help people who had it as bad as we did." I gripped my hands tight, feeling snot drip from my nose. "I'm sorry."

She didn't speak for a long time. Just looked at me, like she was measuring something deep inside me.

"Intentions matter," she said at last, "but they don't erase consequences. You know that, don't you?"

"You... what did you inject yourself with? I saw you use a syringe a moment ago." I asked.

"That was a syringe to calm my nerves, Wallace. Whenever I'm dealing with something terrible and feel like lashing out, I inject myself with a calming spell. It keeps me from shouting, from getting angry. If I hadn't taken it, I'm sure I would have lashed out at you, and I never want to do that."

"Oh..."

Kreila leaned forward, resting her arms on the table, her eyes locking on me.

"Allen is dead. I tried to operate on him, to save him, but it was too late. He was doomed the moment he stumbled in here."

"No…" The words barely left my mouth.

Everything inside me twisted. I thought about everything Kreila had given me, all the chances, and I felt like I had thrown them away. My hands trembled in my lap. I couldn't look at her.

"I thought that you would have it under control…" I mumbled.

"No, Wallace. I don't always have it under control. And I don't save everyone. But whether I could have saved him or not, you should have been here to help me. You could have bought me time, even in the smallest way. Instead, you were gone. That's why I'm disappointed.

Her voice cracked slightly. Just once. She steadied it before continuing.

"Even if your training isn't finished, you can still help. You chose to steal, and that was selfish, Wallace. If you truly want to be a doctor, you must always be ready to answer when someone calls for help. Morning or midnight, rain or snow—you'll never know when it'll happen."

"I'm sorry. Please forgive me," I said quietly.

"I know you love the twins, and I'll never tell you to stop loving them or spending time with them. But I want you to think about the kind of doctor you aspire to be. Do you want to heal this city, or become another vulture feeding on its corpse? Learn from this, Wallace. Decide what kind of doctor you want to become."

"Yes, ma'am." I nodded, grabbing a handkerchief to wipe my face.

"I won't be teaching tomorrow. I need to rest. You're going to help the servant clean, and tomorrow you'll read the book on stopping blood loss." Kreila stood, walked over to me, and gripped my shoulders.

"I accepted you as my apprentice because I believe in you, Wallace. I still do."

She turned and headed up the stairs. Her steps were slow, tired. I waited until I could no longer hear them.

All I could do was rest my head on the table and cry in regret. That con artist would be laughing if she knew what happened. The twins were probably celebrating, and here I was—crying and cleaning up blood.

Chapter 21

I spent that night turning over everything Kreila had said. I wanted to find a way to earn her forgiveness, to prove I was serious about becoming a doctor. But how could I be a good doctor without abandoning Michael and Melena? They loved me. They needed me. I still believed stealing was the only way to pull us out of poverty. Yet those words from that con artist kept echoing in my head—that someday, I would have to choose.

No. I'd been through too much to give up. I survived without parents, without clothes, without food. I believe that with time, I could prove everyone wrong. I could handle both, keep both sides happy. I just needed to figure out how. I never wanted to hear Kreila say she's disappointed in me again.

The next day, I woke to find Kreila sitting downstairs, reading one of her romance novels with a cup of tea in hand. She looked up at me and gave a small, almost gentle smile.

"Food is in the kitchen," she said, her smile faint but real.

After eating, I went back to my room and cracked open the textbooks she assigned me. Slowly, piece by piece, I started to understand Elvish. Most of the medical texts were written by elves.

The rest came from mages far to the west in Elaria, with their massive mage colleges and endless libraries.

After a few hours of studying, I heard a knock at the door downstairs. I went down and saw Kreila opening it to a group of kids. The tallest one, standing in front with copper skin and freckles, looked straight at her.

"Hi there, we're looking for Wallace," the boy said. I didn't recognize any of them.

"Oh, okay, just a moment." Kreila closed the door and glanced up at me standing on the stairs.

"Do you know these children, Wallace?"

"No, but I can go see what they want."

"Alright then. I'll be by the window, just in case they try anything." She leaned near the window facing the front.

I opened the door to find three kids about my age. Their clothes were torn but still clean. The copper-skinned boy in front was a bit taller than me, with messy hair. He stuck out his hand.

"Hi, Wallace! I'm Ronald!"

"Hi, Ronald. Who are you?"

"We were told to come talk to you. Melena said she'd explain later." Ronald grinned slightly.

"How do I know Melena sent you?" I asked, eyeing the strangers.

Ronald handed me a small letter. I unfolded it and immediately recognized Melena's awful handwriting.

Come to the tavern, you dunce, where are you?

"Yep, that's exactly what she'd say. Okay." I nodded.

"Ask your mom if it's okay. Melena told us to tell you that too," Ronald added.

I glanced toward Kreila. She looked down at me, then leaned over and patted my shoulders.

"You can go play with your friends, Wallace, but don't forget what we talked about. If they're up to trouble, you come right back. Do you understand?"

"Okay, ma'am." I nodded.

"Walk in packs, Wallace, not alone. And remember how to draw quickly?"

Without hesitation, I pulled a syringe from my sleeve.

"Good. Stay safe, Wallace." Kreila gave a small smile.

I stepped out of the shop with Ronald and his two friends, all three of them staring at me.

Ronald pointed toward the other two. "We're all from the birds' nest. Melena paid us to come get you."

"Paid you?"

"Yep! Now come on, I think they'll give us extra if you get there quickly!"

The four of us walked quickly to the tavern, slipping through the crowd until we reached the place where Michael and Melena were already in the middle of an argument.

"Wallace!" they both shouted, rushing over to hug me. They clung to me so hard it felt like they were trying to squeeze my organs out.

"What happened? You ran off so fast!" Michael asked.

"Kreila needed me home for something. I don't want to talk about it right now," I mumbled.

"Did you get grounded?" Ronald asked from behind me.

"No, I wasn't grounded." I turned toward him.

"Well, sounds like you did."

I glanced at the twins. "Who are these people?"

"Michael was talking too loudly about the coin. Then these three followed us here today and said they wanted money too. But not before I tackled Ronald for tailing us," Melena said with her usual pride.

"He seemed to like it too!" Michael scoffed. I looked back at Ronald, who had covered his now-red face.

"So we let them stay. I had some ideas of what to do," Michael said with a grin. "Come on, let's all sit down here."

We stayed there talking for hours, from sunrise to sunset, with our new tagalongs quietly listening in.

The twins argued that I should be the one to hold onto it. Too many sketchy eyes hung around the Bird's Nest—despite Ronald volunteering to hide it himself. We knew we couldn't be careless. If the three of us started running around in new clothes, flashing jewelry, and hanging out with dozens of women, Kreila and the heads at the orphanage would notice fast.

So we made a smarter move. We decided to renovate the bar— clean it up and make it look presentable.

Michael and Melena still splurged here and there. We hit fancy restaurants and taverns when we could, but we always made sure to stash enough coin for the occasional bailout in case a scheme went sideways.

The best part? We didn't need to steal as much anymore. Not when Ronald and the other kids from the orphanage started following the twins to the bar. Michael let it slip that we had gold after bragging to a girl he was trying to impress. Word got out. And they wanted in.

Ronald turned out to be the most invested of the other kids. He was a year older than we were, but he jumped at any chance to get new clothes and books. Quiet most of the time, he still asked constantly how he could help. He liked the idea of pitching in, probably because his story wasn't much different from ours. Dropped off by his parents at the birds' nest when he was five, he'd been chasing a better life ever since.

Of course, Michael and I knew his biggest reason for sticking around was Melena. Ronald was known for keeping to himself, barely speaking. But somehow, whenever Melena was around, his words narrowed down to just two phrases: "yes, boss" and "no, boss."

That's when the twins and I had an idea. Instead of the occasional stick-up or small con, we could form a gang. Pay the kids. Give them a real shot at making a living.

We hated to admit it, but they had a better chance working with us than surviving out there on the streets.

We got in touch with taverns and brothels across the city, offering to deliver letters for cheap. The other members helped us move goods and messages from one end of the city to the other. For a few coins, I'd tell folks I was a doctor who didn't ask too many questions—so long as I wasn't killing or hurting anyone.

The twins and I stuck to that rule as best we could. No killing. Maybe a broken bone or a few bruises here and there, but no killing. We didn't want anyone's soul hanging on our conscience.

There was one loose end, though—the maid.

Captain Lyons eventually realized some of his gold was missing. We hadn't left enough behind to get caught, and it took him a few days to even notice, which made tracing it back to us almost impossible. So he turned on the maid. Said she should've done a better job. Not only did he give her a black eye, but he also had her imprisoned for theft.

I couldn't stop thinking about her face—the way she smiled when I gave her that potion. The way she clapped her hands and giggled like someone had reminded her she was still worth something. And now? Bruised. Shackled. Forgotten.

The twins and I felt awful. Some poor old woman had to pay the price for something we did. So before they could put her on trial, an anonymous Dr. Miricale showed up, paid her bond, and slipped her a little extra coin for good measure.

But it didn't undo what happened. It didn't change the bruise. It didn't erase the shame I felt. I kept replaying the moment she took the potion from me, so eager, so trusting. That's when the question started forming: how many times could we do this before we became just like the scum we stole from?

That question stuck with me. Even as the gold piled up. Even as we laughed and planned for a future. Because sometimes, when the tavern got quiet and the buzz wore off, I still heard her voice in my head; soft, grateful, and so human.

Chapter 22

Four years passed since our first big heist. A lot had changed for the three of us. I kept learning under Kreila and was finally getting the hang of things. She even started taking days off to travel, letting me run the store on my own. Nothing I couldn't handle.

Patients rarely stayed overnight, so most nights I was by myself. One fool tried to rob the place while I was alone. The guards found him knocked out, tied up with a rope, and his clothes burnt with acid. By then, I was a confident spellcaster—could handle myself in a fight, slip in and out when needed, and even chop off a limb to save someone's life.

One time, I had to amputate an old man's foot to stop an infection. He lived. I even helped him get a peg leg, but only after he cussed me out good.

Kreila hadn't changed much, but I guess when you reach her age, you settle into who you are. She was pushing eighty-two then. You wouldn't notice it if you just saw her at the front of the shop, but I saw it—how she moved more slowly, how she spent more days writing her books than healing. Some nights, I'd find her asleep at her desk, a single candle lighting up the room. Whenever that happened, I'd get the servants to help carry her to bed.

I started noticing how her hands shook when she reached for delicate tools. How her voice, though steady, carried a weariness it hadn't before. Sometimes I wondered how much time we had left. And what I'd do when she was gone.

Barron started showing up more often, though after a while, he mostly came to talk to me and drop off gifts. He'd share business advice and explain how his caravan operated. Whenever Kreila was away, he'd show up to place big orders and leave me generous tips. I tried not to ask for anything, but he always insisted. Said it made him happy—said he enjoyed watching me grow.

Kreila would come back from her trips to find me in my room, lounging on brand-new furniture that made hers look like antiques.

The twins had their growth spurt, of course. They were nearly a foot taller than me—and I was 5'10". Every now and then, they'd pet my head or lean down to talk to me like I was some toddler, just to show off. I paid them back by kicking Melena in the shin and Michael right in the balls.

They looked like copies of each other—both well-built and muscular, always training. Melena picked up her strength from running drills with the guards and practicing how to move unnoticed by doing exactly what she was told to watch out for. She got her kicks from pulling dirty pranks on gang members or on Michael and me. I'd find my potions or gear missing from the store, and if I pissed her off, she'd scare the soul out of me by nearly assassinating me in a dark alley.

Her favorite target always ended up being Ronald. He grew up alongside us, just a bit shorter than the twins. Ronald had a knack for sneaking around. He told us he'd often steal extra food from the birds' nest and pick pockets in his free time. Quiet as ever, he was still one of the most helpful, and he earned the bonus of hugs from the twins and me.

After about two years of their back-and-forth, they became evenly matched. They were bitter rivals, and whenever Melena seemed to have the upper hand, Ronald would counter and send her to the ground. One day, as a reward for his victory, she gave him a kiss on the cheek. Since then, it has become their tradition.

Ronald knew that dating her would be a death wish. Still, he kept showing up for every duel.

Michael, of course, spent most of his free time working out, just so he could run and fight if needed. He had a full lineup: ex-boyfriends, ex-girlfriends, current partners, and side pieces. He got so good at acting and magic that he could pull off pretending to work for rival gangs just to get information.

The orphans who'd asked to join us four years ago brought their friends along, and what started with three petty thieves became something bigger. MWM—Merry With Mead. That wasn't just the name of our tavern; it was also the first initials of the twins and me.

We had the whole place rebuilt, nearly from scratch. The walls, floors, and ceiling changed from that old, nasty but homey dark green to a clean red oak finish. We added fresh oak furniture and even had a steel chandelier hung from the ceiling. We weren't even old enough to drink legally, but no one in this part of the city cared or enforced that sort of thing.

We picked roles for everyone. One of us ran the bar, someone else handled the door, and we had older girls work as waitresses. From what I could tell, the food and drinks were about average for the city: cold mead chilled with enchanted tools, and warm chicken roasted over our brand-new brick fireplace.

What made the place even better was when we found out it had an abandoned sewer bunker right below it. After hiring a few of our members and some extra help, we learned that the tavern and the bunker were built by a gang of dwarves a long time ago. The halls, rooms, and storage areas were made from old red bricks. So, we renovated the bunker too, making sure it had multiple exits and entrances in case we ever needed to get out fast.

We added new furniture and reinforced the brickwork to make the place livable. It also gave us a spot to disappear when we needed to lay low. Mostly, we used it to stash stolen goods and illegal food.

I told the twins and the gang we were staying away from selling drugs. I already knew that road led straight to chaos, and we still had some kind of moral compass. No killing unless it was absolutely necessary. No working with slavers. And if we stole, it was only from rich jerks or the usual brutes. We made it clear—we wouldn't take from anyone who looked like they were barely scraping by. We didn't want to be the gang that made the city worse, that put people on the street, or left a kid going to bed hungry.

But not everyone agreed.

One night, after the tavern closed, I got into it with Michael. He thought we should start taxing smaller gangs for protection. I told him that's just another word for extortion. Melena didn't say much, just leaned back in her chair and watched us argue like it was a sport. I could feel the cracks forming, everyone wanted to grow, but not everyone cared how.

"We're not thugs," I told him. "We're not slavers. We help people."

"We're not saints either," he shot back. "At some point, you're going to have to choose: be rich or be right."

There was a silver lining in what we did for the city, though. Orphanages that were falling apart suddenly had new books, clothes, and furniture from "anonymous" donors. A few homeless amputees got new wooden limbs. Some run-down homes across the ghetto got repairs that helped them hold up against more than a light breeze.

I even fixed up old man Wallace's shop. Got him new equipment and proper windows so he didn't have to work outside anymore. Wallace got a new cane and a bed that didn't feel like concrete. Hannah got new clothes and some jewelry. It felt good seeing a close friend happy. Getting a hug from her was even better.

To surprise Kreila, I told her I'd been saving my allowance and finding good deals at the market. Over the years, I gave her new dresses, lab tools, and even new romance books. She didn't like to admit it, but any book that had romance and drama would make her smile with glee. Especially if it was characters kissing characters, they shouldn't be. I never told her where I really got those things or how much I paid. I didn't want her to know about the gang. If she ever found out, I didn't know how she'd take it.

One time, I joked that I stole from rich jerks for sport. She laughed and said as long as I was only stealing from the rich, then it was fine. But she always made it clear—her work was meant to help and defend, not to start fights.

Still, I could tell. There were times she looked at me like she knew more than she let on. Like she was waiting for me to come clean. I couldn't bring myself to. Not yet.

I took a page from Doctor Stantion and started selling fake potions. But I had my rules, which made me better than your average scammer. If some rich scum came looking for medicine for a headache, I'd overcharge. If one wanted a love spell to get some girl to fall for him, I'd give him a charisma potion that lasted five minutes. I'd tell him it would last five months. Most never came back to complain, probably too embarrassed. Plus, I kept moving around and switching up my outfits.

Thanks to Michael, I learned how to change my voice too. Gods above, I once stuffed some pillows into my clothes, put on a different voice, and passed as a woman. It worked. Sales were great that day.

It was one scorching July, miserable for everyone. People were begging the sun god for mercy, and buying up anything tied to ice magic. The tavern and Kreila's shop had cold stones powered by magic, but they only worked a few hours at a time. Then they'd shut off, and we'd all be back to roasting. I had to sleep practically naked just to stop sweating through my bedsheets.

One brutal summer morning, I got a letter from a place called the Drunk Lions. They were asking about a job and a potential alliance—something that could help us reach the big leagues. MWM was still small at that point. We weren't enough of a threat for the bigger gangs to target us yet, so any shot at making more money sounded like a win.

But I'd heard of them before, rumors mostly. They burned down whole blocks to settle a score. That their brothels doubled as blackmail rings. That their mercs smiled while torturing debtors. If even half of it was true, then this wasn't an opportunity. It was a warning.

I didn't tell the twins everything. Just said to stay sharp and let me handle the meeting. But in my gut, I already knew: if we said yes, everything would change. And not necessarily for the better.

I suited up, grabbed my tools, and headed to the Drunk Lions Tavern. The Drunk Lions was a three-pronged operation—running brothels, taverns, and a small mercenary force to keep everything in check. The company owned dozens of slaves, so security wasn't just a precaution; it was a necessity. I reminded myself to keep calm. Don't get too involved. Don't come off too soft. Otherwise, they'd see it as weakness and try to take advantage.

Chapter 23

The tavern was massive, two stories of freshly laid red brick with brown oak support beams. It sat in the middle part of town, making it busier and cleaner than the ghetto where MWM was located. Noise spilled from every direction: inside, the clash of tankards and raucous gambling; outside, crowds bustled and merchants shouted their prices. I wondered how people could move around in this kind of heat, especially during this time of year. By the time I arrived, it was noon, and the sun was still blazing. But I guess beer and wine hit the spot no matter the season. When I stepped inside, the interior echoed the same fresh craftsmanship. Brown walnut stools, bars, and tables looked like they'd just been nailed down. The bar stretched across an entire wall, manned by two bartenders rotating shifts, pouring glass tankards of beer, and serving beef pies. The whole place smelled like alcohol and meat, trying to overpower the summer heat.

The patrons were a mix: rich locals and armored adventurers, all looking for a drink. From upstairs, I could hear chips clattering and voices shouting. That was probably where the gambling was going down.

One thing I noticed was the staff. They all wore forced smiles, had baggy eyes, and carried bruises and cuts that were barely hidden. They looked clean enough, but I spotted a waitress off in the corner, fanning herself as sweat soaked her clothes. When I looked closer at the rest of them, something else stood out. Each had a stamp burned into their skin—a lion with a number. The mark was on their elbows, the backs of their necks, even their chests and heads. These were the slaves the Lions owned. Must've hurt, I thought.

I walked up to the bar and asked to see the boss. The bartender pointed to a hallway at the corner of the room. As I made my way over, I could already hear someone barking orders behind the door. I knocked. The shouting stopped instantly. A mercenary in chain armor opened it.

"Who the hell are you?" he asked, the rattle of his chainmail loud in the silence.

"I'm Doctor W from MWM. I got a letter from your boss." I kept my voice tough and steady. Don't seem weak, I kept muttering to myself.

"Oi, boss, you asked for a doctor, yeah?" he yelled over his shoulder, then gave me a nod.

"Alright, come on in. Try anything and you're dead," he said.

"Don't plan on dying, so I'll keep that in mind," I replied with a grin.

The door swung open, revealing dark wooden walls and flooring with a polished shine. In the center of the room sat a man behind a massive desk, decorated with ornaments studded with jewels. Behind him, two flags hung on opposite sides of the wall. Both showed a purple and gold design with a lion gripping a tankard in its claws. Two large windows filled the space with daylight, and a silver chandelier hung overhead.

The heavy-set man, dressed in bright royal robes, was skimming through papers and occasionally biting into a piece of steak beside the stack. When he noticed me approaching, he lifted his head and smiled.

"Ah, there you are, Doctor. I was hoping you'd show up before nightfall. Got stuff to do, and I'd rather see the work handled before then."

As I neared his desk, I caught a glimpse of another mercenary standing off to the side near the windows. He was in black leather armor, twirling a knife between his fingers. The large man extended his hand toward me.

"The name's Samuel Clemson. Have you heard of me?"

I gripped his hand with a firm shake. Good thing I had my gloves and mask on. The smell of steak hit me right away, and I noticed fresh grease stains on my glove from his palm.

"I hear you sell drinks, slaves, and arms to anyone willing to pay. That's about it, to be honest."

"Well, you got most of it. Not much else to say. I own a couple of taverns and a brothel. I run the taverns, my wife handles the brothels, and my brother commands the mercs. Gotta have mercs these days. City guard doesn't offer any protection. Not from the Table, anyway."

"The Table?" I asked. "Thought that was just some bedtime story to keep kids off the streets."

The man chuckled. "I wish it was just stories. But it ain't. You and your crew must be new. Never heard of you until recently. And the fact that you think the Table is a myth tells me you haven't been around long."

"I assure you, my team and I work like we've been doing this for decades. Table or not," I said.

He paused, then let out a long, raspy laugh that filled the room.

"You dumb fool. If the Table wanted you dead, you'd be dead before you walked out that door."

He took a drink from a tankard, beer spilling into his bronze beard.

"Let me teach you something, kid. The Table doesn't play games. Your gang is probably too small for them to care about, much less owe thanks to. Queen Verona owns this city. Hell, she runs the entire country. Ain't anything the Eltons can do about it."

He downed the rest of his drink in one long pull.

"Verona is immortal, just like the former King Darius. When Darius was in charge, he picked the wealthiest gang leaders and traders to run the country. They kept the people in line and made sure they bought their drugs, goods, and slaves. Anyone who stepped out of line was killed—or worse.

A bunch of crusaders from across the continent tried to stop them. All of them ended up dead, or wishing they were. Even with the king gone and the Eltons back on the throne, the Table still has its grip on the country. Half the parliament is on the king's payroll and blocks any real move to bring Verona down.

Now King Kendrick Elton is getting old, and everybody knows it's down to two options—either his grandson or Verona takes the crown. You want some advice, kid? Don't mess with Verona or the Table. The less attention you draw, the better."

His words rang in my ears long after he stopped talking.

I had known the Table was powerful, but this? A queen with her claws in parliament, immortality whispered like fact, whole cities under her heel?

We weren't just playing a dangerous game, we were ants crawling across a loaded crossbow. And people wanted in on this? What kind of madman chases a seat at a table that kills everyone who breathes near it?

And what kind of fools were we to think we could keep floating underneath the players who were gods in men's skins?

He shook his head. "But that's not why you're here. First, I've got a few deals for you and your crew. Just help move and protect some goods, in and out of the city. I'll pay you, and maybe we can build up to a full alliance."

"Why did you choose us exactly?" I asked.

"Well, now that Barron Blackwood raised his prices, only the big boys can trade with him. Shame, really. I got a good number of slaves from him."

My heart sank. If my mask hadn't been on, Clemson would've seen the color drain from my face. No. Not Barron. He said it was just weapons and wine. He told me that to my face. I had to stay calm. Couldn't lose it.

The room suddenly felt too small, too hot. My ears rang, and for a split second, I wasn't standing in some lion's den—I was back in the warehouse with Kreila, sipping tea while Barron joked about his hunting dogs and fine wine. Only now, all I could see were the faces of the waitresses in this tavern, their branded skin.

He said it was just weapons and wine. He told me that to my face. And Kreila—Kreila had always vouched for him. How could she not know? Or did she know and... choose to ignore it?

My throat tightened at the thought. Did I trust her judgment so blindly?

"Barron Blackwood? Any idea why he raised his prices?" I asked, trying to keep my voice steady despite the storm boiling underneath.

"Don't know the full story, but the word on the street is he's trying to join the Table. I can see why. Barron runs one of the biggest slave and drug trades in the city. It was only a matter of time before he started gunning for a seat."

A part of me wanted to run home and cry. Or scream. Or hit something.

How do I tell her? Does she already know? And if she doesn't, what happens to us when she finds out I knew and said nothing?

I felt like I was falling, and there wasn't a floor in sight.

"You alright, lad? You're shaking like you've seen a ghost."

"Oh, I've just got to piss. Think this morning's vodka is hitting me harder than I thought."

He chuckled. "That's no problem. Gotta get one of the slaves in here for the next bit anyway. Larry, show him to the bathroom and bring Isabelle in here."

"You got it, boss." The mercenary opened the door behind me. "Toilets are down that hallway. Last door on your left."

I followed the directions. Lucky for me, my mask was still on, so I didn't have to smell the toilet. But it was hard to keep it on. I was breathing heavy, my heart racing, and my head couldn't lock onto a single clear thought. Barron Blackwood was a slave and drug dealer. All this time, he'd talk to me and Kreila about his stories—hunting, deals, trade. Was he out there hunting people and peddling poison?

And I'd shaken that man's hand. Shared drinks with him. Trusted his money. I felt dirty. Worse than dirty. I felt complicit.

"Shit!" I shouted, slamming my fist into the wall beside me. Pain bit into my knuckles from the wooden paneling.

I slowed my breath, forced myself to calm down. Kreila could take care of herself. If Barron wanted to hurt her, he would've done it already. But why did he say he was interested in me? What did that mean?

I didn't have the answers. Not yet. I just had to finish the job and get home.

I stepped out of the bathroom and made my way back to Clemson's office. I knocked once, and the mercenary opened the door to let me in.

The room was just as I left it—dark wood, polished floors, bright from the windows—but now there was someone new. A woman knelt in front of Clemson's desk, clad in red and black brigandine armor. A steel-red mask covered part of her face, hiding what was underneath.

But I knew burn scars when I saw them, and it was bad. She didn't want anyone to see it, but the damage was there.

Her armor had no sleeves, probably because of the heat, which exposed more burns running down her right arm. A spear and shield were strapped to her back, and her dark leather boots blended right into the floor.

"Ah, there you are, Doctor," Clemson said. "This is Isabelle. She's going to be working with you on the job."

He held a metallic whip in one hand, engraved with gold markings. His fingers curled tight around it.

"Isabelle, say hello to the doctor. And you do everything he says, got it?"

"Yes, master," she replied in a deep voice.

She stood up and turned toward me. I finally got a full look at the woman standing before me. She looked about my age, maybe even the same height. But her dry, tanned skin and brown hair gave her an older edge. Bruises spotted her arm, adding to her worn-down look. She seemed tired. Like she hadn't had a break in years. And judging by those scars, she'd been through hell.

Something in the way she avoided eye contact told me she'd given up on kindness a long time ago. Maybe, even forgotten what it looked like.

Still, she stood tall. There was something iron in her spine—forced into shape, maybe—but iron nonetheless.

She deserved a break.

Isabelle extended her right arm to shake my hand. "I am Isabelle. I will do as you command," she said with a tone that carried pride, though I could tell there was weariness underneath. It was the kind of pride that came from survival, not joy.

As our hands met, I noticed her grip was tight, unrelenting, not a formality, but a challenge. A message.

I don't break easy.

"Just call me Doctor. It's easier that way."

I met her eyes. Brown, tired, with dark bags underneath. She looked like a beaten wolf—worn down, patched with exposed wounds, barely holding it together. And still, she stood tall.

"My other servants keep getting sick," Samuel said. "I've lost almost fifteen of them. Puking, defecating themselves to death. One of them's knocking on death's door. I want you to figure out what the hell's going on and fix it. Get them back to work."

I hesitated. It wasn't the task that bothered me, it was the way he said 'get them back to work' like they were tools, not people.

But I knew better than to flinch. Not here.

"Not a problem. Lead the way, Isabelle."

She gave a silent nod and motioned for me to follow.

Chapter 24

She led me out of his office and into the tavern. In another corner, beneath the stairs, there was a door. As she opened it, the summer heat smacked both of us. I already had a gut feeling about what was wrong. Probably heat exhaustion and bad water. It made sense—slaves drinking whatever they could get their hands on, getting sick from it.

The back area behind the tavern was worse than I expected the slave quarters to be.

The large barns had a front door. They were old, barely holding together, with mold spreading in patches. Black, rotten, inside and out. As Isabelle showed me around, I noticed the rocky dirt beneath our feet, probably tearing up the slaves' soles. Only a few of them had shoes. The rest were darting around, likely just trying to keep their feet from giving out.

"Damn," I muttered under my breath.

In the middle of the field, I noticed a set of five barrels. They looked just like the sheds—rotting. I peeked inside one. What I thought was water sat at the bottom, murky and filled with hair. Mold too, probably. I turned to Isabelle.

"Is this all the water you're given to drink?"

She nodded. "This is all the water we get to bathe, clean, and drink."

Gods above, this place was terrible. I pulled a black bandanna from my mage bag and handed it to Isabelle.

"Put this around your mouth, please. I already see a dozen problems with this place."

She nodded. "Yes, sir," and took the bandanna, wrapping it over her mask.

"Please don't call me sir. I'm not old, and I'm not ready to grow old."

She tilted her head. "Are you not a doctor? Doctors are usually adults, I thought?"

"Let's just say I'm a quick learner," I chuckled.

I thought it was funny, but her face didn't move. No smile, no reaction. Just silence behind the black bandanna.

I should've known better than to joke here. Nothing about this was funny. Not to her. Not to them.

I started walking around the field and spotted what looked like two outhouses. The smell was awful—urine and feces from around forty people cooking under the sun. My stomach already wanted to tap out, but I didn't have to get close. The problems were clear from where I stood. One outhouse was filthy, inside and out. The other one didn't even have a roof.

"Can you take me to the one in the worst condition?" I turned to Isabelle.

"Yes, doctor," she said, motioning for me to follow.

As we approached the barn, the smell hit hard—like the outhouse, but layered with sweat. Inside, bunk beds lined the walls. Men, women, and children twisted in pain. I could hear the groans, the coughing, the sounds of bodies shutting down. They all wore basic tunics and pants, most with holes. Some didn't even have shirts.

A young girl suddenly jumped out of bed, wincing as she ran. She pushed past us, bolting toward the outhouse before slamming the door behind her.

It felt like walking into a nightmare. Not the scary kind, but the kind that just breaks you slowly. You know there's no fixing it. Only surviving it.

It's cholera, probably from that filthy water. The heat makes them desperate. They drink it, and then it starts—body aches, stomach cramps, and a brutal guessing game of which end it's coming out of. Could be every hour. Could be every few minutes.

Isabelle pointed to a small child curled up in the corner. "That's Connor. He's been the sickest, the longest."

We walked over to his bunk. As expected, the stench was strong—even through the lavender I'd stuffed into my mask. He was lying in the fetal position, his clothes torn, with brown stains around his pants.

This was a horrible job to take. But I'd rather it be me than some other con artist playing doctor.

"Hey, Connor, can I talk to you?" I asked gently.

He turned to face me, and the drowsiness in his eyes flipped to terror. He backed into the wall, breathing hard, hands flying up to cover his face.

"Hey, Connor, it's gonna be okay. I'm here to help you feel better."

"Maybe it's the mask," Isabelle said. "He gets anxious a lot."

Gods, please no. That meant I had to take the mask off. The wave of stench waiting for me was gonna hit like a brick wall. I had a spell to keep me from catching anything, but still—this would probably be the end of these clothes.

I pulled a syringe from my sleeve and jabbed it into my hip. It always hurt, but you get used to that when you're a plague doctor. Even with the spell, my eyes started to water. I did my best not to breathe through my nose.

"See? It's just a mask! Don't worry, kiddo," I said, forcing some enthusiasm into my voice and hoping the gods wouldn't ask me to go the whole day without it.

Connor looked up again and loosened his posture, just a little.

"Who are you?" he asked, voice shaky, speech broken by his accent.

"I'm Doctor W. I'm here to take a look at you."

I placed my mask back on before I collapsed. Then I pulled a small syringe from my sleeve—a spell designed to help me identify illnesses with certainty instead of guessing.

Connor's fear returned. He turned away from me, clutching his legs. "No, no, no!"

By now, some of the other slaves had woken up and were watching me, concern in their eyes.

I looked over at Isabelle. "Don't worry, I've played this game before. I just got to—"

She wasn't looking at me. Her eyes were locked on Connor. She knelt beside me and placed a hand on his shoulder.

"Connor, it's Isabelle. Can you look at me?"

He turned slowly, his body trembling. Isabelle reached out and cupped his cheek.

"Be strong, Connor. You're growing, and that means you have to be tough. I know you can do this," she said gently.

Her low, brooding voice softened into something almost maternal. Like this kid meant everything to her, she leaned in closer and held his hand.

"I'll be right here with you, Connor. I'll try to get you something for being brave. I promise."

I watched her closely, this towering woman who could snap steel and yet held this boy's hand like she was cradling glass. Something in me cracked.

I could only see half of her face, but gods, she was gorgeous. It wasn't just looks. It was like her soul was kind, but her body had been through hell. The way she spoke, the way she moved, it pulled me in. I'd never seen someone that scared and that muscular be so gentle. I caught myself thinking I'd love to hear her talk more.

Connor turned and held Isabelle's hand. Then, slowly, he shuffled toward me, eyes shut, clutching his left arm.

"Thank you, Isabelle." I nodded. "Don't worry, kid. This'll be over in three. Two. One."

You gotta be quick with kids. Take too long pulling blood, and they'll lose it. With a little skill and a touch of magic, I was so fast he probably didn't even feel the syringe hit his arm.

"See? You did it, Connor. I told you that you were strong," she said, patting his back.

I looked at the blood in the syringe. It was turning dark brown. The book Kreila gave me had a chart. Color meant everything. But honestly, I didn't even need it this time. The signs were all there. Cholera. The rotten buildings, the water, the clothes. One of them caught it, and now it was probably spreading through the whole place.

I could almost hear Barron's voice, laughing at how weak this all was.

I started thinking through a game plan. But first, the kid.

I reached into my mage bag and pulled out a small potion bottle. The green liquid inside shimmered and shook in the glass.

"It's apple flavor. Don't worry."

I pulled the cork off and handed it to Connor. He took a whiff and smiled. Green apples are practically the only flavor I've managed to nail down. Everything else tastes like piss pretending to be fruit. It'd be a shame if all the other kids ended up hating apple too.

He chugged the bottle in one go and turned to me. "Will it make me better?"

"Yes. For now, it'll stop the bathroom runs and the aching. But I'll have you drink some more in a bit, alright?" I said, trying to match Isabelle's softness.

He nodded. "Thank you, sir!"

As Isabelle and I stood and turned around, I noticed the whole barn had sat up. They were getting closer, all of them speaking broken Paljavish.

"Please, master, please!" some of them shouted, waving their hands.

Luckily, I had a spell for this too. It's called being loud.

"Alright, everyone. I just need to go talk to your boss real quick. I'll be right back, I promise!"

They looked defeated but stepped aside.

Isabelle patted my shoulder and stepped forward. "Follow me, doctor."

She held my shoulder a moment longer than needed. Her grip said thank you. Her eyes said more.

We knocked on the door and entered. Samuel was sitting inside, reading a book that looked like it was about money and numbers.

"Oi, what did you find out?" he asked without hesitation.

"Cholera. And it's bad. It'll spread to everyone if it's not handled quickly."

He closed the book and looked at me. "Alright. What do you have to do?"

"Hell, first off, the whole place practically needs to be burned down and rebuilt. The disease is coming from all the rotten buildings and beds. Mix that with the heat and toxic water, and they're screwed. They drink, get sick, crap and vomit themselves, get thirsty, and repeat."

"Hmm. Is that right? What will it cost me?"

"Five copper a person. Plus, you'll need to clean the whole building and rebuild the barns outside. New water barrels, too. Ones that get checked often. I can cure them, but the rest is on you. I know some—"

He cut me off.

"Five copper is too high. They're slaves. They ain't worth that much. Just cure them. They'll get used to it. Bodies evolve or whatever," Samuel said with disgust.

There it was, the real him. The rot beneath the wealth.

"Sir, that isn't going to stop the problem. It'll just push it down the road. They need better conditions, or they'll die. Especially when summer ends and it gets colder," I said, my voice rising with frustration.

He started laughing. "I'll find more. Besides, it'll weed out the weak ones. Rebuilding all that out there would cost me a small fortune, and those barns have been around since I was a teenager. And with your asking price, I can't do it."

I looked at Isabelle. She looked defeated, her face creased in a deep frown. I couldn't let it end like this.

"One copper a person. Will that help them get the supplies they need?" I shouted.

"Better price for sure. But getting the rest of that stuff, that's a problem for later. They'll get used to it, doctor, I'm sure. I've been in this business for a while. They get accustomed to it. The illness fades. And the ones who die were probably on death's door anyway. Why do you care so much, anyway?" he asked.

I clenched my fist. I wanted to kill the brute right then and there.

"Give me one copper a person, and I'll do the rest myself," I said quietly, almost like I didn't want anyone to hear my cowardice.

Samuel's posture shifted. He sat up in his chair.

I turned to Isabelle and saw the shock on her face.

"You're a soft one, aren't you, doctor? Willing to throw away your time and money for free," he sneered, leaning back. "If you're in charge of MWM, it won't survive with a golden heart like that."

"I've done my homework on you and your other leaders. Young upstarts are trying to play with the big gangs. You're smart, but naïve. What you do won't make a difference in this town. A person with a heart, no matter how intelligent, won't last long. But I'll admit, it'll be interesting to watch you try. At the very least, I can scavenge what's left of your crew when you're crushed."

He threw his hands toward me.

"One copper a person, and you do the rest? Sure. I'll do that."

He reached into his desk and pulled out a coin bag.

"But before I do, let me teach you something, boy."

He dropped the coin bag on the desk.

"You fellas needed money, right? Punch the girl beside you, and I'll give you a gold for it."

"What?!" I gasped.

"Now, now, this is a lesson I'm teaching you. Go ahead, punch Isabelle. Or are you a coward? Too good for a peasant's annual salary?"

I turned to Isabelle. She looked timid at first, but then she stood tall and locked eyes with me. It was like she already expected it, like she'd seen this test before. Isabelle flexed her muscles, bracing for the hit. Even if I doubled my strength, I doubted I'd leave a bruise.

I knew exactly what I needed to do. I was going to hit her in the stomach and get the gold my people needed. I reeled my arm back and stepped into a fighting stance in front of her. I threw my fist toward her gut with all the force I could fake. A flash of shock crossed her face, and I saw her close her eyes.

But when my fist landed, Isabelle's eyes snapped open. That same look of confusion returned. My punch felt like a love tap. Honestly, a pillow would have hit harder. She looked down at my fist, then up at my face, clearly puzzled. She couldn't see my expression, but I hoped she could tell I was smiling.

"Welp, there's your punch. Hand over the gold," I said, stretching out my hand toward Samuel.

A loud, visceral laugh exploded from him, like it was the funniest thing he'd ever seen.

"You clever little fox. I could use a smart weasel like you!" he said, still laughing.

"Finally," I thought to myself. Time to get some of the tension out of the room.

"That was funny, doctor. Like your punch. You're weaker than I thought." His tone turned sour as he leaned forward in his chair. "To make it in this city, you need power, boy."

He reached to his side, pulled out a silver whip, and clenched it tightly.

"Isabelle, throw him to the ground. Now!" he barked.

Isabelle didn't hesitate. Her leg swept out beneath me, and she kicked my legs forward. I fell hard onto the wooden floor and barely had time to collect my thoughts before her hands wrapped around my throat.

She gripped me like she meant to tear it out.

I looked into her eyes and saw horror. Her gaze twitched, her expression filled with rage—like I had killed Connor. But after a second, her hands started to shake. Her breath came faster, panic creeping in.

"Punch the doctor in the face as hard as you can!" he shouted.

"No! Get off me!" I shouted back, struggling under her weight. But she drove her knee into my ribs, pinning me. Every movement made it feel like my chest might shatter.

I wasn't even able to draw a syringe fast enough to dodge her punch, but I didn't need to. She missed by half a foot, striking empty air to my left.

Her grip slowly began to loosen. She looked furious, but now tears were sliding down her cheeks. Her eyes shut tight, and she kept pulling back. She still had me pinned, but I could feel she was trying to stand.

"You do as I command, and you punch him in his naive, stupid face as hard as you can!" Samuel shouted.

He raised the whip above his head, and I saw it glow a dark red.

Isabelle began slamming her fists down around me, blow after blow. She shattered the wooden floor beneath us, but not a single punch hit me. Her knuckles started to bleed. She was furious, but also torn apart inside. Worse than that, I saw the branding on her shoulder light up, glowing the same dark red, and smoke began to rise from her skin.

"No," she whispered.

"Do it!" Samuel screamed.

I didn't want to hurt her. She was fighting to protect me. She was good. God, her skin was burning, and still she refused to give in.

I slowly reached for a syringe hidden at my wrist.

"I'm sorry, Isabelle," I whispered. I had to get her off me, no matter how. I knew casting a knockout spell at close range while she was in that trance would bring her serious pain. She might suffer for days.

"I'm sorry," she said, too, grinding her teeth. She had been holding back so hard that she might have broken her hands.

My hand trembled. I couldn't bring myself to hurt her. Gods, she didn't deserve this. My sleep syringe would only work if the target wasn't in a blood rage, and every other spell I had would cause her serious damage. The knockout flash would hurt both of us, but it was the best option I had left.

I screamed as I tried to pry her hand off my neck with one arm. With the other, I drew my syringe and readied it.

Just then, the entrance door flew off its hinges. The guard standing in front of it was launched backward with a loud slam. The door shattered as it collided with him. Two men entered the room.

One of them was massive—part giant, from the look of him. He wore heavy steel armor molded to resemble a muscular chest, nipples and all. His helmet bore the face of a bearded man with hollow eyes glowing red. In his hands, he held a massive Warhammer, surrounded by a dark red aura.

Behind him stood a half-elf with dark skin, clad in green padded armor and trousers. He had a bow drawn and aimed directly at me. His red eyes locked on my syringe, and in that instant, I understood—if I moved the wrong way, no one would ever find my body.

"What the hell is happening here?!" the armored man shouted.

Before anyone could respond, the sound of a lute strumming and drums pounding echoed from the room behind them.

Everyone turned toward the doorway.

I glanced back at Isabelle. Black leather arms had wrapped tightly around her waist.

Then, without warning, she was lifted and slammed into the floor hard enough to shatter it. As her body hit the ground, part of her hood slipped off, revealing long black hair. The attacker wrapped her arms around Isabelle's throat and pressed a blade to her neck.

"Mel—" Before I could finish, the loud orchestra from the main tavern cut off.

Michael entered the room wearing his black padded acting clothes, a lute in hand, and a hand drum hovering behind him. His voice boomed through the space, commanding instant attention.

"Everyone, drop your weapons now. Or we all die right here."

He strummed the lute, holding a single string. Smoke began to curl from his fingers.

"If everyone doesn't calm down right now, I'll blow up everyone in this room."

"Daniel. John. Lower your weapons, now," Samuel said.

The two men slowly lowered their arms, eyes locked on Melena, as if daring her to make a move.

I got to my feet, trying to shake the chaos off and pull myself together.

"Put your knife down, and let's talk," said the half-elf, his voice laced with a dry chuckle. "Do you three really want to die today? Because I sure as hell don't. It's been a good week."

Melena released her grip on Isabelle and shoved her off.

"Touch him again, and I'll feed you to the dogs," she snapped.

Isabelle stumbled up. Her hands were bloody and filled with splinters.

Samuel, seeing the tension drop, lowered his whip and sank back into his chair.

Michael let go of the string on his lute. The smoke stopped. He stepped into the center of the room and gave a slow, theatrical bow.

"Now that we've calmed down, would you mind telling me why I hear our doctor screaming in here?" Michael asked, his voice dripping with sarcasm.

As he spoke, Melena walked over to me and patted my shoulder, giving a small nod. I nodded back, letting her know I was alright.

I looked over at Isabelle. She had her hands on her knees, breathing deeply. Her eyes met mine, full of tears. That sad look on her face— she wanted to apologize, I could feel it.

The half-elf turned toward Samuel.

"Why did he need to be pinned to the ground anyway?" he asked, glancing at Isabelle, then at me. "Doesn't even look like a fair fight."

What a dick.

"You're all taking this too seriously," Samuel said. "I was just trying to teach the doctor a lesson in manners and respect. He tested my patience and acted like he owned the place. So, I told Isabelle to put him in his place."

"All I wanted was to stop your slaves from dying. You called me weak and thought making her punch me was teaching me respect?" I said, the anger bubbling back into my throat.

"We heard a good chunk of it from outside. Something about the doctor here being a hero—who was supposed to be indifferent, by the way," Michael said, glaring at me.

"I won't let those people—"

"I don't care," Melena cut in. "We are here to do a job, and nothing else, doctor."

"See, those two get it," Samuel said. "All you had to do was follow orders, and we could've avoided this entire fiasco."

He looked around the room.

"Where are my guards?"

"They're asleep in the other room. With the rest of the patrons. Also getting some well-earned sleep," Michael replied, with just enough pride to be smug.

"I threw that one. Knocked out that one when you weren't looking," Melena added, pointing to an unconscious guard slumped in a corner. Then she nodded toward Isabelle.

We heard groaning from one of the mercs on the floor, rolling in pain.

"He shouldn't have stood so close to the door. That was a dumb mistake," the armored man said.

Samuel sighed.

"How about this. You do your job and your charity work, doctor. Then you leave. I don't ever want to see any of you again. Unless you're here to trade, get lost."

"Fine by me," I said. "I'll start my work. It'll take three days. In that time, I'll have some people build them livable quarters."

I looked over at Isabelle.

"Alright. Do what you came to do and bugger off. You'll get your one copper per person. Otherwise, I don't care," Samuel said, gesturing toward Michael. "Go wake up my people and get out too."

"Nah. We're gonna stick around and protect the doctor. Make sure you don't try anything," Melena said with a grin. "When he leaves, we'll leave."

"I don't care. Isabelle, Johnson, and Daniel stay here. The rest of you, get out of my sight."

He waved us toward the door. As the twins and I stepped out, I heard footsteps behind me. I turned and saw Isabelle, wiping tears from her face.

"I'm sorry, doctor," she mumbled.

I lifted my mask. I wanted her to see a real smile.

"Don't worry about it. Just buy me a beer and come help when you can. Besides, I can't do this without you."

I handed her a healing potion.

She gave me the smallest grin. After all the pain, the torture, and everything she'd endured, she still found a way to smile at me. It didn't matter that it was faint. It made my day.

I wanted to hug her. But I told myself I'd wait until the others weren't watching.

Chapter 25

About an hour passed, and the twins had gathered some of our members who'd been waiting outside the Drunk Lions Tavern for orders. They all looked eager to fight, even though their clothes were ragged and mismatched. We looked like teenagers trying too hard to be intimidating. I split the eight of them into two teams of four.

"You four, go get barrels of water. Bring me six. The rest of you head to the market and buy clothes. Focus on quantity, not quality. Anything's better than what they're wearing. Make sure you get clothes for men, women, and kids."

I turned toward Michael and Melena. "You two are my bodyguards, right?"

Melena shook her head. "I'm your bodyguard, but you won't see me. I'm not getting anywhere near those sick people. But know this, if anyone crosses the line with you, I'll gut them. I mean it."

"How did you get into Samuel's office anyway?" I asked.

Melena gave a smile and pulled out a potion bottle labeled invisible.

"I keep the potions you give us, Wallace. I wanted to hear how things were going with Samuel, so I followed you and the slave girl inside. I stayed by one of the windows, and when you were attacked, I knocked out one of his guards. You saw the rest."

Melena spoke with pride, but there was something else in her voice—almost like she was glad she'd been there for me.

Michael raised his hands. "I'm trying to negotiate with Samuel. We need this alliance, both of you. Other street gangs are already watching us. We need money, and we need to grow fast. So, I don't get why you're doing all of this for cheap. Practically free, Wallace."

I looked toward the ground. "I'll take it out of my stash. No gang money. I can't let those slaves suffer while I could help."

The twins exchanged glances.

"I don't like it," Melena said softly, "but now isn't the time to be a hero. We need more muscle before we challenge slavers openly."

Michael nodded. "If you want to fight slavers in this city, we'll drown in enemies. The Table's on their side."

They were right, but my mind flashed to those faces in the barns. I swallowed hard. "So… you're okay with me doing this alone?"

The twins shook their heads.

"No. If I had it my way, I'd see those people released, Wallace. But if we try to be the liberators of slaves in this city, we'll drown in enemies. The Table keeps that slavery in line, and not even King

Kendrick can stop the Table," Michael said as he came up to me and hugged me.

"I know, Wallace. It's hard. But all we can do is our best. I'm proud of you for sticking up for yourself."

"When did you two learn about the Table?" I asked.

"We've been scouting other bars for info and found out about them yesterday. I thought it was a joke, but after hearing what happened when you talked to Samuel, it's hard to say now," Melena said.

"Regardless, we won't be far, Wallace," Michael added.

I took the chance to hug Melena as well. "Thanks." She hugged me back.

As I reentered the slave field, I saw Isabelle talking to the two men from earlier. As I got closer, I noticed the three of them wrapped in a hug. The two men towered over Isabelle, at least a foot taller than her. A small grin appeared on Isabelle's face.

They all looked at me as I approached. The steel man stepped forward. His booming voice echoed through the space. If Isabelle was the wolf, then this man was the bear.

"You're the plague doctor, right? Got another name besides Doctor?" he asked.

His red eyes locked onto me, sharp and intimidating, like one wrong word and I'd be torn in half. I froze for a second, but then I felt the half-elf and Isabelle come closer. Somehow, their presence made me feel safe.

"I use Doctor as my name just in case. People tend to come after you in this city. It's how you stay safe," I said with a chuckle.

"Daniel, ease up on the man. Isabelle didn't break his jaw for a reason, I'm sure," the half-elf said.

The steel man groaned and extended his hand. "I'm Daniel. This is Johnson."

As I shook Daniel's hand, he was worse than Isabelle. It felt like he was trying to crush my bones on purpose. When he finally let go, Johnson stepped up and offered his hand.

"They try to break your hand as a sign of dominance. Don't worry," he said

The half-elf shook my hand too, and I was grateful his grip wasn't nearly as tight as Isabelle's or Daniel's.

"Are you two slaves too?" I asked.

"No. Isabelle is being trained to be the driving force behind Samuel's growth plans. Johnson and I were hired to train and protect her," Daniel replied.

"It's a dumb way of saying we aren't her parents, but we are in spirit!" Johnson laughed.

"We are not her parents. I don't know how many times I have to tell you that," Daniel said, grimacing.

"God, Daniel, don't say that. You're embarrassing her. See, this is why I'm the mother figure in this relationship, and you're the father, ignoring his responsibilities," Johnson said, grinning.

I turned toward Isabelle, who had her face in her hands, sighing in frustration.

"Doctor, you have a job to do. Follow me, please."

I looked back at the other two and saw Johnson slapping Daniel on the shoulders.

"When are you going to be a better father, my dearest husband?"

"Doctor, go with Isabelle. We have to talk to the boss," Daniel said. Then he turned to Johnson and gripped his arm. "We're leaving."

I watched as Daniel dragged Johnson behind him toward the other building. Then I turned back to Isabelle and followed her. This time, I kept my eyes on her back instead of anywhere else. I didn't want to piss off either of her parents.

She led us back to the first farmhouse and looked at me.

"I'm going to be here for multiple days to get everyone better. Let's do the kids first. If my team shows up, just help them out the best you can," I told her.

"Wait. I'd like to ask you something, Doctor." She crossed her arms. "We didn't do anything for you. You're doing all this and losing money. Why are you helping us?"

I took off my mask before we entered, trying to ignore the smell.

"Because it's the right thing to do." I looked down. "If I had the money or power, I'd try to free you all. This place is a nightmare. If I can't take you out of here, then I can at least make it a little more bearable. None of you deserves this. I'm sure of that."

She lowered her arms and bowed.

"Thank you, Doctor. I hope to pay you back for this."

"Isabelle, I have one favor to ask now. Call me Wallace. My name is Wallace."

She stood up straight. "Okay, Wallace. Let's get moving then."

Any birthday gift money I had for Kreila was gone. I'd planned to get her a beautiful necklace, but if she knew where the money went, she wouldn't mind. And if she didn't know where it came from, even better.

After draining my bank account, my team managed to bring new clothes, water, and tools to help rebuild the farm.

I spent the next three days working those disgusting farms. I had to bathe three times a day just to keep from gagging. The little copper I was paid went toward new clothes for myself—anything to avoid smelling like piss and dung. I worked alongside the slaves, curing their illnesses and teaching them how to care for their wounds if they got hurt.

I caught myself staring at Isabelle as she worked. She looked like she could snap me in half. Watching her all day, her muscles slick with sweat, was... unexpectedly appetizing.

I also tried teaching them basic first aid, although that part didn't go as smoothly as I'd hoped. When I asked for a volunteer to demonstrate what to do when someone is choking, I looked at Isabelle. But of course, Johnson stepped up instead—far too enthusiastic about the whole thing.

With many of the gang members and slaves working together, we were able to rebuild the outhouses, restore the farm, set up clean beds, and more. I paid for a couple of nearby workers to deliver fresh well water to the slaves every few days.

As happy as I was to see the slaves wearing real clothes and playing with actual toys for the first time, deep down I was screaming. Everything turned out to be more expensive than I planned. I had budgeted five gold for the entire project. It ended up costing fifteen. That meant I was basically broke for the next few months.

Still, a lot of those thoughts faded whenever I saw Isabelle smile. She spent time with the kids, helping them into their new clothes. She looked genuinely happy to help. Even though she was clearly exhausted, she kept pushing through. I went up to her several times, urging her to take breaks. Most of the time, she listened. Her answers started as "Yes, Doctor sir," and slowly turned into "Let me finish this, Wallace."

On my final night there, I gathered the slaves around a campfire with Isabelle by my side. My last lesson was how to make soap and bathe properly. Real soap, the kind that smells fruity or like some polished gentleman, was expensive. But with animal fat, water, ash, and oil, I showed them how to make something simple and cheap that still cleaned well.

Using advice Kreila gave me a while back, the slaves were able to make a batch that smelled faintly of fresh flowers. To be honest, it was more like catching the scent of a flower garden from across the city. Still, it worked. It was cheap, and it was what we had.

Isabelle stayed up that night helping me teach. Every day I spent on that farm, she mirrored my movements and techniques like she'd been watching me closely the whole time almost like she'd been staring at me too.

As the final night came to a close, I looked back at the slave farms. It wasn't fancy, but everyone had new clothes, proper equipment, and a place to sleep. I wished they didn't have to stay here at all. I'd dreamed of freeing them, but I knew it would end in blood.

I walked over to Isabelle. She was helping an elderly man make his first batch of soap.

"Isabelle, you got a moment?"

She nodded and walked with me toward the tavern door.

"Wallace, I was hoping to talk to you. I wanted to apologize."

I cut her off.

"Now, why would you need to apologize for something you couldn't stop? I saw your scar and the stamp. I could tell you were in pain. I don't blame you for knocking me down, and I wouldn't have blamed you if you hit me either."

"Thank you, Wallace. Where did you learn all your skills? I thought I heard you mention a university?"

My face went red.

"Well, I am a doctor, but it's from a university no one's ever heard of. It's far east, in the Paljavan Republic."

Isabelle rolled her eyes and shook her head.

"Are you some kind of con artist?" She stared at me like she was ready to kill me.

"Well," I said with a grin, "I also had a plague doctor down the road teach me everything I know. Her name's Abigail Kreila. I've been her apprentice. On top of my college hours."

"Johnson was assigned to spy on you over the past two days. It sounds like being Kreila's apprentice is true, but I'm unsure about the rest," Isabelle said with a sigh. "But if you were a con artist, he would've said something by now—or the people here would still be sick."

She extended her hand.

I reached out and shook it. "It was great working with you, Isabelle. Take care of your people."

"Thank you for your assistance, Wallace. I hope I can help your people and your family someday. I don't like being in debt to anyone," she replied.

"You're not in debt to me, Isabelle."

"Then just know that everyone here thanks you, Wallace. Even though they aren't here to say it, Johnson and Daniel appreciate your work too. Please stay safe."

We shook hands again. This time, her grip was gentle—not bone-crushing like before.

"I'm always happy to help. As long as you tell Johnson to stop spying on me," I said.

"I'll inform him of your request, but I believe he may ignore it." There it was again—that cute smile with just a touch of sarcasm. "Also, if he thought you were a threat, he would've killed you by now."

She was copying me, and she was good at it. Still, I didn't like the idea of a peppy half-elf spying on me. If it had been anyone else, I would've thrown a fit. But not her.

As I waved goodbye and neared the tavern's front door, I spotted Johnson sitting at a table. As I passed, he gave me a smile and a wink.

Terrified, I bolted outside.

I waved her goodbye and exited the tavern. As I stepped out, Michael and Melena spotted me and came over.

"Well, good news. After your little stunt, I managed to negotiate with that snake. We help protect some of his shipments—wine, supplies, that kind of stuff—from other gangs. In return, he's providing actual weapons, gear, and coin."

I stared at him, stunned. "You got us back into his deal?"

"I've got a smooth tongue, Wallace. Ask Penelope," he said with a grin.

I kicked him in the shin for that smug remark.

Chapter 26

I got home after my last night helping Isabelle and her crew. My body was sore, and I was dead tired. I had pushed myself harder than I should have, trying to impress Isabelle by lifting more boxes, but all I did was mess up my back worse than I expected. The twins went back to their tavern, and as usual, it was another late night.

I noticed the house was lit with candlelight, which meant Kreila must have come back from one of her monthly trips. A knot formed in my stomach, Barron's shadow felt heavier now, and I didn't know how to start telling Kreila what I'd learned. If I spilled everything, would she see me differently? Would I betray her trust? I wasn't sure how to break the news about Barron. I didn't know where to start. If I told her everything he was involved in, she might ask how I knew. But if I kept quiet, she could end up being his next target. I paused at the doorway, biting my lip, fighting the guilt of spending money on Isabelle's farm when Kreila deserved my attention. I decided I'd feel out the situation once I saw her.

I unlocked the front door, and as I stepped in, I heard movement upstairs. I went to Kreila's room and knocked.

"Come in, Wallace," she said softly.

When I walked in, she was laying out clothes and putting them away in her drawers. Her movements were careful but tired, as if the weight of years pressed on her shoulders even in this quiet moment. She was already in her nightgown, and the room smelled like chamomile and faint hints of lavender, the soft glow of a candle flickering in the corner casting dancing shadows across the faded wallpaper.

"Where have you been? The Captain said you were gone a few days," she asked.

"I was with the twins. We had a lot of customers at the bar this weekend, so I wanted to help out and be around them," I said.

I guess it wasn't exactly a lie. I was helping the twins. Securing that deal with the Drunk Lions counted as helping them, didn't it?

She nodded slowly. "Makes sense. Still, those two worry me. Wallace, you're not even adults yet, and you're running a whole tavern. A drinking spot in the ghetto, no less. I'm still shocked you three pulled it off."

"Hard work," I told her. "Late hours and giving up my off days to help them build it."

I sighed, starting to feel uneasy under all her questions.

She gave me another look. "Wallace, what's wrong? You look worn out. You seem upset," she said gently.

I felt the tension coil tighter in my chest. The words I wanted to say tangled up in my throat, but the heaviness of what I had to confess pushed me forward.

I was stuck in that moment. I was exhausted, not just from the day's work but from worrying about her and Barron. I moved ahead carefully.

"I was with the twins today, and I heard a rumor from one of the tavern goers. I think they were probably criminals or mercenaries. They mentioned that Barron's company was trading drugs and slaves across the continent," I said.

She stopped folding clothes and stared at me.

"Let's talk downstairs. I'll make you some tea to help you sleep."

We headed down to the dining room. She walked past me and started boiling water.

"If criminals or mercenaries are showing up at your bar, Wallace, I don't want you there. I'm worried about what you might get dragged into. Gangs use taverns as meeting points or places to plan things. If the bar is where you said it was, in the east part of Elton, then that's probably the worst area for crime."

"I appreciate the concern, ma'am, but we've got it under control. We've got security, and all the staff know how to get out of a fight if it comes to that. And you taught me how to fight too, when I need to."

"I'd rather you not need to use it at all, Wallace," she said, staring at me. Then she sighed.

The tension between us grew. I felt torn, wondering if I was walking the same dangerous path Barron had taken, slipping too far into the shadows I once despised.

"What was it you wanted to tell me about Barron? Slave trading, was it?" she asked.

I leaned in toward the table.

"The tavern goers said the Blackwater Caravan trades in drugs and slaves. They said Barron is cold and calculated, but that's all I know. I wanted to ask what you know about him."

She raised her arm and dropped a syringe, summoning a servant to bring the tea.

"I've known Barron for a long time, Wallace. Twenty years, actually. He was charming, but he always wanted me to work with him. About fifteen years ago, just as I was leaving for one of my monthly trips, he stopped me and asked for help. I told him I had to go, but he kept insisting that I stay. He even offered me a pouch of gold. Still, I left. When I came back a few days later, he showed up looking visibly angry."

The teacups arrived at the table, and the smell of honey and chamomile filled the air, taking our noses hostage.

"That's when Barron asked me to meet him at his palace. As a precaution, I told Steven and some friends where I was going. I could hold my own, but just in case, I wanted people to know where to find me if things went sideways. Barron sat me down in the dining hall and told me what he had been working on. He told me why he was frustrated. He had been trying to become immortal, to stop himself from aging."

My heart skipped a beat. But it made sense. Barron claimed he was in his eighties, yet he barely looked like he was in his mid-forties. Aging doesn't just slow down on its own. To beat it, you'd need something powerful—something unnatural.

"Barron said that the day he came to me, he felt like he was on the edge of a breakthrough. He believed he could drastically improve his immortality. But what I was doing at the time was important. I still can't tell you what those trips are about, and I don't tell you or him because it would put you in danger."

She looked down at her teacup.

"Barron told me he wanted to be immortal so he could fix the country. He said the Eltons were powerless and that the former queen, Verona, was still pulling strings through corrupt leaders. He wanted power by any means necessary so he could take control. His goal was to sit on the throne as the new ruler and reshape the nation in his image—no more royal houses, no more parliament. Just him and whoever he chose to help him was in charge. That's when he said he needed me. He believed I was the one who could help him gain the power to take over the country.”

She frowned and kept staring into her tea.

“He hinted that I could have his power too. That I could stop aging, and become his immortal advisor. He even hinted I could be his queen. But I turned him down. I told him immortality was a curse. Watching your friends die, living without end, with no real peace—that kind of life would break him. He respected my answer at first, but over time, he kept reminding me of the offer. I think he’ll make the same offer to you soon.”

The blood drained from my face.

“What do you mean? Why would he want me?”

She stood up and moved her chair beside mine, turning to face me. I adjusted my seat to meet her gaze.

“If he can’t have me, he’ll want the next best thing. You’ve done well, Wallace, and he knows it. Barron sees that you’re young, sharp, and capable. I believe he plans to influence you, to pull you into his company. I don’t think he would ever hurt you, but I do think he’ll be disappointed if you say no. Still, the decision is yours. I won’t force you to take up the shop or follow in my footsteps. That choice is for you to make when the time comes.”

Her hands began to tremble, and she reached for mine. I held her hand gently. Then she looked me in the eyes.

"I know I'm getting older, Wallace. I'm slowing down. I can't handle much work anymore, and I want you to start working here full-time. I'll teach you everything I can, as quickly as I can."

She smiled.

"Most of my days will be spent writing and teaching you. I understand you spend time with your siblings, but there will be moments when I need you to stay here with me and help run the store. I have savings put away to keep us afloat in case I can't work, but I want you to know we'll be alright, no matter what."

"Nothing will happen, and I'll make sure of that," I mumbled.

"Ha! You sound like me from the past!" she said, chuckling as she let go of my hands. "When I was young, I thought I could cure a god if someone asked me to."

I laughed with her, trying to cover the sadness welling up inside me. I understood what she was really telling me. Kreila was getting old. Her body was slowing down, and soon she wouldn't be able to work anymore.

"I have some stories I want to tell you before we drink our tea and rest," she said. Her voice softened, and the candlelight flickered against the worn pages of the book resting on her nightstand.

"Could you please grab the book from my nightstand? It's the one with green lettering."

"Of course, I'll be right back," I nodded.

I walked into her room and headed straight for the nightstand. I saw the book with green letters on the cover: The Witches of Eltonia. A small smile crept onto my face.

As I turned to leave, I hesitated for a moment, letting Kreila's words echo in my mind, her fears, and Barron's looming presence. Then something on her pillow caught my eye. I moved closer and picked it up. It wasn't just a strand of her hair—it was a whole clump that had fallen out.

Chapter 27

Kreila screamed from the floor below like someone jumped at her. I jumped out of bed without thinking. Still in my underwear, I reached into my nightstand and grabbed my emergency syringes. I had one for acid to melt, one with light to stun, and another for healing wounds.

Moving with the speed of a lion, I sprinted down the stairs, syringe in hand, ready to throw it at whoever had broken in.

"Oh well, it's nice to see you too!" said the elf, raising his hands above his head.

I glanced at Kreila. She didn't seem to be holding anything—just looked shaken by the elf's sudden appearance.

"Your—" She stopped herself, stumbling slightly over the word.

"Yep, it's Thomas!" he said with glee, waving his hands in the air.

"What in God's name are you doing here, boy?" Kreila asked, her voice sharp.

Thomas's smile faltered for just a moment, a flicker of something unreadable crossing his face before he recovered.

"I just wanted to stop by and visit. Passing through, really. I also got a raven recently from this area. Would you happen to know anything about that?"

His voice was light, but there was a tremor beneath the surface, as if the cheerful tone was a mask.

He looked at me, then at Kreila, then back again. His eyes scanned me from head to toe, like he was sizing me up.

"Wallace, good to see you too! I'd give you a hug, but hugging another man my age in his underwear might strike fear into my father."

"Hello, Thomas. Goodbye, Thomas," I muttered as I turned and ran back upstairs.

I came back down wearing just a shirt and some brown pants. When I returned, Thomas spotted me and smiled. I hadn't seen him in years, but I couldn't understand why Kreila looked so shaken. Just like the twins, he approached with those long arms of his, towering over me. Another one taller than me. I really needed to fix that with magic, I thought to myself.

His bright teal eyes, warm brown skin, curly hair, and pointed elf ears gave him the look of a foreigner. As he reached out, I opened my arms to greet a friend I had only seen once in the past four years. He wrapped me in a massive bear hug, lifting me clean off the ground. He squeezed tight, trying to crush every last bit of air from my lungs.

Then he dropped me back onto the floor and gave my shoulder a firm pat.

"Kreila says you've been doing well in your training. Said you'll be an Abigail junior in no time," he said with a laugh.

Despite not knowing him that well, he gave off the energy of a big brother I hadn't seen in years—maybe even one I'd lost.

"What have you been up to, Thomas? It's been a long time," I asked, still trying to catch my breath.

"Oh, I've been spending time in the Tylvan Union. Being around a bunch of old elves teaches you a lot," he said. "I've been making charms and wood carvings. When we have time, we travel and sell the pieces we make. Most foreigners don't really know what's a fair deal and what isn't, so it's a good living."

He laughed, his smile warm and genuine.

"I made something for both of you to keep."

He reached into his pouch and pulled out a small wooden carving shaped like a bear's head. It was dark green and worn as a necklace. Despite its rough shape, it had a charm to it. The green wood was rare and expensive in Eltonia, since the trees only grew far to the east, deep in Tylvan territory.

He handed one to me and one to Kreila.

"My dad wanted you to know, Kreila, that he appreciates everything you've done. He said you should never hesitate to ask for help. I made this so you'd have something to remember him by."

For God's sake, how many old men are in love with Kreila? She must've been a heartbreaker in her youth.

I held the necklace in my hand and felt a faint trace of druid magic. It wasn't strong enough to do anything useful, but it gave off a scent— clean pine, balsam, and warm cedar.

"It's got a scent that never fades as long as you're wearing it. Think of it as instant cologne or perfume," Thomas said. "You'll smell like the woods. The good parts of the woods, at least."

"Thomas, you're too kind. I appreciate the gift, sweetheart," Kreila said. "But please get back to your father. I'm sure he'll be needing your help soon. Don't make him worry."

Thomas's smile tightened for a heartbeat, a shadow crossing his face. "No worries, Mrs. Kreila. I'll be safe. I just need to stick to a couple of roads, and I'll be fine."

I caught the hesitation in his voice, and my instincts screamed that something was off.

"Why do you sound so concerned?" I asked, turning to Kreila.

"Oh, umm, it's because…" she stuttered again.

"I'm popular with people," Thomas jumped in. "I get swarmed sometimes—folks wanting to buy charms or women hoping for a kiss. It happens all the time!"

His eyes lit up as he flashed a bright, confident smile.

I've done my fair share of con work in my free time. I've learned how to read people—when they're angry, sad, calm, or somewhere in between. There was real joy in his voice and warmth in both his and Kreila's smiles, but I could tell what was going on.

He wasn't supposed to be here.

He was either in danger or being followed. I didn't want to call them out on it, but it was obvious they had a history—one deeper than either of them wanted to explain.

Before leaving, Thomas glanced around nervously, lowering his voice slightly. "If anything happens, remember the raven. It's more than just a bird."

"Okay, okay, I'll get a move on. But just remember, Kreila, if you ever need us, you know how to send ravens."

With one smooth motion, he hopped over the counter and wrapped Kreila in a hug strong enough to crush an ork. After nearly destroying her bones, he jumped back over the desk and launched himself toward me, pulling me into a tight embrace.

"Love you, Kreila. As for you, Wallace—we'll see," he said with a grin. "Catch you next time I'm in town!"

He waved goodbye and was gone.

Since I put on the necklace, I'd been smelling like a log cabin in the woods. I glanced over at Kreila, who was holding hers up to her nose, taking in the scent.

"He put a lot of effort into making these," she mumbled, eyes thoughtful. Then she looked at me.

"I've known his family for a long time, Wallace. I helped deliver one of his sisters a few years ago—before I met you."

"You mean when I broke your window?" I said with a grin.

"Yes, your attempted burglary," Kreila replied with a smile. "One of these days, I'm sure he'll try to get you to meet his family."

"What are they like?" I asked.

She hesitated before answering, as if weighing how much to reveal.

She spent the rest of the day talking about her younger years—how she and her husband, Steven, would sometimes wander into the woods to pick flowers. One day, they came across Thomas' parents, wounded after a bandit attack. Kreila and Steven helped them escape, even killing the bandits who were chasing them.

After the rescue, the elves showered her with gifts and continued to visit her from time to time. But after a few years filled with hardship, the visits stopped. Thomas and his family were always on the move. Their trinkets attracted attention from humans eager to get their hands on rare and expensive artifacts. They spent most of their time among the other elves in Tylvan, but eventually moved to Eltonia to start a new life.

Then the king grew paranoid, and they were kicked out.

Her voice grew quieter, tinged with regret. "The coven and the family... everything changed after that."

Once she finished telling me about Thomas and his family, she began to share more of her past. Back when she was part of a witches' coven, they worked together to create rare and powerful potions. But not every day was serious—sometimes, they crafted spells to make themselves more attractive, hoping to charm a local man into marrying them.

Kreila said she was the first to marry. After that, her coven sisters raced to be the next bride. One of them eventually married a young nobleman from the far east. Kreila told me she still stays in touch with one of her coven sisters, but the rest have passed away—some during adventures, some from old age. The one who survived is a half-elf now married to a dwarf.

Her voice softened, tinged with vulnerability. "I left the coven because the magic stopped feeling like mine. Steven showed me another path, one full of love and choices."

To cheer her up, I decided to put on her makeup. Using lipstick and red powder, I tried to make her look a few years younger. Thanks to my years of conning and impersonation, I managed to make her look marvelous.

When I showed her the mirror, she burst into laughter, saying I had done far better than she expected. Kreila admitted she thought she'd end up looking like a court jester, but she praised my work with a smile.

As I watched her, I realized how much she was hiding behind that strength, the quiet fears about getting older, about what would happen to the shop, to her legacy.

As the evening wore on, she showed me a few of her old trinkets from her younger days.

One was a pipe flute covered in ancient elven carvings. She never quite learned how to use it properly—something my ears weren't too thrilled about.

Next, she pulled out an axe handle. It was worn and weathered, its age clear from the faded wood and chipped edges. It had belonged to Steven, who used it working himself to the bone as a lumberjack. All of it was for her—so he could buy her jewelry and perfumes. Even though Kreila earned more than he did, Steven insisted on getting her gifts with his own hands.

The last item she revealed was a white gold ring. She said it was a family heirloom from Steven's side. Ever since the day she proposed to him, she's never gone more than ten seconds without wearing it.

She sighed, fingers tracing the ring's smooth surface. "Sometimes I wonder if I'm holding on too tight to the past. But it's all I have left."

We were both overjoyed, surrounded by the quiet comfort of old memories and the lingering scent of balsam and cedar.

Chapter 28

It had been a few months since the drunk lions incident, but the twins told me the deal they made with them was helping the gang grow. The crew even got new equipment and training on how to stab and how to steal. We were still small, but people around that part of the city knew who we were.

I had hoped to visit Isabelle, but the last few months with Kreila had been packed. And I am pretty sure Samuel is not trying to let a slave take breaks just to spend time with me, especially not for free.

The summer was starting to fade, and the leaves had begun to turn orange and brown. I was sitting around one morning, just reading books stacked over beakers and bottles—ones Kreila had assigned me. The day dragged on, and I would often read for so long that I would forget to take off my glasses before slamming my head into the desk in frustration. By the time evening came, I had only sold two potions. The rest of the day was just more reading. Kreila went out for her trip again, which I could now confidently say was her way of going to see Thomas.

The books she gave me were a bore. When I was younger, the writers had some spark. They made the pages fun, sometimes even exciting. But as I got older, the books she picked for me lost all that. No more wild art or interesting stories—just line after line of dry facts I already knew. Learning fast can be a curse in disguise.

I started to drift off at the front desk, eyes barely open. That's when I heard shouting—loud, panicked voices coming from down the block. They were getting closer. Then the door slammed open and several men rushed in. Most of them were gagging, and a few turned right around to vomit outside.

They were all wearing the purple and gold sigils of the Drunk Lions, dressed in everything from light leather to full steel armor. The yelling continued, from "Help him up" to "What about the other guys at the bar?" coming from behind the crowd.

Twelve men came in, all familiar faces. Daniel and Johnson were among them. Johnson was helping Daniel stay on his feet, nearly carrying him. Daniel had vomit on his steel armor, and Johnson's leather was stained with something foul.

"You, Wallace, we need your help now!" Johnson shouted.

"What in the hell is going on?!" I shouted back.

"Don't know for certain, but I think we all got poisoned or hit with some kind of spell. I think this was planned. They killed our healer first."

I started putting on my gloves and secured my plague mask.

"Who are they?"

"Rival mercs, probably. From the Red Fang Syndicate. They're known for using rare toxins, extracted from venomous insects deep in the swamps, mixed into powders that can be thrown or smeared. This poison causes burns and internal rot, and the symptoms show within minutes, spreading through the bloodstream fast. No time for other questions. Just help Daniel first."

He leaned Daniel over the desk, which creaked hard under the weight of his armor. As Johnson took off Daniel's helmet, I saw why he had kept it on. His head was burned so badly that part of his jaw was fully exposed. His skin was bright pink, raw, and all the hair had been scorched off. In some places, it looked like his skin was peeling away completely.

"Fix this right now, boy!" he barked, just as another merc threw up in the corner.

Assholes are going to make me summon a servant to clean that up.

I pulled a syringe from the slot on my wrist and jabbed it into his arm to get a sample. The liquid inside turned brown almost immediately. The vial confirmed it—it was poison, and a strong one too.

Good thing Kreila's work holds up. She's stronger anyway.

I reached beneath the counter and brought out two brown bottles, the contents rattling with each step I took.

"Here. One for you, and one for you. Drink it! I'll get more."

They barely let me finish before Daniel and Johnson had their lips on the bottles, drinking like they hadn't seen water in weeks. Johnson was polite enough to place his bottle back on the desk. Daniel, though, dropped his. The glass shattered on the floor—another mess for my faithful servant.

I sprinted to the inpatient room and grabbed a bucket along with several more potions. While I gathered supplies, I could hear more disasters piling up for the loyal magical servant I don't pay.

When I returned, one of the mercs was gagging. I slid a bucket by his feet and let him handle the rest. I handed out potions to the ones who looked the worst off. Once I ran out, I switched to the syringe. The potions worked, and my magic through the syringes worked too—but using the syringe drained me way more than brewing a potion. Still, I was focused on speed. Kreila did not need to come home to a wreck and a magical servant strike.

After a few minutes, the worst of them started coughing—a good sign the potions were kicking in.

"You all are gonna have bad times in the outhouse," I said, "but until then, you'll live."

I pointed to two of the mercs who looked like they were still about to drop. "You two need to sit down or lie down. One of the two."

Before they could move, two other mercs grabbed one of them by the shoulders.

"No. They come with us," one said.

Daniel slid his helmet back on and took a deep breath. "No time. They're gonna need us back at base now. Isabelle is there with only a few guards."

This issue then became my issue.

"At the same place? The Drunk Lion?"

Johnson stood up beside Daniel and let out a loud belch. "Yeah, we need to go right now!"

The mercs flew out the door, sprinting away from the city block. A few lagged behind, either still slowed from the poison or being carried.

I dropped my syringe to the floor to summon my servant, then ran up the stairs. I quickly threw on my armor and strapped on my winged boots. Grabbing the silver broom, I bolted back out the door—and caught sight of a broom hovering just above the floor, sweeping vomit into a bucket.

"Sorry, man. I've got to go. You are the best!"

As I ran outside, I heard the soft whap of a broom smacking a desk in frustration.

I let some magic move from my heart to my hands, then to the broom. As the energy flowed, it began to levitate slowly. Luckily,

Barron taught me how to use this thing—before I found out he was a snake.

I gave the broom's end a light pull, and it rose higher and higher, until I hovered about two feet above the shop.

"Eyes forward. Look for the bear fountain," I told myself.

The Drunk Lion tavern wasn't too far, but getting through the crowds was another issue. I could see the rooftops and chimneys in the morning light. Tall houses made of wood and smaller ones built from clay stretched for miles. A few neighbors glanced up and waved. I waved back.

Flying brooms were rare and expensive, but enough rich scum had them that it wasn't shocking to see one anymore.

I focused my direction north and tightened both hands around the broom. I could feel the magic flow through me, like water spilling from my fingertips. I took a deep breath, slid my hands slightly down the broom, and started to accelerate. I kept adjusting my grip until I was moving at a decent speed.

The winged boots would keep me from falling to my death, but bruises and broken bones were still fair game.

I headed for the north side of the city, slowing just enough to scan for landmarks. I searched for statues of a bear—the symbol of loyalty. As I flew, the wind whipped past, but the mask kept bugs and flies out of my face.

Eventually, I thought I heard shouting off to the left. When I turned, I spotted the Drunk Lion tavern—and chaos.

Dozens of bodies were scattered around. The tavern was under attack by red-masked men clad in leather, all wielding knives, swords, or crossbows. There were about twenty of them, surrounding six Drunk Lion members. At the front stood Isabelle, blood-covered and panting.

As a bandit lunged at her, she raised her spear and let out a fierce shout, charging straight at him. He tried to dodge the tip, but she stopped short and smashed him in the face with the side of the spear. While he was stunned, she swept his legs and brought him down. Then she drove the spear clean into his chest.

I quickly lowered myself to the ground and noticed that all the Drunk Lion defenders looked either injured or exhausted. My hands moved fast, sharp and precise, as I hurled syringes at them. I didn't care where they hit—so long as it wasn't the head or the heart. That was the rule.

As soon as the syringes struck, I saw some of them take deeper breaths. A few of their wounds began to close right before my eyes. With renewed strength, the Drunk Lions roared back into action, lunging at the bandits with axes and swords.

That was when the bandits turned their focus toward me. Two of them charged with swords raised.

As they sprinted my way, I drew two syringes from my wrist and flung them. To my left, one of the bandits screamed as a syringe struck his hand, erupting in green acid that ate through his skin on impact. He dropped his weapon and hit the ground, wailing.

The second bandit to my right wasn't hit directly. I only saw acid splash behind his shoulder and sizzle into the dirt.

"Damn. I missed."

He saw the opening and didn't hesitate. He swung his iron blade toward my arm. The sword tore through my leather and left a river of blood pouring down my right side

I screamed and stumbled back, clutching my arm, then grabbed another syringe just as he moved in for the next hit. As he prepared to swing again, I hurled it straight into the center of his chest.

The moment it landed, he froze. His sword lowered. He dropped to his knees, coughing violently. He clawed at his neck, trying to figure out what was choking him.

It was a coughing spell. It wouldn't kill him—but it would make him hack so hard he could barely move.

I stepped toward him, pulled out a syringe, and jabbed it into my injured arm. Heat radiated from the wound, but it quickly cooled. I watched as the cut closed, and the leather on my sleeve slowly stitched itself back together.

I approached the screaming bandit as small bits of skin and blood melted from his hands. He looked up at me, wide-eyed, just as I injected him with two syringes. I watched his hands begin to heal, slowly. Then I heard him collapse, coughing violently.

Turning back to the bloody town square, I saw the Drunk Lions pushing the attack. On one side, Isabelle was dodging strikes from three different bandits.

Without hesitation, I flung a syringe across the city block. It struck one of them in the leg. Within seconds, he dropped to his knees, coughing and gasping for air.

The other two froze in confusion. Before either could react, one of them got cracked across the skull by the pole of Isabelle's spear. The third looked down just in time to see an arrow pierce through his chest. He fell instantly.

Shouting erupted from the nearby street. I looked up to see Daniel leading the charge, swinging a massive steel sword with so much force that he split a bandit clean in half. Johnson was close behind, loosing arrows with precision and speed. Each shot hit its mark—backs, heads, he didn't blink before drawing the next one.

As the rest of the Drunk Lions poured into the square, the bandits finally broke ranks and sprinted toward the side streets. But they didn't get far.

Isabelle lifted her spear to her shoulder and hurled it, striking one poor lad in the back and pinning him to the ground. The rest didn't escape either. Johnson and the others released a volley of arrows, dropping them one by one, hitting legs and spines. The remaining defenders chased them down to finish the job.

Before I ran to check on Isabelle, I pulled some rope from my bag and tied up the hands of the two coughing bandits. One of the defenders gave me a nod as he dragged them to the wall.

I was exhausted. I could barely feel my arms, and the magic running through them had gone from warm and fluid to almost nonexistent. I had to resist the urge to take off my mask for air. I still needed my face covered—especially with criminals still lurking around.

I looked up and saw Isabelle being greeted by Johnson. He placed a hand on her shoulder, and green mist began to rise from his fingertips. Slowly, her wounds began to seal.

As I walked up to them, I suddenly felt a massive slap on my back that knocked me flat to the ground. Looking up, I saw Daniel staring down at me.

"I was trying to say good work, but it looks like you're too weak to take a pat on the back," he snorted.

I pushed myself back to my feet just in time to see Samuel and a few others coming out of the tavern. Two thieves in leather armor stepped out behind him, blood on their knives and MWM branded on their shoulders. We must've had people posted inside to help defend.

Samuel walked right past the victorious defenders and came straight to me.

"Doctor, Doctor, Doctor! I take back everything I said about you!" he shouted, slapping both of my shoulders. At least I saw him coming—unlike Daniel.

"You did a better job taking care of those thugs than my own men!"

He turned toward Daniel and Johnson.

"Where the hells were you guys?!"

Daniel took a step away from Isabelle and toward Samuel.

"That meeting with the Crimson Dogs was a trap. They poisoned us all and jumped us. We lost three in the fight." He shook his head, shame heavy in his voice. "One of them was our healer, so we couldn't cure the poison quickly. We found the doctor there, and he cured us. Then, somehow, he got here before we did."

"Broomsticks are expensive for a reason," I said, still trying to catch my breath. I held up my silver broom. "It's fast—as long as you're not afraid of falling."

I was terrified of falling. Why did I say that?

Samuel was grinning from ear to ear. "I take it all back about you being a weak kid. You saved my bar and my business from those monsters!"

He grabbed my shoulders and started shaking me. I nearly vomited, just like the others had earlier.

The two MWM members approached. I looked at them while still being rattled by Samuel.

"Tell your boss what happened. Wait for me to come with you, and we'll take the safe way."

The feminine one gave a nod. "We stuck to the rules, boss. Bruises and scrapes, but no corpses. Well... it was more like we wounded them, then a merc slashed 'em."

I felt proud. We were bruised and bleeding, but we didn't kill unless we had to.

Samuel finally stopped shaking me and looked me straight in the eyes.

"I'm gonna treat you nice, doctor. I'm gonna give you a reward that'll make you want to come here every night, I'm sure of it. Come on inside!"

Still trying not to vomit, I raised my hand.

"I'd love to, sir, but I should go home. My arms feel like they'll fall off, and I'm trying not to hurl. Magic and flying will do that to you."

He laughed. "Do whatever you want to do. Just come here tomorrow morning for your rewards."

Then he turned to the tavern staff and mercenaries.

"You lot, clean this up. Daniel and Johnson, my office. Right now."

As everyone began moving to their duties, I noticed Isabelle quickly taking charge of the cleanup.

"You three, secure the perimeter. You two, let the other taverns know what happened. The rest of you, help me get these bodies onto a cart to burn them."

Once she gave the orders, she adjusted her leather gloves and wiped blood off her chainmail.

I started walking toward her. I wanted to help, especially since no one had thanked her. But as I got closer, my body suddenly felt like stone. I bent forward, hands on my knees, gasping for air.

Back when the fight broke out, I had tossed syringes like candy and told myself I'd deal with the fatigue when I got home. But it didn't wait. It hit me now.

Two of my members walked up beside me.

"Boss, you alright?"

I nodded weakly and reached for one of the potions strapped to my belt—something to restore stamina. As I did, I looked up.

Isabelle was standing right there, watching me.

"Wallace, what's wrong? You look tired."

I looked up at her and saw the blood and sweat dripping from her armor and face. Isabelle was breathing hard, but even so, she extended a hand toward me. I took it, and she helped lift me to my feet.

Looking into her eyes, framed by that battle-worn helmet, made me feel like I had to act tough again. One of my crew stepped in and helped steady me on her shoulder.

"Here. I can't do much else right now, but take this. It'll give you back some of your stamina," I said, still gasping for air.

I handed her a small bottle filled with a deep purple liquid. Isabelle looked at it, then tilted her head to one side, as if unsure.

She glanced at me, looking for confirmation.

"Yes, it works. Why in the world would I try to poison a merc whose parents know where I live?"

She smiled and shook her head.

"They're not my parents."

Chapter 29

I had the two members carry me to Merry with Mead to see the twins. I told them everything that had happened and how Samuel offered to give me gifts. I also made sure to reward the two members who fought to protect the drunk lions by doubling their pay. The twins told me to bring the money back to the gang if I was given a large amount of gold, but we agreed to take a small cut for ourselves.

As evening approached, I walked back home. It smelled like vomit and an outhouse. The servant had cleaned up some of the mess, but as my magic faded, he must have disappeared. I spent the rest of the night resummoning my servant and having him help clean the house before Kreila returned. I remembered she would be back sometime tomorrow, so I decided the smell of vomit and dung would have to battle a dozen lavender candles to the death.

After scrubbing the floors and occasionally getting smacked on the back of my head with a broom by a complaining servant, the place was finally clean. Though honestly, the war between vomit and lavender would probably rage on through the night. I then scrubbed myself down in a bath twice over, and finally lay down to rest for the evening.

As I woke up the next morning, I got myself dressed and lit a few extra candles to prepare for Kreila's return. Barely an hour later, she arrived, scanning the shop.

"Good morning, Kr—" I started.

"Wallace, what happened yesterday? Something smells off," she interrupted.

"Well, I had a family show up and make a mess. I think they all caught food poisoning. What you're probably smelling is that mess... and me trying to clean it."

Kreila shrugged. "Your attempt is admirable. Just please don't forget to open the windows sometimes. The faint smell of that family's mess is barely there, but for God's sake, I'm being smothered by lavender."

I started walking around the shop, opening windows to help air the place out. I also summoned my servant to clean one more time—lucky for me, they don't tend to complain when Kreila is around. I slipped a few coins into the profit pouch to make sure Kreila didn't think I'd done it all for free.

Once I helped her with her luggage, she sat down at her alchemy station and started making potions to replace the ones I had used the day before. I told her I needed to walk to the Merry with Mead to help out in the morning, and that I'd get back to my studying once I returned. She waved her hand to signal her approval.

I began my trip to the Drunk Lion. As I approached the entrance, I noticed several mercenaries walking around the bar, and even saw two of them on horseback patrolling the streets. When I went inside, it looked like the slaves were still cleaning up the mess. I spotted Isabelle in one corner, directing the slaves as they rebuilt broken tables and chairs.

I gave her a wave as I entered, but she was focused on the work and didn't notice me. With my mask on and wearing my light leather uniform, I knocked on the office door and was ushered in.

The office, as expected, was packed with heavily armed mercenaries, all of them in full armor. Behind the desk, Samuel was writing what I assumed were concerns and complaints. He looked up and grinned from ear to ear as I walked in. Standing up, he came over with open arms.

"Well, there he is! The helpful doctor!" His shout was probably loud enough to be heard outside. "I could use a dozen plague doctors like you. This city would be mine if I had that."

He stopped across from me with a coin purse in one hand and scrolls in the other.

"What in God's name even happened out there yesterday?" I asked.

"Rival bandits who call themselves mercenaries. They tried to kick us out of this part of the city and take our properties. They call themselves the Crimson Dogs. Those bandits only made it as far as they did because they hit all my properties at once—we were spread too thin. Daniel and Johnson are off making a deal with them, trying to get the Dogs to learn their place."

"Instead, of course, they poisoned the men I sent and ran them off. Both sides took heavy losses. But I have more money, and I can replace the people I lost. The Crimson Dogs can't. So I sent Daniel and Johnson to launch a counteroffensive before those dogs could lick their wounds."

"You should know that whatever poisoned them was expensive. They didn't even have to drink it. All they had to do was make sure everyone touched something. Maybe a handshake, a piece of paper, a doorknob, anything."

"Hmm, thanks for the tip, kid. They aren't as stupid as I thought. Clever bastards. Regardless, you're here for your reward!" he said with a sinister grin.

"First off, here's fifty gold. Spend it as you like. If you weren't there, I would've lost far more."

This was good. More than I expected. But I wanted to give some credit to his soldiers. "Your soldiers did most of the work killing those dogs. I wouldn't have been able to help if it weren't for them." Seeing Isabelle impale several bandits? She deserved a medal at the very least.

"Yeah, yeah. This wouldn't have happened if they weren't lazy and stupid. When I hired those people, I expected better. Now it feels like

I was taken advantage of. At least the ones who survived are proving their worth by killing what's left of the Crimson Dogs. They'll earn some of my forgiveness for that." He shook his head.

"Your second gift is an invitation, handwritten by me, to House Marshe. I noticed you use a lot of magic, and House Marshe makes some of the best magic weapons in town. Probably better than that broomstick!" He burst into laughter.

"House Marshe?"

"You've never heard of them? They're an old house of retired adventurers who married into one family. They've got walls upon walls of magic goods. You can only get in with an invite or someone important by your side. They don't let just anyone in."

I hadn't heard of House Marshe before, but I knew most of the named houses across the city were known for something. House Genoakay was famous for its bards and scholars. House Danson dealt in old religious artifacts. A few other named houses existed in the city, ranging from bankrupt homes of forgotten heroes to houses powerful enough to own their own cities.

"Lastly, I want you to choose anyone I own, including staff, mercenaries, or slaves, and you'll have the opportunity to do anything you want with them for a full twenty-four hours. Do your chores, fight, or spend a night, it's up to you. It doesn't matter who it is, unless it's my wife, my brother, or me," Samuel said.

I paused for a moment to think about what I would do. But it was already clear who I was going to choose. Isabelle deserved a day off from Samuel. Plus, I knew exactly how to use her to make today even better—without me having to touch her.

"Can I have Isabelle for a day? I like how she fights. She can be a bodyguard for a trade meeting I have to do today."

Of course, I didn't have anything to do today besides tossing the coin purse to the twins. Beyond that, I planned to read and stare at the store door until someone came in.

"Oh, you are a lucky man, doctor. I bought her eight years ago for a good price. At the time, I needed a new slave driver—someone to keep the rest in line and kill anyone who messed with me. Daniel and Johnson agreed to train her, but only on the condition that she wouldn't be put back on the market or be given a job fit for a prostitute. I never really planned to. She's hideous with all those burns and scars, and she doesn't come off as friendly. Daniel and Johnson don't like her being sent on jobs they don't know about, but they're gone for now, so you can do whatever you'd like with her," he said with a sinister smile.

His eyes flickered cold for a moment as he added, "Just remember who owns her. And what happens if she steps out of line?"

Anything deplorable was out of the question. I saw Isabelle as a friend, and forcing anything like that would be cruel—something I wouldn't be comfortable with anyway. Samuel's comment about her not being friendly was almost funny, considering she had helped the slaves the last few times I'd been around. She was decent to them, too. That's exactly why I wanted her by my side for the day—to get her away from this disgusting brute.

"Yes, I've made up my mind. Bring Isabelle out if you can," I said.

"Done. One of you, go grab her and bring her here right now," Samuel ordered. As he spoke, two mercs headed to the front to find her. After a short wait, Isabelle walked into the office and bowed before Samuel.

"What do you need of me, sir?" she said, polite but firm.

Her eyes flicked toward me briefly, there was a sign of something darker, a hint of fear she tried to hide.

"The doctor here is your boss for the next twenty-four hours. You are to do anything he wants you to do. If I hear that he's displeased, or you try to resist him, I'll make sure you regret it. You know better than to try to escape. Two days without being near the silver whip would hurt you so bad you'll be begging to come back." He laughed maniacally.

"Sir?!" She turned toward me, her eyes full of shock and anger.

"You're going to be my bodyguard for the day. It'll be easy. Just grab your best armor and come with me. I'll explain more on the way," I said, hoping she wasn't scared. I wanted to make her feel comfortable being with me for that long. Saying nothing would probably make it worse.

"But why—" Isabelle started, but was cut off.

"Because he said so! You do what he asked and get your stupid armor," Samuel shouted.

"Yes, sir," she said, her voice trembling slightly. As she walked out the door toward her slave quarters, I waved to Samuel and thanked him for the gifts. I opened the door and saw Isabelle slowly heading toward the slave farm.

"Isabelle, wait!" I jogged after her. She turned toward me, her face twisted in pure anger.

"I'm not just another slave fighter here to follow your orders. And I'm not getting dragged into whatever gang problems you've got going on. I don't need eyes on me, and I sure as hell don't need bandits coming after me for something you did. Why would you do this, Wallace?!"

I'd pissed her off, no doubt. So the only thing I could do now was tell the truth.

"I'm… taking you on a date…" I mumbled.

She tilted her head. The anger was still there, but now there was a flicker of confusion.

"What do you mean by a date? Wallace, I—" she started.

I stepped in closer, lowering my voice so others wouldn't hear just how embarrassed I was.

"Look, I know this sounds weird, but this isn't for me. My teacher, who has been guiding and mentoring me for the past six years, has been like a mother figure. I love her more than she knows. The problem is, she keeps bothering me about finding a girl to spend time with and bring home so she can see... I've taken an interest in someone." I started to frown.

"She's getting sick. She's trying to hide it, but I've noticed it in her movements lately. I want her to feel excited, to believe the girl I've been spending time with is real—not something I made up. I chose you because... because you're an amazing fighter. You're kinder than Samuel says you are. And I think you're... pretty."

As I finished, I turned my face toward the ground in embarrassment. Why did I say that? The word pretty just slipped out, and I hadn't meant to say it. It was true—I did think she was gorgeous—but I had no idea how to tell her. Just saying it, while trying to keep my legs from trembling, felt like the hardest thing I'd ever done.

When I looked up at her, her jaw was open, her eyes wide. She looked stunned, as if I had just started speaking a language she'd never heard before.

"You're asking me to go on a date with you? Is that your request? I don't know how to date, Wallace. All I've seen are people taking their partners to the tavern. I wouldn't even know what to do."

I decided to bring her some confidence through honesty. "I've never been on one either. But I've read about it... in novels I pick up sometimes. All we have to do is spend time together doing something. I was going to bring you to my teacher's shop and just talk, have tea, and eat some sweets."

My insides were tearing themselves apart. Why the hell did I admit I read romance novels? I liked adventures with daring heroes, not stories about soft-hearted fools who had no business even looking at women. I'd only ever read one book that could be considered romantic, and it was Doctor Love, the doctor who healed broken hearts... and broken hearts.

Looking at her, I could see the confusion, but the anger was gone. She just looked stunned.

"Okay... what do I need to do?"

"Wear whatever you want, as long as it's not covered in blood or mud. You should probably take a bath too. Kreila can smell a flower from several miles away. I'll wait out front at the tavern until you're ready."

She nodded and headed toward her farmhouse.

Shit. What am I supposed to do? I've never done this before. How do you date someone? Michael's not here, so I guess I'll just repeat things he would say. Would that even work? No, not with her. She's a warrior. Michael usually flirts with innocent girls in fancy dresses.

Isabelle already knows how I look. I didn't want to come off as timid, but looking like a cherry about to burst probably didn't help. No. I'm Doctor Wallace from Kreila University. I'm competent. I'm confident as long as she isn't looking directly at my face.

I began pacing outside the front of the tavern, waiting anxiously for Isabelle's arrival. I kept debating what she might wear—something unique or something simple? As much as I might have wanted to see something revealing, I couldn't take her to Kreila like that.

Another minute passed, and the tavern doors swung open. Isabelle stepped out wearing splint armor. She had on a dark red, padded top and pants, with several strips of steel strapped along them. The metal covered most of her arms and legs, and a chest plate protected the crimson fabric across her torso. Her whole outfit looked new and spotless.

Of course, I didn't want to get caught staring for too long, so I looked up at her face. She wore her standard half-mask, covering the right side. Aside from her hands and the visible part of her face, she was covered head to toe in armor. If that's what made her feel comfortable, I wasn't about to complain.

Isabelle approached and stood across from me, giving a nod. "Are you ready?" Her voice was muffled beneath the chainmail helmet.

I gave a nod behind my mask. It covered my entire face, and the leather garb I wore wrapped me entirely in thick layers. Kreila was going to laugh at us. But if it made Isabelle smile, it was worth it.

"It's not too far, just around two miles south. It won't take long." I tried to keep the fear out of my voice.

"Let's make our way there now." She nodded again and began walking at my side.

I was about to turn my outfit into a sauna with how much I was sweating. Luckily, there was a nice cool breeze today.. All that sweat was just nerves. I wanted to ask her something, anything, to pass the time. She walked beside me, quiet, seeming lost in thought.

"So I was going to ask Daniel and Johnson this, but how did those two know where I live?" I asked, genuinely curious.

"Uh, Johnson knows these streets very well. I suppose when he trailed you a few months ago, he figured out you had a shop. I guess the meeting wasn't far from your place, so he remembered it," she said. "Was that a problem?"

"Oh no, not at all. In fact, business is good as long as they don't wreck the place," I replied.

"I see. If I may ask, Wallace, how did you end up becoming a plague doctor?" she asked gently, the soft rattle of her chains following her words.

"Well, to keep it short, I was abandoned when I was eight. I don't remember much before then, just being dropped outside taverns and brothels, dragged around by two people. I don't even know their names or faces."

"Oh, that's terrible…" she said, her voice touched with concern.

"After they abandoned me in an alley, I met Michael and Melena. We decided to survive the city together and made our own kind of family. We stole, ate disgusting leftovers, and huddled in taverns for warmth and safety. One day, I caught a bad fever and was close to death. I broke into Kreila's shop trying to steal potions, but I passed out on the floor before I could do anything. She found me and healed me. I was blown away by her magic.

"The twins got to stay at an orphanage, but I became her apprentice. Kreila has been almost like a mother to me ever since. Though, don't let her hear that. I've got the feeling she'd snap back with some heavy sarcasm."

I worried for a moment that I'd talked too much, but I wanted her to trust me. And sometimes, that meant revealing a few layers of myself.

"That's sweet, what she did for you. She raised a good doctor," she said with a nod.

"I appreciate that. How about you? If it's not too personal, how did you end up with the Drunk Lions?"

She tilted her head down, took a deep breath, and sighed.

"I don't like talking about it, but to keep it short, my parents sold me as a slave. They spent the gold on gambling. That's how I ended up under Samuel. Since I was decent at reading and writing, he made me a slave driver—a leader meant to organize the other servants and make sure they followed orders. And to harm them, if needed, to keep up efficiency.

"Johnson and Daniel have been my tutors, though most of the time they act more like guardians. They help keep Samuel from crossing certain lines or using me for whatever he wants that day." She grasped her arm briefly, then let it go. "I'm sure that may change someday."

"What do you mean by change?" I asked.

"That I can't answer. For both our sakes," she replied, shaking her head.

"Isabelle, if I may ask one more thing... is there a reason you always wear the half-mask?"

"It's not that it's a private concern. It's just a story I don't like talking about."

"No worries, Isabelle. I won't push. Besides, we're almost there. But before we get there, I want you to know—your tutors turned you into a great fighter. I'm surprised the bandits didn't run in fear with how amazing you looked out there."

"Thank you, Wallace. That's nice of you to say."

We fell into silence for a few moments as we turned the corner of another street. The two-floor white building ahead always brought me a deep sense of comfort. It felt perfect knowing that, inside, a warm cup of tea and a bowl of stew were probably waiting for me.

Luckily, it wasn't even noon. With any luck, spending time together might help us both relax.

Chapter 30

I took a deep breath and looked at Isabel's barely visible eyes.

"Thanks for doing this again, by the way," I mumbled as we approached the door.

"Well, I wasn't really given a choice, Wallace," she whispered.

There was no bitterness in her voice. Just truth. The kind of truth that had shackles wrapped around it.

As I opened the door, I saw Kreila behind the front desk, writing in a book with mint tea in one hand and a quill in the other. She looked up and noticed our concealed faces.

"Wallace, is this a friend of yours?"

I focused all my energy on sounding confident, not scared to death.

"Kreila, this is my friend Isabelle. We're on our second date, and we were passing by the area, so we wanted to say hello," I said, trying not to panic.

Isabelle quickly raised her hand and placed it at her side. "Hello, Mrs. Kreila. It's nice to meet you."

Kreila's eyes widened. She shut the book and walked toward us, studying Isabelle like she was reading her energy. Then she stepped back, moved past us to the front door—and that's when I heard Captain Townsin's voice approaching.

"Good morning, Kreila. I was hoping to get some tea—"

He didn't get to finish. Kreila waved her hands, cutting him off.

"Nope. We're closed for the day, Townsin. You'll have to come back tomorrow. Ta-ta!"

She said it with such joy, turning toward us with one of the brightest smiles I'd ever seen. It was contagious.

"Why hello, Mrs. Isabelle! I love the name. And you look fantastic today too. I knew Wallace had good taste. I taught him everything he knows, by the way!" She giggled and shook Isabel's hand.

Then she turned to me with a cold look in her eyes.

"Wallace, go take those ridiculous garbs off and change into something date-worthy, or I swear to the gods I'll use your blood to make a new brand of potions…"

She glared like she'd actually follow through in the next few seconds.

"Right away!"

I spun around and rushed up the stairs to my room. I didn't have much that was clean, so I grabbed a white long-sleeved shirt and pulled a dark green tunic over it. My pants were a soft brown, and I slung a satchel over one shoulder.

As I was heading out, I remembered the necklace Thomas had given me. Found it, threw it on, and grabbed my glasses too.

When I came back downstairs, I spotted Kreila pointing at all the glass jars and plants around the room. The scent was a blend of rosemary, dried citrus, and something earthy. The whole space felt like it belonged to someone who loved deeply and lived loudly.

"That plant right there is a rare type of mint. It grows in the far east, the coldest part of Paljava. It's hard to keep alive during summer, but once you do, it's like being kissed by a goddess of mint and honey."

Both Isabelle and Kreila turned to look at me.

"See, Wallace? You look precious!" Kreila chuckled

"I'm going to make you all the best tea you'll ever have. Not for me, though—red wine sounds more like my speed right now."

She sat us across from each other at a rectangular wooden table, big enough to seat five. From the kitchen, I could hear Kreila humming as she got to work. The soft sound of bubbling water mixed with the airy whistle of the kettle.

"She seems sweet," Isabelle said. "I didn't think she'd be this excited."

"This is what I was hoping for. This is all going great," I replied, though I could feel the knot tightening in my stomach. I was trying to remain calm, but something about being here with her made it hard to keep the act going.

But of course, it did.

Kreila reentered the room with a glass of wine in hand and sat down at the head of the table. She lifted the glass, took in the scent of the red grape wine, and smiled at us.

"Well, I think we should get this out of the way, Wallace. You're shaking and fidgeting with your hands. I'm going to be your wise teacher in bonding, okay?"

She tilted her head and smiled at me.

I didn't bother looking down at my hands. I already knew she was right. Isabelle looked stunning—so calm and composed—that I didn't want to come off looking like a fool. Truth was, I wasn't sure what I meant to her. I knew what she meant to me, and that scared me. I wasn't good at this. Not the feelings, not the reading between the lines. But I wanted to be. For her.

"You see that goddess under that armor? Isabelle is your friend. She's here because she wants to be. Don't be shy—you've already gotten her to a second date. I doubt your face is going to scare her off, even if you're blushing like crazy."

She chuckled, then stopped herself.

"Take a deep breath, son, and look at your friend. Smile. It's infectious, Wallace."

She slid her chair back to the head of the table.

I tried to keep my composure and looked Isabelle in the eyes. I couldn't tell what she was feeling right then, but I figured I'd go for the best move I could think of.

I puffed out my chest.

"I didn't know I'd have two goddesses in the house at the same time. You both look quite stunting!"

I meant to say stunning. And I definitely didn't mean to sound that shaky. This was bad.

Then I heard a snicker, followed by another. I looked at Kreila and saw the smile on her face—though her mouth wasn't moving.

Suddenly, laughter burst out of Isabelle. It was the first time I'd ever heard her laugh, and it was beautiful. Not just because of the sound, but because it cracked through the shell she'd worn like armor.

As she giggled, I felt like I had hit both of my goals in just a few minutes.

"Stunting? Stunting?!" Isabelle kept laughing.

Kreila clapped her hands. "See? That was easy!"

She nodded, and right then, I heard the teapot start to sing.

"Wallace, come help me with the tea, please!"

But it wasn't a request. As she walked toward me, she grabbed me by the ear. None of my "Ow!" complaints made a difference.

Kreila moved the teapot, but I noticed something strange—the water inside was golden. She reached for a jar way in the back. It looked like mint, but it was glowing, almost like it gave off its own light. I could feel cold radiating from the glass.

She took a few of the leaves and dropped them into the pot. Then she looked at me and spoke softly.

"Wallace, do you see those burn scars? Some parts of her face barely have skin on them. Poor girl…"

"She didn't tell me what happened, but I noticed it too," I said.

"Wallace, listen to me closely. I want you to say something sweet to her. You may not realize it, but she seems a little nervous too. Don't overthink it. Just let her know what she means to you. Compliment her. Let her feel that you're grateful she's here."

Then Kreila hugged me and let go, finishing up the tea.

Getting hugged was nice. But getting a hug after encouragement like that? Even sweeter. And for the first time, I let myself wonder what Isabelle's life had really been like. How many days did she spend being ordered, used, and ignored. How many nights she cried, and no one came. I didn't want to be just another man she tolerated. I wanted to be someone she could breathe around. Someone who never made her flinch.

I started thinking of sweet things I could say. Things that wouldn't come off too strongly.

Kreila approached, holding floating teacups while a servant behind her handed them out.

"I'll wait till you're done."

As the two of us walked back into the room, I realized what she'd said was true—Isabelle was fidgeting with her hands, arms locked tight. I needed to calm her down, to make her smile again. I'd do anything just to hear that beautiful, ridiculous laugh one more time.

I sat across from her.

"Hey, Belle. Have you ever had tea before? If you did, it wasn't real—because my teacher makes tea so good it'll kick us out of our chairs."

Why did I call her Belle? That wasn't her name... but I thought it sounded cute.

She tilted her head slightly. "Belle?"

"Kreila made something nice for you. And I wanted to tell you something."

I'd already made up my mind. I placed my hands on the table and looked straight into her nervous brown eyes.

"Isabelle, I don't care what's beneath the mask. I don't care what those animals say or think about you. You're my friend because of your heart—not your face, not your body, not your skills. It's your soul. It's kind. And I'm grateful just to be around you.

"I didn't bring you here just to meet my teacher. I brought you here because I wanted you to have a day away from all of it—away from the barking orders, the unbearable masters, and the constant work. My only request isn't just to spend time with me. It's for you to finally relax and enjoy yourself.

"Seeing you smile helps too."

There was a pause between the two of us. I could feel her staring into my eyes, and I was doing everything I could not to drop dead right there.

Did I do it right? Was that too much? Maybe she's even more uncomfortable now. God—I was the one shaking again.

From the kitchen, I could hear Kreila humming joyfully. Was that her way of telling me I'd done well?

Before I could figure it out, Isabelle slowly removed her mask.

And I saw her face.

Kreila had been right. Several patches of skin were burned so deeply that it looked like they had reached the muscle. It was the kind of damage even Daniels couldn't ignore. It looked painful—horrible.

Her eyes were watery, her face red like a bunch of radishes. She looked down at the floor, then back at me.

On one side, her warm brown skin and gentle smile showed me a girl who probably hadn't been called beautiful in a long time. On the other, red and pink burn scars covered nearly a quarter of her face. The injury stretched down past her jaw, all the way to her shoulder.

And she was perfect.

"Thank you, Wallace. That was kind of you to say," she said softly. "I must admit, I haven't met many people like you. But I'm glad I did. You're nice to be around."

She paused, her voice turning quieter.

"It's a shame I have a time limit... but I'll enjoy it while it lasts."

Kreila entered the room with a plate of cookies in her hands, and warm, ruby-red teacups floating behind her. Even after seeing it a hundred times, it was still impressive—especially when her summon wasn't complaining like mine always did.

She sat down. The teacups and cookies settled in front of us. Kreila gave Isabelle a brief glance, then turned to her tea.

"This is expensive tea. Please enjoy it and don't make a mess. Otherwise, that's gold down the drain," she said with a smile.

I raised the teacup to my lips and took a quick sip.

An avalanche of peppermint hit me, crashing through every sense. But it didn't stop there. Beneath the peppermint came a wave of strawberry. The sweetness coated my tongue, while the peppermint filled my throat, my nose, and my head.

It was intense.

The tea had been brewed quickly, but the taste told a different story. That meant the ingredients were rare and costly. Kreila hadn't been bluffing. This was her way of showing us she appreciated our company.

As I lowered the cup, I noticed Isabelle staring at hers like it was a long-lost child. Then she turned and glared at Kreila, who wore the smuggest look I'd ever seen.

Kreila knew exactly what she had made. And she was proud of it.

"Madam Kreila, how did you make this? This might be the greatest thing I've ever tasted!"

Her eyes sparkled with amazement as she took another sip. It was just as good as the first.

"I'll never reveal my methods, Isabelle. Otherwise, people will try to mimic my art," Kreila chuckled, holding her cup of wine to her face. She took a slow sip from her teacup, then gently slid it toward Isabelle, inviting her to taste the perfection again and again.

"Good news—Wallace is actually pretty good at mimicking my work. So keeping him around is the closest you'll get to me making tea for you all the time."

Isabelle turned to me, smiling. "Really?"

"Kreila's giving me too much credit. But yes, I'm better than your average tea maker. Sometimes you have to make good tea just to help people take their medicine," I said humbly.

As Isabelle and I sipped our cups, Kreila glanced at me.

"So, how did you two meet?

I didn't want to tell her the truth about slavery. If she found out, she'd get attached fast and try to free Isabelle. As kind as that was, Samuel and his investors wouldn't take it lightly. They'd put a price on her head, and Kreila would never sleep peacefully again.

"I treated her teachers when they stopped by. They offered to buy me a beer, and that's when I found out they had an apprentice. And that's how I met Isabelle."

Some truth, some lie—just enough to keep her off my trail.

Isabelle turned her head toward me, and I gave her a wink. My quiet way of asking her to play along.

"My teachers thought he was annoying. Always talking about money and drugs," Isabelle said.

Dear gods. She was taking this seriously.

Was this her way of messing with me?

"Really? What else happened?" Kreila asked, staring at me.

"That's not true. I talked about medicine and charity. Once I mentioned that I'm a doctor, you wouldn't leave me alone," I said, firing back at Isabelle.

"Wallace, you are not a 'doctor.' You just say that to seem impressive," Isabelle replied with a small grin.

Kreila snorted.

"I'm not just smart. I'm stronger than most doctors. I'll beat you in a test of strength any day of the week."

Oh no. I shouldn't have said that.

Isabelle's eyes widened. She looked at me like I was prey. Without a word, she scooted her chair in, planted her elbow on the table, and raised her hand—ready for an arm wrestle.

Luckily, I don't play by the rules.

From my sleeve, I pulled out a strength-enhancement syringe and jabbed it into my hip.

"I'll take your challenge," I said, squeaking from the sting.

As I held Isabelle's hand, Kreila drank the rest of her wine in one gulp.

"Hold on, Isabelle. Let me make sure this is fair."

She stretched her arms and, without warning, threw a syringe into mine. Suddenly, the strength-enhancing spell I used was dispelled.

"Cheating gets you nowhere, Wallace…" Isabelle said, staring straight into my soul.

"I've changed my mind. I don't want to break Kreila's table."

I tried letting go of her hand, but she gripped mine tighter.

"Don't worry, Wallace. This table is stronger than you think," Kreila said with a smile.

"Ready… and go!" she shouted.

Kreila took longer to count down than I lasted in the match.

Despite my best effort, Isabelle slammed my hand into the table. She won. Easily.

At least she didn't try to break my hand—but it was definitely bruised.

As Isabelle smiled at me, Kreila burst into laughter like she'd just seen a jester get pied in the face.

"I was holding back. Didn't want to hurt her feelings," I muttered, trying to save what little masculinity I had left.

But before I could breathe, Isabelle placed her hand back on the table.

She wanted a rematch.

I whimpered, "I'd rather not spill the tea with my power."

Kreila and Isabelle laughed, and we spent the rest of the evening trading stories about each other.

Kreila made sure to fact-check all my so-called tales of heroism. She also shared some of my more embarrassing moments—like the time I dropped teacups or made tea so bad it nearly knocked someone out.

Isabelle told stories about watching her guardians fight, and what it was like living among mercenaries. She gave me part of the truth, but I knew the whole picture. The mercenaries got to sleep in warm, comfortable beds. Isabelle lay on straw and old animal fur.

She was clearly proud of her skills. And even though she tried to act tough, I could hear it in her stories—Daniel and Johnson genuinely cared about her. And she cared just as much about them.

I didn't want to see that smile of hers fade. But I had no idea how to help.

The next morning, with Isabelle sleeping in the intake room, I put my plan into motion. When we returned to the Drunk Lion Tavern, I made my move.

"I want to have Isabelle act as my part-time bodyguard. She would help protect me during my work with MWM, maybe scare off a few assassins. This wouldn't be a daily thing—just once or twice a week."

I stood in front of Samuel, hands behind my back.

"I know she's valuable to you, so I'm not here to argue over a servant you own. Because of that, I'll gladly pay for her time. I'll pay you directly."

Isabelle stood beside me, watching quietly as I laid it all out. She already knew about the plan and had agreed to it—on one condition. She wanted to use those days to relax more than to fight. She wasn't interested in getting tangled up with MWM, and I couldn't blame her for that.

"So you want to hire her for a day or two? Ha! That's a bad deal for me, even with the pay," Samuel chuckled. "But for you, let's work something out. Five silver a day?"

Well, there went a good chunk of my monthly pay. Half of it, gone just like that. But any price was worth it if it meant spending time with her.

"Deal."

Chapter 31

My eyes were blurry. The room was dark, and it smelled of balsam and cedar, just like the charm Thomas gave me. When my vision cleared, I scanned my surroundings, but I wasn't home. I was in what looked like a laboratory, except the tools, bottles, and potions were far too expensive and pristine. The stone walls and torches gave me the impression that I was in a castle.

I tried to move my legs, but they wouldn't respond. I was paralyzed, stuck in the corner, watching. A figure sat at a table with their head resting on the surface. They wore what looked like a plague doctor's outfit, the mask hanging from the belt and studded with jewels. The rest of the garb was light blue and white.

"Wait a minute," I whispered.

Before I could process anything else, the door on the far side burst open.

"Abigail!" A man stepped into the room, his voice filled with urgency. He wore dark green silk robes, his shoulders draped with a white bear pelt. A golden crown dangled from his belt. The dark-skinned man strode toward the plague doctor with excitement.

"Abigail, Abigail, wake up! You've done it!"

That was Kreila he was shouting at. The plague garbs were already enough to tell me it was her before the man of royalty even walked into the room. But when she lifted her head, I noticed her hair looked different; mostly brown, streaked with shades of grey.

Kreila exhaled deeply and asked, "How long was I asleep?"

"A few hours. You must have worked yourself so hard that you passed out. I'll have a servant fetch you water and food."

"I would appreciate that, Kendrick. That's very sweet of you."

Kendrick? The man's clothes matched the green banner of Eltonia, with the bear sigil and his crown. That's King Kendrick, the ruler of Eltonia. Why was Kreila here?

"How is Philip?" Kreila asked.

"He is okay. He managed to open his eyes and talk for a few minutes, but he keeps drifting back to sleep. The other healers have been watching him and say he needs to rest."

"Verona and her table will want me dead even more now than they already do…" Kreila muttered.

"You saved my son and his wife, and now you have saved my grandson, too. Kreila, this kingdom owes you everything it has. I'm in your debt, Abigail."

Kreila didn't answer. She just smiled faintly and shook her head, a tear sliding down her cheek.

"Yes. I've done everything I can. Soon, it will be up to you and him…" Kreila gripped her hands tightly.

"What do you mean, Abigail? What's wrong?" The king cupped Kreila's cheek, wiping away her tears.

"I already explained the poison Verona used on Philip, and how the Violet dragon mushroom was the only cure. I told you it was dangerous to use."

"Yes, but you said you could do it, and you did! You told me that making the cure with that mushroom would take days, but you finished it in just an hour—just enough to save Philip."

"I made the cure, but I didn't make it right…

The king straightened, fear creeping into his face.

"No. What do we need to do now? What is going to happen to Philip?"

"Nothing. He's cured. But the mushroom released fumes from its cap. A small cloud of it slipped through my mask." Kreila's head hung low.

"I've caught the Violet dragon disease, Your Majesty. It's fatal."

My breath hitched. Kreila... dying? My stomach churned. She had never told me.

"No, no, no! I will find another doctor. I'll send ravens to every kingdom and college on this continent. I will get you your cure!" the king shouted. As he did, a surge of energy rose from his cloak, raw and overwhelming.

Kreila's voice softened, almost maternal. "Kendrick, there isn't a cure. No one has created one in centuries. It's so rare that no one bothers with the research, and so deadly that no one dares to study it. But it's okay. Philip didn't catch it; only I did. Otherwise, he wouldn't be awake at all."

"I'll find something, I swear, Abigail. What do you need?"

"With potions and magic, I can slow it down, but I can't stop it, Kendrick. I'm sorry…"

Kendrick turned from her, his shoulders sagging. He pressed a hand over his mouth, trying to still his breathing.

"Kreila, that godless Verona has taken almost everything from me. My son, my grandchildren, and she almost took Philip. And now…" He buried his face in his hands. "This is all her fault. Gods, why? Soon it will just be me and Philip. I'll have to send his little sister somewhere to keep her safe, but I can't keep her here. I wish my wife were here. She would know what to do…"

Kreila stood, walked to the king, and wrapped her arms around him.

She didn't speak right away. When she did, her voice trembled, but her words were steady.

"It's going to be okay, Kendrick. I'll be okay. I'm going to dedicate my years to working on a cure or at least something to slow this down. Just promise me you'll take care of Philip. Keep him safe. I'll come to the palace from time to time to see him until he grows up. But until then, promise me you'll watch over him. I gave my life for him after all."

"Abigail, I will pray every day to Ezella herself for the rest of my life. I want you to live, and I want your legacy to be known. Everyone will know you're a hero."

Kendrick pulled Kreila into another embrace.

"I love you, Abigail, and I know, from the bottom of my heart, that everything you have done will save us all again someday. I don't know how, but I will pray every day until someone comes to carry your will forward."

That word, "love," hung in the air longer than anything else.

"Thank you, Kendrick. I love you too. I'll keep my eyes open, but for now, I need to head home. Steven will be expecting me." Kreila stepped back from the king's arms.

"I'll come to see the prince tomorrow. But for now, you need some rest too, Kendrick." Kreila started toward the door, but the king placed his hand on her shoulder, gently turning her back.

"Abigail, you're an angel. I want you to know that if you ever need anything, please tell me."

Kreila lifted her hands and held the king's face.

"Now go rest, otherwise I'll have to knock you out with tea again.

"I told you, your tea makes me kick in bed whenever I drink it. I almost kicked you off the bed once." The king chuckled.

That line. "Off the bed." The intimacy in it. The familiarity. The way they smiled at each other.

They looked into each other's eyes as they slowly closed the distance. The king leaned in and kissed her.

I didn't know what to say. My head spun with questions. Her illness, the prince, Verona, and now an affair. What was happening? Why was I seeing this?

Kreila, always composed, always firm, yet hiding this? Hiding him? She was already under the weight of her sickness and my mess. She was tired. Would confronting her be wise? No. It would only push her further into panic. I wanted answers, but I didn't know how to explain what I had witnessed.

I didn't get long to think. My eyes grew heavy, my breathing slowed, and within seconds of rest, the smell of eggs and tea filled my nose.

"Wallace, are you awake? I made something for you."

Hearing Kreila's voice rattled me to my core. What else was she hiding? Beneath the warm smell of breakfast lingered the scent of balsam and cedar.

Chapter 32

As several more days passed, I decided to keep quiet about the strange dream. Bringing it up to her would only worry Kreila. She was clearly doing her best to hide her illness. Still, the charm Thomas gave me wasn't giving off the same aroma anymore. My guess was that Thomas wanted me to see something through it, or maybe the charm was reacting to something else entirely.

I turned my attention to Samuel's invitation to visit the Marshes' house. MWM could always use magical equipment to help us get out of trouble. Michael was the only other one in the gang who knew how to use magic besides me, but his magic was way more complex. He played in a way where he let the magic from his soul pour out through his mouth and into his fingers while he played the lute. What pissed me off was how fast he picked things up. It was like he had been born a mage.

Still, I would be an idiot to turn down a tour of a powerful magic house with things for sale. It might pay off to know the Marshes later, especially if the rumors about their collection were true.

I got dressed in my plague garbs and slipped on my mask. I practiced changing my voice to sound older, making sure everyone would believe my name was Robert. Nobody in that mansion needed to connect me to MWM, and I wasn't about to let some rich person figure out who I really was.

One summer morning, I headed toward the other side of the city. As usual, the freshly paved roads and passersby dressed in fancy clothes and drowning in perfume greeted me as I stepped into the area. My plague garbs weren't elegant like theirs, but that didn't matter. My outfit was meant to show my occupation, not my wealth.

After walking several blocks and asking for directions, I finally found the Marshe house. The grey brick mansion looked old, but it was still a mansion. Blue banners hung from the upper walls, each marked with a white hammer, the emblem of House Marshe. Out front stood a statue of a smith hammering an anvil, likely an ancestor of the house. A small crowd gathered near the entrance, whispering and gossiping. Some wore cloaks that screamed magic, their presence sharp and heavy. Others had garments that radiated strange energies— cold, hot, and something in between.

As I neared the mansion door, two guards stepped forward, pikes in hand, steel armor shining like it had just been forged. They raised their hands to stop me.

"State your purpose, citizen."

I pulled out the invitation Samuel gave me. "I'm here to check out the Marshes' magic items for sale. Got invited by Samuel of the Drunk Lions."

The guards studied the letter, then nodded.

"Go on inside. Any funny business and we'll know. City rules don't apply in the house."

"And what do you mean by that exactly?" I asked.

"Steal from us and there will be no trial. Only a rope or a blade will serve justice." The guard's tone was low, dangerous.

"Fair enough."

One guard escorted me toward the massive wooden doors, towering over ten feet high. They were carved with rows of hammers and anvils etched deep into the dark wood. He pressed his palms against the surface, and a dark blue glow lit up under his hands. Slowly, the heavy doors creaked open. The guard gestured for me to step inside.

The walls were painted a deep, dark blue, covered with sigils running up and down like crawling runes. Portraits of men and women lined the hall, their eyes following me as I moved. Display pieces of swords and shields hung between the paintings, each one screaming history. The two-story building glowed with the light of lavish candles, and every guard inside wore fine attire. Their armor wasn't spotless, but that just meant it had seen battle.

A man in expensive blue garbs approached me, posture sharp and rehearsed.

"Welcome, sir, to the Marshe estate. Please stay within the approved areas while touring and viewing our esteemed magic weapons. If you would like a glass of wine, seek out one of the workers. They all bear the Marshe sigil on their necks." He tilted his head, revealing the mark burned into his skin.

I looked closer. The branding was eerily similar to the mark Samuel put on his slaves. The staff here weren't here by choice, that much was clear.

The branded man gestured for me to follow and led me into a room to the right. Inside, magical items gleamed behind glass boxes, each protected by a shimmering shield spell. The room buzzed with wealthy guests, all dressed to the teeth, pointing and whispering about the artifacts like they were priceless trophies.

I stopped at one of the displays. Behind the glass sat a golden sword. The plaque claimed it belonged to a mighty angel. The price: three thousand gold. More than MWM had scraped together in years. I almost choked when I saw the number.

Nearby, a guest pointed to a glass case holding a golden skull. A staff member immediately unlocked the shield and opened the case. The woman pulled emerald coins from her purse. Emerald coins.

Most folks thought they were a myth. Only the richest of the rich ever touched them, and they were worth far more than gold.

The twins only gave me four hundred gold to see if anything was worth buying, but the moment I saw the prices and those emerald coins flashing around, I knew we were nowhere near rich enough to afford a thing here. Still, I kept walking, checking out more of the magical artifacts.

One sword on display claimed to have belonged to a knight who once served under the great hero himself. The Church of the Holy Light hailed that hero as its champion, saying he traveled the continent, slaying demons and purging evil until people started believing he was a god in disguise.

The artifacts ranged from weapons to clothing. A white and golden dress was labeled as having been worn by an elven princess a thousand years ago. A dusty book was said to be the diary of an ancient Elton princess. Every piece had a price that would drain ten lifetimes of our earnings. The cheapest thing I found was a broken wand going for eight hundred gold.

Then I stopped. My eyes landed on a book with a sigil I recognized. A heart cradled in two hands, the nails sharp as blades. The plaque beneath it claimed the book once belonged to the great Thorin Oberon, a renowned vampire known for his medical research, with his name carved into medical textbooks everywhere.

Servants drifted through the room, balancing plates of cheese and fine wine, offering them to the patrons. I approached one, doing my best to mask the fact that I was just a seventeen-year-old under this mask.

"May I have a glass of wine, please?" My voice cracked slightly, but the slave didn't seem to care. They handed me a glass of grape wine that smelled divine, like it had been pressed from the finest grapes in existence.

I kept searching the room for more artifacts tied to Thorin. Every doctor across the continent knew his name. I couldn't afford a single thing he created, but just seeing his work laid out like this felt unreal.

I raised my mask slightly to take a sip of the wine, but before it touched my lips, the glass vanished from my hand in a blur.

"Hey, what's your—" I spun around and froze. The tall, imposing figure in front of me looked more amused than angry.

Barron stood there, holding my glass of wine.

"Kreila would be displeased to know you were here drinking wine, young man. Especially in a place where you have no business being." His deep voice carried humor, like he was holding back a laugh.

My pulse quickened. I lowered my mask quickly.

"Barron, sir, I was just... Actually, you're right, I should leave." I turned to go, but his hand clamped down on my shoulder.

"Now, now, Wallace, don't be afraid. I won't tell Kreila you were here. But I am curious—how did you get into this mansion?"

I froze, scrambling for an excuse, but nothing came out. I just stood there, silent.

"Hmm. Could it be you stole someone's invitation, Wallace? Considering your history with theft, it would make sense." Barron smirked slightly. "No matter. I'm glad you're here. In fact, I was planning to bring you here myself someday. I wanted to show you some artifacts I think you might need one day."

Barron turned his gaze to the glittering artifacts scattered around the room.

"Doctor Thorin is believed to have been the greatest doctor in our history. I suppose being a vampire gives you plenty of time to try out new techniques, don't you think?"

"Yeah, I guess so. Every doctor wishes they could learn from him or his family."

"I'm sure I could get you an invitation to meet them, Wallace. I have no doubt they'd be interested in hearing about Kreila's apprentice. She was famous enough at one point that I'm sure they know who she is."

"Really?"

"Of course. Abigail shows up in several textbooks across the city's libraries. She figured out how to make expensive potions both more efficiently and at a fraction of the cost. The high elves hate her for it. They couldn't keep charging hundreds of gold for potions she could brew for ten."

"That's incredible."

"Come, walk with me, Wallace. I want to show you the garden behind the mansion. I have special access." He motioned for me to follow, and we slipped through the crowd toward another set of massive doors.

When we stepped outside, we entered their flower pasture, but the sight was far from what I expected. All the flowers were wilting, their colors fading into brown and gray. Stone benches stood scattered around the garden, each one occupied by a lone figure sitting in silence.

At the center of the garden stood a bronze dragon, water spilling from its mouth into the bowls below.

"Hm. Looks like House Marshe is struggling. This side of the building is showing real wear. I never knew it had gotten this bad."

"What do you mean?"

"Oh, House Marshe has been locked in trade wars with several other houses across the continent. They've been losing for years.

That's why they're selling off so many magical artifacts—to claw back some of their wealth."

He pointed toward the dragon statue.

"That thing used to be covered in rubies. Seems they've sold them off too. When I was young, I managed to buy this trident from them."

With a snap of his fingers, a long golden trident appeared in his hands. Its surface gleamed, edges sharp enough to pierce straight through flesh and bone. Barron twirled it once before snapping his fingers again, and the weapon vanished into thin air.

He pointed to an empty bench nearby and gestured for me to sit.

We sat side by side, both of us staring at the bronze dragon as the water dripped steadily into the bowls.

"Wallace, what would you say to working for me after you finish tutoring under Kreila? I could use a doctor like you. I see something in you, boy—potential I could show the whole continent someday."

"I'm not sure, sir. Honestly, I still don't know what kind of doctor I want to become."

"Well, if you choose to work under me, I can tell you what you'll gain. A house larger than Kreila's, servants to meet your every need, and a personal meeting with Thorin's family. You'll have everything you could ever want."

"That's an amazing offer, sir. I'd have to think about it."

"Take all the time you need. But when you do decide, and you want to work for me, let me know. We'll come back here and buy some of Thorin's books to help you study, son."

"Son?" I asked.

"Ha! Of course. I think I'm the closest thing you've ever had to a father, Wallace. You told me you never knew your parents, and I've been by your side for almost eight years."

"I'd be honored, sir, but I still need time to think."

"Of course. It's not a decision I'd want you to rush."

His offer settled on my shoulders like lead. My thoughts drifted back to what Samuel told me—Barron was a slave trader, and he wanted to join the table. If he wants to join the table, does that mean he plans to kill the Eltons, too? Either way, I decided it was time to ask him about his disgusting trade.

"Can I ask you something, Mr. Blackwood?"

He nodded.

"I saw the servants with branding on them. I've seen a lot of slaves across the city in rough shape."

"Ah, yes. That can be hard to see sometimes for a boy your age."

"Barron, do you own slaves?"

Without a pause, he answered.

"Yes. But I prefer the term indentured servants. Slaves is derogatory."

His reaction stunned me. It was like he had answered this question a hundred times—or maybe he expected me to ask.

"Why? Why force them into a life they don't want? Don't they want to be free?"

"Wallace, you should know this. Any slave owner who treats their slaves like animals—I denounce them. My servants, like those in the Marshe house, are well-housed and kept clean. I don't keep them because I want to deny them freedom. If anything, living under me is better than surviving in this city without me. They provide the labor I need, and in return, they get food and shelter."

"And if they want to leave?"

"They won't. Because they know there's nothing out there for them. Serving me is better than anything else they'd find."

A knot twisted in my stomach. He spoke like a savior, but all I could hear was a man polishing his chains.

"That sounds like you won't let them go."

"Wallace, here's a lesson my father taught me. Slavery in this country was legalized under King Darius after the demon invasion was pushed back. At first, everyone hated the idea, but eventually they learned to obey the rules. The homeless, the downtrodden, the uneducated—they were given a purpose: to serve those who needed guidance. That's why, of all the nations hit during that demonic incursion, Eltonia rebuilt the fastest. Even now, with that fool King Elton trying to argue otherwise, our roads stay clean, our food is plentiful, and our cities rise faster than anyone else's."

"But Barron, I was homeless. Do you think that means I should've been a slave too?" I wanted to throw his words back at him, to force him to face the hypocrisy of wanting to hire a doctor he would have considered beneath him.

"No, Wallace. You and your siblings weren't like the others rotting on the streets. You were willing to learn, willing to grow into something more. Others refuse to change, whether out of weakness or stupidity."

He leaned forward, voice low but steady. "I want people in my company who are strong, people who can survive the darkest parts of this nation. You survived because you are strong, Wallace. And the strong will be the ones to create a new great age for the future."

His words curled around me like incense, sweet but suffocating. And for a moment, they almost felt uplifted. But I wasn't going to bow to someone who kept people in chains. Isabelle would never forgive me, and neither would I. I appreciated that he saw me as someone with potential, but I couldn't shake the knot in my chest. Hells, maybe I'm not so different from Barron. I have my own demons—demons the twins and I use to make gold.

"I don't know, sir. But… thank you for thinking of me that way." I stood up and turned toward him.

"I understand, son. It's a lot to take in, I'm sure. You're young, and life will teach you its lessons with time. Still, I hope you learn them well. Come now, even if I can't get you the original versions of Thorin's books, I can at least find new copies. Besides, someone refuses to sell me an artifact I've been after anyway." Barron shrugged.

"What artifact was it?" I asked.

"A powerful lute. Dark red wood, studded with gems. Legend says its strings were spun from the hairs of a deity of lust and wine, long ago."

As we walked across the property, I noticed cracks in the perfection. There were dents in the polished marble of the manor. The windows at the back were locked, but the locks looked old and rusted—easy to break with the right tools. A few guards in the garden were slumped in their seats, fast asleep. Then I saw it: a manhole, leading straight into the sewers. No doubt about it. Curious.

Chapter 33

A few months passed, and the autumn calm finally kicked in. I'd learned how to make small batches of hallucinogenic cigars that the Merry with Mead tavern could sell. I found the recipe in a dusty old book about druids in the fey lands getting high on whatever they could scrounge. One of the bookstores I usually hit had it tucked away like it was nothing. The twins and I set up a makeshift lab in the bunker beneath the tavern so I could start producing them.

I still wanted nothing to do with folks who robbed people blind. So I made the cigars as non-addictive as I could. I laced a little old magic into them, just enough. I told the staff to only sell them to people who didn't look desperate. If someone kept coming back too often, like they were getting hooked, they were to tell me immediately. If it ever got to that point, I planned to whip up a potion that would make them feel sick every time they lit one. Fortunately, it never came to that. Most of the buyers were adventurers just passing through. We never saw them again, for better or worse. Still, it was one way I helped bring extra coin to the gang.

Kreila had gotten stricter with my training. She snapped more when I messed up and wasn't as patient as she used to be. She was running me day and night. The twins handled most of the gang's day-to-day. I backed them up with supplies and coins when I could. I wasn't stupid, I knew what she was doing. She was preparing me for something. Something final. She had started cutting her hair shorter and said it was just a new style she wanted to try. But I saw the way her hands trembled sometimes when she thought no one was looking. The way she rubbed her joints like they ached from the inside. I knew better, but I didn't have it in me to talk to her about it. Truth be told, I think she didn't want to talk about it either.

Isabelle was glad to get a break twice a week. We tried to spend our weekends together, either touring the town or just relaxing at the shop. It was my chance to breathe a little, too, away from Kreila's nonstop training. She even admitted it was hard to keep me focused when I had a cute girl hanging around.

Isabelle had gotten more comfortable being around me. She was talking more, laughing at my jokes, and venting about how stressful work had been lately. Whenever she did, I would slide her a few extra coins to help out. She always hesitated, though, saying she didn't feel right taking money from my cut of MWM's profits. Sometimes I caught her staring at the fire in silence. I never asked what she was thinking about, but I could guess. It was the same look I wore when I remembered the pain. She hadn't told me everything. I hadn't pushed. But the way her fingers brushed her arms when no one was watching, like tracing scars I couldn't see, told me enough.

Kreila helped her too. She gave her oils to soothe her skin in case the burns ever flared up or got itchy. There was something tender in the way Kreila did it, something that reminded me she still had softness left, hidden under all that steel.

Nobody could ever confirm my actual birthday, but some mages managed to narrow it down to early October. The twins' birthdays landed sometime in September of the same year. When I finally turned seventeen, Barron showed up, like clockwork, bearing gifts. He always came heavy with gold and the kinds of books I liked—tales of adventure and heroes.

One of his gifts stood out: a tunic crafted by the Eltonian school of medicine. He said he wanted to see my skills grow past what Kreila could teach and even offered to cover the cost. But there was a catch. I'd have to work for him and his company. That offer echoed in my head every time I brewed a potion or recited a spell. Did I want that kind of life? One tied to men like him? Was I just trading one leash for another? I dodged the issue and told him I'd think about it, kicking that problem down the road for future Wallace to figure out.

As winter crept in, the twins told me they needed my help with an upcoming project. They wanted me to whip up dozens of potions with different effects—and they needed them fast. I convinced Kreila that I was just brewing a batch for practice and for selling to adventurers at the Merry with Mead tavern. She wasn't thrilled, but she gave me the go-ahead. For two days straight, I worked nonstop trying to brew as many potions as possible.

Each bottle I corked felt like a step closer to something I couldn't name, a future I wasn't sure I wanted.

Once I'd finished, Michael and Melena called me to the bar. It was time to plan the biggest heist we'd ever pulled.

The three of us were down in the bunker beneath the tavern. We could hear footsteps and the muffled voices of the others moving around upstairs. The room was dim and quiet, perfect for what we were about to do. We spread out blueprints of a mansion across the table. The place had multiple floors and entrances, with guards constantly patrolling the grounds. The map marked out the treasure room and the gang members assigned to specific areas. Even the parchment smelled like danger.

"Sorry to spring this on you out of nowhere, Wallace," Michael said, leaning over the table. "But we have to move fast. House Danson and House Marshe have been butting heads for decades. They kill each other's people constantly, and half the time they don't even know who started it. It's gotten so bad that they just hire gangs to do the dirty work for them."

He paused and tapped the map.

"The last time they really went at it was over ten years ago. Two of the Marshes killed a Danson kid, not even realizing who he was until it was too late. That kicked off a war. They fought to a standstill, throwing mercenaries and gangs into the fire just to avoid lifting a finger themselves. Both families come from old money. Their ancestors were adventurers, the kind who brought back gold and relics and laid the foundation for their houses."

"Barron took me to the Marshes. They've got slaves and emerald coins. They won't even notice a few missing books or swords." I felt a grim satisfaction knowing we'd chosen a house that deserved to be robbed.

Michael looked up at me with a grin. "Now, both of them hired us to gear up for a fight against the other."

I frowned. "Both? At the same time?"

"Other gangs in the city are whispering about being hired by one side or the other. The Marshes and the Dansons had teenagers in love. The only name we got is Susan Marshe. The other one doesn't matter," Michael said, his voice even. "They tried to keep it quiet, but Susan found out the Danson boy was cheating on her. So she killed him."

He leaned back and continued. "When both families figured out what happened, they blamed each other for the mess. Now the Dansons want revenge. They're saying the only way to peace is to bring back Susan's head. The Marshes won't go for that, of course. It was a shame, too. I got a look at Susan Marshe. Pretty blonde one with red eyes."

"So are we taking a side? That could land us in a gang war," I said, looking between them.

Melena shook her head. "That's where their investors come in. Both houses have backers who don't want a full-on war."

Michael grinned. "The investors talked them into having dinner together at an old tavern hall in the center of town. They've hired cooks, waiters, and guards to help run the event. Once they're off to meet their guests that evening, we hit the Marshes' estate while it's nearly empty."

He sounded proud of himself.

The room stilled for a second. I felt the weight of it, this wasn't a job, it was a gamble with blood.

"I did some scouting around the Marshes," Melena added. "They usually move with escorts and a dozen guards. But with most of the family heading to that dinner, they're gonna bring every bit of security they've got. That means the estate will be light. Nothing we and our crew can't handle."

She smiled, something dangerous flickering in it.

"A few months ago, I got the chance to check out the mansion myself. There's a sewer tunnel in the garden, and the back windows? Old and rusted."

"Well, that's good to know. I'll add it to the plans. Shouldn't be hard to find a map of that part of the sewers," Michael said.

"Why the Marshes specifically?" I asked.

"While I was spying on them, the Marshes seemed like the weaker of the two houses," Melena said, her voice steady. "They've got money, but not enough to match the kind of heavy security the Dansons roll with. Which means every single guard they have is going to be escorting them to that dinner."

She leaned forward and placed her hands on the map. "Best part is, they don't know the sewers like we do. That gives us a back route into the estate. If things go bad, we make a run for the sewers. It's a maze down there, and we know it better than anyone. Our members are expected to memorize the sewer system. It's basically a requirement if you want to move up the ranks."

I stared at the map, heart ticking louder than I wanted. "What if someone doesn't make it out?"

"What's our backup plan if this goes south?" I asked. I didn't like the nerves crawling up my spine. This wasn't just another job. This was the big one.

"That's where all your potions come in," Michael replied. "We'll have everything we need to get out of trouble—invisibility, smoke, healing, whatever you've brewed that we can stuff in our packs. You'll be our support and magic expert. We're gonna need someone with skills once we're inside that place."

He paused for a beat, then added, "Plus, we hired a wizard merc. She doesn't care what we do as long as she gets paid."

"I like the plan," I said slowly, still unsure. But inside, I was already splitting in half. I thought of Kreila and her fading strength. Isabelle and the calm she gave me. I didn't know who I was doing this for anymore. "But this is the most dangerous mission we've ever done. I'm worried someone's gonna get killed, either one of us or one of the Marshes. If they find a body in their mansion, this whole thing could explode into a war."

"If it is, then it won't be for long," Michael said. "The Marshes pretend to be as rich as the Dansons. It's all for show, just to intimidate them. But at the end of the day, they're a straw house waiting to be kicked in."

He leaned back with a shrug.

"The two houses don't even know we accepted their offers. All we said was that we'd think about it and get back to them."

"We've been planning this for weeks," he went on. "But if we wait too long, they'll probably wipe each other out. And if that happens, we get left with nothing. Better to hit now, before their mansions turn into fortresses."

Michael was starting to convince me. His logic made sense. Timing was everything. But something deep inside me wanted to run.

"Sorry, I haven't been around more—" I began.

Melena waved me off. "You getting better at magic helps us. Means we'll have a mage with real experience, not some merc we have to keep paying."

I took a deep breath. This could get us into serious trouble. Or it could change everything.

If we played this right, we could be rich enough to walk away from the gang for good. No more back alleys or stolen coin. We could live in mansions of our own. Build something lasting. A dynasty, even. I could finally buy out every slave from Samuel... or better yet, end his whole operation. But would I even be the same person by then? Would Isabelle still want anything to do with the version of me who made that dream happen?

"Alright," I said. "What do you need from me?"

"Just get some rest. We've got all the supplies now that your potions are here," Michael said. "We just need to wait a week. The peace talks start in two days. Until then, we'll keep reviewing the plan and watching the Marshes daily. The crew coming with us are the most experienced. They'll be fully briefed on the layout and their roles."

"You can make extra potions if you want. The more the better," Melena added, patting me on the back. "Just make sure you watch your trail back to Kreila's. We don't want to bring any heat to her shop."

Michael nodded. "Stop by the bar to get updates, drop off supplies, and go over the plan again. Also, you'll need a new outfit. No plague doctor mask. We're not leaving any clue behind."

I nodded and wrote the details down in my journal so I could review them later at home. I planned to make as many potions as I could and bring them to the tavern. My hands moved out of habit, but my mind spun. To keep things smooth with Kreila, I told her I was making good coin selling potions to adventurers across the city. That way, I wouldn't have to explain why I was draining her supplies.

Chapter 34

The night before the heist, I couldn't sleep. I was too tense. I didn't want any casualties, any clues, or any regrets. The twins and I talked about how much we could rebuild the ghetto with the money. The homeless, abandoned, and broken of Elton could finally see us as heroes. I could free Isabelle and actually make a difference. I could stack enough gold to help Kreila retire and finally rest.

Either way, I was only ok with the plan if we were using the gold for something good, especially with war creeping in. There were going to be houses burned down and clinics packed with the wounded.

After enough daydreaming, I made a cup of chamomile tea and knocked out.

It was a cold fall night. Seven of us, including Michael, Ronald, and me, stood under the manhole behind the Marshes' mansion. It was Monday night. Nobody was out this late, and the few who were had already headed home. I wore a new leather outfit. I wasn't another plague doctor. I was just another thief in the dark.

Once the job was done, we all had fresh clothes to change into and planned routes to dodge the busier roads.

After a few minutes of waiting, Melena came running down the sewer tunnel toward us.

"They're gone, and most of their security too. We need to get in now and get out," she said, catching her breath. "We all know our target rooms, our partners, and the time limit. Five minutes. One of us robs, the other counts and watches for guards. Let's move."

"Let's grab what we can and not get greedy," I whispered. But already, my nerves were creeping in. What if we were wrong? What if someone stayed behind?

We were all strapped with potions. Healing, smoke, and those that boosted strength, speed, and more.

The mansion was huge, but we could tell it was fake. The red brick structure had its flaws. Mold clung to its sides, the fountains were partially broken, and the flower garden out back was barely alive. The house looked dark and nearly abandoned, but we still had to be cautious.

We crept around to the rear, staying low beneath the windows. Melena knocked out a blue-armed guard in the garden. It wasn't hard—man was practically asleep in a chair. My partner was Ronald, one of our best lockpickers, so I was on lookout.

On the first floor, outside the house, there was a line of windows leading to bedrooms and trophy rooms. As we unlocked the windows, we glanced at the other team, gave a quick nod, and carefully slipped inside.

The room we entered was nearly empty, but it belonged to a minor Marshe noble. The light blue walls and oak wood furniture looked old but still held their quality. That told us they were the real deal—solid and expensive.

Ronald and I grabbed whatever jewelry we could find. Sapphire rings, emerald necklaces, silver bracelets—enough to turn a good profit on the street. But my hands felt clumsy. I kept looking over my shoulder. My instincts didn't like this. Something about the silence was off.

A minute passed. I pressed my ear against the door, then slowly cracked it open. The hallway was painted green with silver-framed paintings meant to remind the Marshes just how powerful they were. I spotted a guard about twenty feet away, facing the other direction. No one else was in sight.

Without wasting time, I pulled out a syringe and nailed him in the back. He dropped silently, fast asleep. Ronald and I dragged him back into the bedroom and laid him on the bed. I didn't have time to tuck him in.

Another minute passed. Ronald slipped into a smaller room. This one didn't have nearly as much jewelry as the last, but a few pearls and some coin purses were still worth grabbing.

We moved fast toward the next spot on our path—the last room before we made our escape. It was supposed to be a trophy room, packed with treasures the Marshes had taken during their adventures.

Ronald started unlocking the door just as he spotted a guard down another hallway. The guard turned and walked away from us, taking a path that led in the opposite direction.

The door clicked open. One more minute left to grab what we could and get out.

Then we heard it. A scream. A girl. Sharp, high, and cut off too fast. Ronald and I froze, staring at each other. That scream came from nearby—same floor. My stomach dropped. That wasn't just a sound, it was a mistake. A big one.

I tapped his shoulder.

"Come on," I whispered.

We sprinted down the hallway toward the sound. A guard stood ahead of us, staring, stunned, as he opened a large door. Without thinking, I hurled a sleep potion into his face. He dropped. The glass shattered against his skin, slicing him up as the liquid soaked in. Blood dripped from the cuts on his face.

I turned and stepped into what looked like an office.

Melena stood inside, shaking. She was splattered in blood. Her eyes were wide, unfocused, stunned.

"Melena?" I whispered.

Beneath her was a blonde girl, young, with a dagger buried deep in her chest. Blood poured from the wound, soaking her blue dress. Her eyes were filled with tears and pain. I froze. That could've seen Susan. Or Isabelle. Or any of the girls we were trying to save with this gold.

What are we doing?

Melena turned toward me with tears in her eyes.

"She… I didn't see her… She was too far away."

She looked like she was about to collapse. Not from fear. From guilt. The job had changed her too.

Gods, this was bad. We needed to leave, and leave now.

I grabbed Melena's hand and turned toward the door, but before we could move, we heard the heavy shuffle of armored boots and the clanging of weapons. I looked around the room for an exit, but there wasn't one.

Ronald started panicking.

"No, no, no. Doc, what do we do now?"

The final minute passed. That was it. Our window was closed.

I was too scared to answer. My legs started to shake. Every instinct screamed to run, but there was nowhere left to go. I yanked Melena's arm to run, but it was too late. A dozen armed guards stormed in, blades and shields drawn. Their armor was heavy, scuffed from battle, and their weapons looked well-used. These weren't rookies. These were killers.

I pulled out a syringe and tried to cast a stun spell, but the moment I threw it, the glass turned to dust in midair. No... magic failure? What kind of spell was that?

Stepping out in front of the guards was a wizard. One of the Marshes' own. He looked calm. Too calm. Like he'd been waiting for this moment.

I hurled another syringe. Then another. And another. Each time, the wizard pointed his wooden staff, and every one of them disintegrated before impact. There was something wrong with him, his presence warped the room, like the air itself bent around him.

"These animals killed Susan! It must've been Danson's. Kill these cowards!"

The guards charged. Swords. Hammers. Axes.

This was it.

I couldn't stop panicking. My breathing went wild. I couldn't catch more than half a second before gasping for the next. I was going to die in a rich man's trophy room. For what? For coins and blood and lies.

"I'm so sorry. I'm so sorry," Melena whispered as we all stepped backward

Then we heard it. A single, sharp string from a lute rang out. The sound cut through the room, making everyone stumble. The guards pulled back into the hallway.

More roaring strings followed. The lute playing grew louder, heavier. But this couldn't have been Michael. This lute had power. It thundered with a force that made your bones shake. It was nothing like the soft, playful notes he usually strummed. The sound wrapped around my spine like ice and fire at once.

"Help me. Help me. Kill me now!" the wizard screamed, his voice shrill and desperate.

The guards nearest to him backed away. Then the wizard turned to face us. His brown eyes were gone, replaced by solid ebony black. I could feel the magic in him rising fast, like something was taking over. The hairs on my neck stood straight. The floor vibrated beneath my boots.

"Do it now!" he screamed again.

One of the guards raised his sword. The wizard pointed his staff at the ground, right in the middle of them all. The guard hesitated—then slashed the wizard's arm just as he had commanded.

The wizard shouted in pain but went quiet just as quickly. The tip of his staff began to smoke. Then it caught fire, flames curling upward from the point where it touched the floor.

That's when it happened.

I heard it—not just a voice, but two. Fused. Twisted. The wizard's and Michael's. Loud as a tempest and cold as judgment.

"Die!"

Chapter 35

"Get up, Wallace, get up!"

I could hear Melena's voice shouting above me. Even if I couldn't hear her, I could feel her trying to shake me awake. My eyes opened, and I saw her blood-streaked face trembling, tears brimming behind her panic. The sound of screaming came from the hallway, and I turned to my side, hearing Ronald howling in pain.

I got to my feet, still dazed from the explosion.

We were supposed to grab the vial and get out. Just in, out, and gone. Not this. Not hellfire and screaming.

"Where's Michael?!" I shouted.

"He's trying to slow down their backup, but we need to leave now!" Melena yelled.

I looked down the hallway behind her and saw chaos. Flames lit the corridor. The wall on the opposite side was blown open. Several bodies were burnt to a crisp, and from the ashes in the center, the wizard who cast the spell looked like he'd been turned inside out. The screaming behind Melena started to fade. My guess: one or two guards survived the blast but died in the blaze.

I ran over to Ronald and checked his wounds. He'd been hit by shrapnel. A small wooden spike had impaled his left leg, and he was rolling around in pain. I looked into his eyes and saw not just pain but terror. Raw, stinging terror..

"Hold on. I'll heal you, then we run."

I gave him one of my potions to numb the pain that was coming. I had to rip the spike out to close the wound with magic.

"This is going to hurt, but only for a few seconds."

I locked eyes with him again, wishing I could say more than 'sorry' with a look.. Then, with all the strength I had, I ripped the wooden spike from his leg. Blood splashed onto me, warm and sudden. His scream nearly drowned out my thoughts.

I jammed a severe healing syringe into his leg. The wound closed, but Ronald's face twisted in agony.

I dropped a syringe to summon my servant, who had never seen combat like this before. They blinked into existence, trembling, but did what they were told. In less than a second, Ronald was hovering above the ground in the servant's arms.

Smoke started choking the room, so I looked to Melena.

"Let's go. Come on!"

The two of us sprinted toward the hole in the wall, knocking through debris as we ran. Our feet hit the grass outside, and we stopped to catch our breath.

That's when I heard it—someone playing a lute, loud enough to go toe-to-toe with the roar of the fire.

"Fall! Sleep! Stun!"

Michael's voice rang out from deep inside the mansion.

His tone wasn't calm or elegant anymore. It was desperately triggering raw magic behind every chord.

"I'm going after Michael. Where is he?!" I shouted.

"He ran to the lobby to try to hold the door! His partner is dead, and mine is in the garden!"

"Get to the sewers! Don't wait for us!" I ordered.

"No! I'll keep watch till you two get out!" Melena shot back.

I took a deep breath and looked down at my arms. Getting Michael meant pushing beyond everything I thought I had left. But it didn't matter.

He would've done the same for me.

As fast as my hands could move, I jammed several syringes into my arms within seconds. Speed. Strength. Stone skin. Empowered lungs. Enhanced vision. Enhanced senses.

Each one burned like a small fire under my skin. I started grunting from the pain. My limbs went numb, but my heart kept pounding.

I injected one more syringe to stabilize myself, then launched into a sprint.

With enhanced speed, I tore down hallways engulfed in flames. Even with all the smoke, my lungs held steady. My vision cut through the haze.

I heard a lute strumming hard to my left. That meant one thing. Michael. I was getting close.

I turned the corner and stepped into the lobby. It was unrecognizable. Marble floors cracked from the heat. The massive carpet curled up, ablaze. The staircase had collapsed, fire eating through every wooden beam. Paintings melted from the walls.

Michael stood in the center. Surrounded by corpses. Some unconscious. Others already gone. He looked like he was seconds from falling over.

"Hey!" I shouted, trying to get his attention.

When I got to his side, I saw him strumming a lute at a that looked forged from blood and fire. It wasn't his.

Strings shimmered like diamonds, and the sound they produced echoed like an orchestra..

His hands were bleeding. Eyes bright red. Magic pouring from every pore.

"Wal?!" he shouted, dazed.

Then he collapsed.

His body hit the floor. His eyes stayed on me as he dropped.

I didn't have time to check all his wounds. I didn't need to. He had burned himself out. Pushed his magic and his body past the edge. Maybe twice over.

Michael looked like he was about to die right there in front of me. And I froze.

Terrified that my face might be the last thing he ever saw.

I stabbed a syringe into him to stabilize him for now. Then I lifted him into my arms. Despite the weight, it was easy. But as I did, the sharp tip of a crossbow bolt punched into my back. My stone skin kept it from going deep. The pain still hit.

I turned toward the door. A new squad of Marsh guards was charging in.

I didn't hesitate. I pulled my final move. With one hand, I threw a syringe at the front door. As it flew, it turned pitch black. It hit the foot of a guard and shattered on impact.

Ooze pooled beneath the guard, spreading into a massive puddle that covered the front door. One guard sprinted toward me with his blade raised, but before he got a foot away, a massive black tentacle wrapped around his head and flung him backward. From the dark pool by the door, several tentacles of pure black ooze rose up and wrapped around the incoming Marshe guards. The tentacles lifted the guards into the air. Then they slammed them hard against the floor and walls of the lobby. The loud crashing of armor hitting marble was rivaled by the guards' screams as bones snapped.

When I cast the spell, I focused on the tentacles bruising and breaking bones. Just enough to disable, not kill.

I sprinted with Michael slung over my shoulders, heading toward the exit we'd made earlier. I was terrified. Everything had gone wrong. Too many people were dying. The screams, the smoke, and seeing Michael and Melena wrecked—it made me want to drop this life for good. I didn't want to die. I didn't want to die in either of the twins' arms. I sure wasn't going to let Michael die in mine. So I kept running. Every inch of my body screamed from the spells I'd layered on myself.

As I turned the corner toward the broken wall, a steel arm came out of nowhere and smashed into my head. Michael and I hit the ground hard. My ears rang. Blood poured down my face again. I coughed and looked up.

A Marshe guard stood over us in full plate armor, holding a mace and shield.

"Danson scum!" he roared.

The guard was terrifying. He was tall, strong, and gleaming in the firelight.

I rose to my feet and faced the guard. He was only about five feet from me. Before I could think, he lunged forward, slammed his mace into my stomach, and sent me flying into the wall. The stone skin kept me from blacking out, but the pain still ripped through me. As I tried to get up, the guard took another swing with his mace. I tossed a syringe of acid at his swinging arm. It melted through his armor, and he dropped the mace, screaming in pain.

"You bastard!" the guard shouted, then slammed me into the wall again with his shield. I nearly vomited as it crushed into my stomach and ribs.

No. This can't be how it ends. Kreila needed me. Michael needed me. Melena needed me. Gods, I never told Isabelle how I felt. Never said how her smile brought me joy in a city full of evil. I started crying in misery. The reaper was coming for me. And he was wearing steel.

The guard dropped his shield and knelt in front of me. "I'm going to chop you to pieces and feed you to the pigs." He grabbed my throat and began choking me with everything he had. I tried to push him off. Tried to lift his arms. It was useless. Even with strength enhancements, he was still stronger than I was.

I looked him in the eyes—blue, cold, full of ambition. He thought I was just a sack of meat for the pigs. Maybe even a ticket to a promotion. I knew what I had to do. And I knew what it was going to do to my soul.

I thought of the homeless man who tried to kill me so long ago. The relief I felt when he dropped to the ground stayed with me. So did the nightmares. Even after all this time, I still saw him in my dreams, walking through the dark with that mangy dog fur coat.

The tentacles were meant to wound. Maybe break a few bones. Never to kill. But now I knew the homeless man would have company in my dreams.

With everything I had left, I pulled out my last syringe. I focused hard. I thought of the biggest splash of acid my body could make. The syringe filled itself with light green fluid. It was hot in my hand.

With all my strength, and an apology in my mouth, I drove it into the guard's neck. I kept my hand there. I didn't let go until I knew every drop had gone in.

The guard's grip on my throat loosened. I gasped, coughed, and blood hit my lips. He clutched his neck with both hands, desperate to stop what he knew he couldn't.

I didn't have time to rest. I yanked out my last healing potion and chugged it as fast as I could. But it wasn't enough. My body was barely hanging on after everything I'd done.

"Don't turn around, don't turn around, don't look at him," I muttered under my breath. I lifted Michael back onto my shoulders. I took one step toward the exit.

Then a hand, weak and shaking, grabbed my leg.

I looked down at the guard and made what I thought was the biggest mistake of my life. His neck was a mess of green acid and crimson blood. The flesh was melting, skin bubbling like boiling stew. His eyes were locked on mine, wide with shock. He stared straight into my eyes like he was begging for something. I wanted to say I was sorry. I wanted to ask if he had a family waiting for him. But I didn't have time. I kicked my leg free from his grip and ran for the exit, leaving his boiling corpse behind.

My feet hit the grass outside. That's when I saw Melena crouched behind the garden bushes. She rushed over

"What happened? Is he alive?!"

I nodded. No words.

We ran to the manhole and slipped below. The sewer welcomed us with its cold, wet dark.

—

The four of us reached the manhole near the tavern. I laid Michael down. Then I dropped beside him, breathing like I was choking on air, doing everything I could not to lose it.

Melena came over and hugged me.

"Hey, it's going to be ok. We're almost there. Come on." Her voice was soft.

I could barely breathe. But I had just enough left in me to make it home.

Ronald, Melena, and I took off our leather garbs and stuffed them into my mage bag. We'd burn them later. Ronald and I undressed Michael together, and all of us changed into fresh clothes. The plan was to look like random civilians dragging a drunk friend home. I pulled out a glass of ale and splashed it over the four of us so we'd smell like a tavern too.

We climbed out of the manhole and limped our way toward the tavern.

When we got there, a few of our people helped carry Michael down to the bunker. Melena and Ronald followed close behind.

"Let's rest up. We'll talk in the morning. Michael's going to be out for a day or so," I told Melena.

She nodded, a frown tight on her face.

I laid Michael down in his room and started triaging him. He was going to be fine. Just needed rest and a bath. I wrapped his wounds and wiped the sweat off his face. He'd wake up sore as hell, head pounding, body aching from everything he went through.

Melena and Ronald were alright too. Ronald would be limping for a bit, but nothing serious.

I was a mess. Head throbbing, ears still ringing, blood drying on my skin. I grabbed a wet towel and wiped the worst of it off. I needed to get to Kreilas before nightfall, but first I took a second to breathe and get some water down.

I dropped off the haul from the heist and burned the leather gear to make sure nothing could be traced. The two we lost inside the palace—our people—hadn't been carrying anything that could tie us to the job.

After about ten minutes of sitting, I stood up and got ready to head to Kreilas. On the way out, I stopped by Melena's room. She was sitting on the bed, her face buried in her hands.

"Melena?" I whispered.

She turned toward me. Her face was streaked with tears.

"Please just go home and leave me alone. I just want to be alone right now," she whispered back.

I walked over and hugged her

"I'll see you in the morning," I said, then stepped out of her room.

"I'm sorry…" she mumbled.

"I know," I whispered.

As I reached the stairs, Ronald passed me in the hallway. He still reeked of smoke and sweat. He stopped and grabbed my shoulder.

"Thanks for not leaving me."

"A shame we couldn't save the other two," I said, frowning.

We both nodded, and I walked out of the tavern. A few of the others watched me as I passed through the bar. They looked concerned. Most of them had known me for years. One of them stepped toward me before I hit the door.

"No, I'll be ok. Just make sure those two are safe," I said, waving him off.

My eyes were barely open. Every step hurt like hell, but I kept going. The streets were quieter than usual. Empty, almost. I moved through them slowly, dragging my body one step at a time.

Eventually, I reached a part of the street where the city opened up in front of me. From there, I could see two pillars of smoke rising into the air. One had to be the Marshe manor. The other, farther north, I didn't recognize.

And right then, I thought about the girl Melena killed. Thought about her dreams. About how they were ripped away before she even got a chance to grow up.

As I kept walking, something heavy settled on my shoulders. The smoke. The fallen guards. Were they still breathing? Were some of them trapped, choking on smoke in that building?

The ones I hurt—were they unconscious? Were they too broken to crawl to safety?

How many people did I kill tonight?

How many families did I destroy?

I couldn't answer that now. I was in too much pain to stop and cry.

I kept walking home, doing my best to straighten up. I didn't want Kreila to see how tired I was. But the urge to cry had been creeping up on me, and I was fighting it the whole way. With everything I'd done tonight, I couldn't stop thinking about the guard I killed. Did he have a family? A wife? Kids? What would they do when they found out he wasn't coming home?

I rubbed my face, trying to push the thoughts out of my head. Just two more blocks. Then I'd be home. I'd take a full bath and go to sleep.

Out of nowhere, pain stabbed deep into my shoulder. I didn't even have time to turn around before I collapsed face-first onto the gravel. My whole body locked up. I couldn't move. Couldn't scream. Could barely blink.

It was time for the silent auction. A slaver must've found me. They were going to take me somewhere no one would ever find me again.

Two men in masks appeared over me. My heart went wild in my chest. This was worse than death. If I died, at least the people I loved would know what happened. But if I disappeared, they'd waste years looking for me, praying I was still out there somewhere.

This was it. After everything I survived—the misery, the pain, it was all for nothing.

I thought of Isabelle. I'd never see her again. She'd keep looking for me, still stuck under Samuel. The twins would blame themselves, thinking it was their fault I vanished. They'd carry that weight forever.

And then Kreila. The only mother I ever had. She'd grieve like she'd lost a son she finally got.

"Alright, what do we have here?"

Two slavers crouched over me. Both wore black cloaks and lion masks.

One of the slavers grabbed my mask and yanked it off. Then she pulled me up by my hair. My body was still frozen. All I could do was stare.

I couldn't fight. I couldn't run. And worse, my vision was going blurry. Even if they weren't wearing masks, I wouldn't have recognized them.

"Looks like a teenager. Black hair, green eyes. Think he'll make for a quick gold."

The two lifted my body and turned me toward an alleyway. A dark figure stood at the end of it, wearing a gold lion mask. The rest of him blended into the shadows.

"Boss?" the man called.

He didn't answer. Instead, something flashed in his hand.

A javelin? A spear?

It flew. Killed the other man instantly.

Then he blurred forward—too fast to follow.

The other slaver screamed. A crunch. Then silence.

I hit the ground again. My body was done.

The gold mask lifted me. I tried to speak.

"Please let me go. I don't…"

But the words didn't finish.

The dark swallowed me.

Chapter 36

Before I could even open my eyes, pain ripped through me like I'd been shredded and sewn back together. I braced for the worst, a pig pen or dungeon, but when I opened them, I saw a white wooden ceiling. The scent of oranges and ginger hung in the air.

For a moment, I thought maybe it had all been a dream. Was I home? How did I even get back here?

But there was no time to think. As the sharp pain in my ears dulled, voices cut through.

"You let him walk alone! You let Wallace go by himself across the hellish city, all while the city begins to burn!"

Kreila's voice shattered the silence like glass. I never thought she could sound that furious.

"Look, like we said before, Wallace knows how to protect himself. If we weren't sure he could walk, we would have had him strapped to our backs!"

That was Michael. He sounded beat, but pissed.

I wasn't about to lie there and let them kill each other with guilt. I pushed myself upright, feet hitting the floor, and tried to stand. A jolt lanced up my spine. My legs gave out as I hit the boards hard.

"Wallace?!" Kreila shouted.

Within seconds, I heard the three of them running around the corner into the room. They saw me collapsed on the floor.

"Hey, what are you doing?!" Michael yelled.

Melena and Michael rushed over and lifted me, laying me gently back onto the bed. Exhaustion hit me again. I had to fight to stay awake.

"Wallace, are you alright? What in God's name happened?!" Kreila asked, her voice trembling.

I couldn't even respond. My body was still wracked with pain.

"I… I saw someone…" I groaned, barely getting the words out.

"Wallace, you told us you were fine after the fight outside the bar. What happened?" Michael asked, glaring straight into my eyes. He threw a glance at Kreila too.

There was something strange about Michael. He moved like the fight hadn't even touched him, like the violence had rolled right off. The ruby lute at his waist shimmered faintly. I could feel the power it gave off. Melena seemed to have recovered, too, at least physically.

Michael's eyes said it all. Stick to the lie. Protect the truth.

But I didn't want to lie. I wanted to collapse into Kreila's arms and beg her to forgive me.

"When strong adventurers get drunk, they can be hard to take down, with or without city guards." I had rehearsed that line before. It was the excuse I kept in my back pocket for nights like this.

Kreila looked into my eyes. Tears streamed down her cheeks. That look almost broke me.

"Wallace, please tell me the truth. What happened? Why were you in a fight?" Her voice was low, still shaken.

Saying it out loud felt like swallowing knives. But if I told her what really happened, she might never let me stay.

"A couple of adventurers got drunk at the bar. They insulted the twins. I had to get them out, but they spat on Michael, and a brawl erupted. We tossed them outside, but they hit me pretty hard. Some knight nearly choked me out if Michael didn't step in.

It hurt to lie to Kreila. But I knew the truth would hurt her even more.

"Luckily, those adventurers looked worse than we did," Melena said with pride.

"All three of you have bruises and cuts on your head and body. Gods, Wallace, your face was terrible. It was covered in blood. Some of your bones were broken, and it even looked like you cracked your skull.”

Kreila’s voice shook. She looked like she was about to cry.

That was when the guilt really hit. Not just because she was upset—but because I had never seen her this undone.

“I told you that the bar wasn’t safe. Why didn’t you stay here like I told you? Wallace, if you were killed or, worse, taken by slavers, I would never sleep well ever again.”

She sat on the bed beside me. Her hands went to her face as the tears came.

Her crying hit me hard. I used every bit of willpower not to cry with her. But I failed. My own tears started to fall.

She had told me before that she cared about me, but it always came out sounding sarcastic. This was different. This was real. She didn’t even have to say the words for me to feel it.

Melena laid a hand on her shoulder. Michael passed her a handkerchief in silence.

“I’m sorry, Kreila. I never meant to scare you.” I said quietly.

I tried to sit up again, aching from every angle. Before I could say more, Kreila pulled me into a hug. Tight. I felt her tears soak my shoulder.

“I’m so sorry,” I whispered as I began to weep.

I noticed the twins had turned their faces away. Looked like they were trying to keep it together too.

After a long moment, they lifted me back onto the bed and laid me down gently.

"Barron found you on the ground with poison darts in your back. He saved you from those slavers who tried to take you. I'm so grateful he was there," Kreila said.

My gaze dropped. Slavers in gold masks. A third figure who killed them. Then being lifted…

Was that Barron? Why would he be out there? Why save me? What was he doing wandering the city at night?

"Barron said he may return this evening and wants you three to stay put for a while. He said the city is getting dangerous right now, and he would return with more details," Kreila said, breaking my train of thought, as she wiped the last of the tears from her face.

"Michael and I live at the tavern, but we have security in place in case something happens. After yesterday, though, we'll probably need to hire extra help," Melena said.

"Why did you three even build a bar in the first place? In the ghetto, where those criminals and murderers live. Why can't you find work somewhere else? Even if it means leaving the city, you could find something safer," Kreila said.

"That tavern is our best chance out of this city, Kreila. Once we get it running strong, we can sell it off and move to another city or country," Michael replied.

"Please don't argue. I don't have the energy to throw syringes," I mumbled, trying and failing to lift the mood in the room.

"Wallace, you need to stay in bed. You slept from the moment Barron found you until noon," Kreila said.

"I'm going to make you some tea to help with your strength. The one next to you has gone cold by now." She picked up the cup from the table beside me and walked out.

Michael and Melena turned to face me. As they did, Michael pulled out his lute and strummed two strings.

Suddenly, everything in my head went quiet.

Then I heard a voice inside me.

"First one's healing, second's the mind-link. You know the drill. Grandma can't hear us now," Michael's voice echoed dryly.

"And of course, he dragged me into it. It's invasive. I hate this magic," Melena added in my head, sharp as ever.

"So, in short, we expected you to return to the bar this morning. When you didn't, we came to check in. Got ambushed by grandma's rant. Still, we were worried. I was about to call everyone we know to start a search party for you," Michael said, somehow without moving his mouth.

"You had us scared to death," Melena added.

"How are you two doing? You look like you're holding up, but after everything that happened, I'm not so sure," I asked.

The twins looked down, then turned to face me with a frown.

"We're functioning. Processing. Pretending it didn't happen yet," Melena said flatly.

"I'm using my acting skills to fake wellness. And failing. She already clocked it," Michael muttered.

Michael's voice cut off. I felt our mental connection snap.

Kreila walked back into the room and handed Michael a dark blue bottle.

"Michael, you look like you've exhausted yourself with that magic. Stop strumming that lute," Kreila said. "You two can stay if you'd like, or head back to the tavern. Just make sure you walk together. I can see both of you are tired beyond relief and need rest."

She handed me a teacup. The scent of honey and vanilla hit me immediately.

Michael uncorked the potion bottle and took a sip.

"Probably best if we stay at the tavern for a few days. Just to make sure those jerks don't come back. We'll be alright. No need to worry about us," he said.

I took a sip of the tea. The mint hit hard, flooding my mouth and nose.

"You two going to hire extra protection?" I asked.

Melena winked. "Yep. We've got it covered. We can get there without any trouble."

"Fine. But please stick together and stay inside at night. I saw two fires from here yesterday. People seem restless. I don't know what's going on," Kreila said with a sigh.

"Thanks for worrying, Grandma, but the three of us are tougher than we look. Don't forget that," Melena said with a flick of sarcasm in her voice.

But Kreila wasn't amused.

"You two need to find a skill and get out of the ghetto. I don't think any of you are safe there. Especially with that lute. Michael, where did you get it?" Kreila asked, pointing at him.

"Oh, this? Something those adventurers left behind during the scuffle. Thought it was their way of paying the tab," Michael grinned.

"That's powerful magic, Michael. It's best that you sell it to a mage college or somewhere far from here. Magic like that can bring unwanted attention," Kreila said, her voice pleading.

The twins walked over and gave me a tight hug, both ignoring Kreila's warning.

"We'll come back tomorrow and check up on you. That, or we'll send a raven," Melena said.

Then they walked out of the inpatient room, and I heard the front door open.

"Thanks, Grandma. You have a good one!" Michael shouted.

The door slammed before Kreila could respond.

Kreila shook her head and sat beside me on the bed.

"Wallace, I know this may be hard to hear. But those two are starting to worry me," she said with a frown. "I heard him strum that lute a moment ago. You should know Michael played it too well. It's overflowing with magic, and I couldn't even tell what kind. I wasn't able to decipher the spell."

She shook her head again.

"You may not have noticed it either, but I saw Melena with a knife. It had some kind of strange aura. She wouldn't let me examine it. She told me she got it during the drunk brawl last night, just like your brother got the lute."

Kreila's voice dropped.

"Wallace, I don't know who those adventurers were, but they had access to strong magic. And I'm worried about how that magic will be used now that it's in your siblings' hands."

She shook her head once more.

"I trust them, Kreila. They've been by my side this whole time, and they'd do anything to protect me," I told her.

"No, Wallace. I know they love you, and I know they wouldn't hurt you. But I'm worried they might piss off the wrong kind of powerful people…" Her voice was softer now, but the fear hadn't left her eyes. And for the first time, I started to wonder if she was right.

"They could hurt a lot of people. Doesn't matter if they're drunk tavern goers or just innocent folks on the street. I can't quite put my finger on it, Wallace, but something feels different. Something has changed."

I looked down for a moment.

Besides that homeless man from so long ago, we've never killed anyone.

Melena looked shaken when she killed that girl. But Michael? He took down several people without flinching, then went out looking for more. I knew they felt something about it, maybe even guilt, but honestly, they were taking it way better than I expected, almost like they were proud of how it all played out.

"I understand, Kreila. But I won't let it get that far. If things ever start slipping out of control, I'll stop them. I'll never let them go reckless, and I'll never give up on them," I said, firm with the weight of everything I meant.

"I hope you're right, Wallace. But from where I'm standing, that moment when they lose control is either just around the corner or already here."

She stood and placed her hands on her hips.

"I'm going to get you more medicine, something to eat, and maybe a few books. I know you're sick of textbooks, so I'll bring down those dragon novels and romance stories you read.

She managed a smile.

Even if I would have rather she not know about my taste in books.

By sundown, I sat at the window, staring at the smoke rising over the city. We had destroyed this place more than we'd helped it. But maybe, with the gold we stole, maybe we could fix it all.

Kreila came back and sat beside me. "Wallace, I never asked, how are you really feeling? Last night must've been terrifying for you."

"I'm okay. Just need some time at home before I go anywhere. I was terrified, Kreila. Scared I'd never see anyone again. Scared to even imagine what they'd do to me. I know sometimes, a quick death is the only mercy a slave gets." I gripped the blanket draped over me. "Last night made me appreciate you all even more. It made me want to say and do things I was scared of doing before, knowing it could all end in a single moment."

"That fear doesn't fade easily," she said. "After surviving death, we often love harder. When my coven faced a demonic cult, one of us died and had to be revived. That was forty years ago, and I still dream about it. But I try to let those memories drift away, like water down a river."

She tried to smile, but failed. Her frown deepened as a tear slipped down her cheek.

"Just know that you are safe now. And someday, you'll be so powerful that people may even be scared to approach you."

"Wallace, I forbid you to leave this house alone. I don't care where you're going, not even if it's the middle of the afternoon. You do not leave this house without protection. Do you understand?"

"Kreila, I can defend—" She cut me off.

"I don't care, Wallace. I lived one of my worst nightmares last night. Watching you get carried into the store with darts in your back and your bones broken was one of the worst moments of my life. I've seen death, destruction, and monsters tearing innocents apart before.

But I can't remember the last time I was that scared. Watching you being carried in like that..." She began to cry again.

"I can't let you leave with the thought that you may not come home. I love you. You're like the son I never got to have." She wiped her eyes with her sleeve.

Seeing her like this was probably the worst moment of my life, too. If Kreila broke down like this just from me being rescued, I didn't want to imagine what she'd look like if I had died. I started to wonder what everyone would look like if they found my corpse. It was fair to say everyone would be crying over my grave. Melena and Michael would probably blame themselves. Isabelle would wish she had been there to save me. Barron would probably just see me as wasted potential. I didn't even want to imagine what Kreila would do.

"Ok, Kreila, I'll stay. I'll send a raven to Isabelle or the twins if I need to go anywhere. And if I do have to leave, it won't be for long, and it won't be far. You can trust me on this. I hate seeing you cry," I whimpered, trying to keep my composure.

Kreila sat up straight and sighed. "I still may need to make a trip soon, with everything going on outside. So if I'm away, I ask that you only leave the house in case of emergencies. I'll have the shop stocked with food and supplies, and I'll close the store until I return."

"The city is at war with itself, and you're still making the trip? How are you going to do that?" I asked.

"I know you have questions, Wallace, and I'll explain them soon. But you should know, my trips are more important now than ever." Kreila said, looking down at her palms.

"Kreila…" I paused. I guess now was the time.

"Kreila, I had a dream a few months ago, and I need to ask you something. Did you work for the Eltons?"

"Wallace, what in the world makes you say that?"

"I dreamed of you, with King Kendrick. You talked about the Violet Dragon. You saved Prince Philip. You… kissed the king."

She froze. Her eyes locked onto mine.

"Kreila?" Her silence was louder than a scream.

"I'll let you rest," she said, voice barely holding. "That tea has medicine for the paralysis."

"Wait, don't leave! Tell me what happened!"

She turned, tears in her eyes. "I've made too many mistakes…

"How long do you have with the Violet Dragon?" I whimpered.

Kreila walked to my bedside.

She stepped close. "A year. No cure. I've tried everything. I might make it to your eighteenth birthday."

"Please don't give up. I'll find a way, I swear—"

"My sweet Wallace. I know you're confused, but please… just go to sleep. Once you rest, we'll talk about your dream."

"I don't care about rest right now! You're dying! I'll find something to fix this. I swear!" Part of me knew I was just saying that because I was afraid, but I couldn't stop myself from trying to believe it.

Kreila didn't answer. She just pulled me into a hug and wouldn't let go. The harder I cried, the tighter she held me.

"Please…" I whispered one last time.

At last, she pulled back. "Your job now is to help me by being the best student you can. Stay close. Keep me company. I love you, Wallace. Always have. Always will."

"I love you too," I whispered as a tear dropped.

Kreila wiped it away with her finger and looked into my eyes. She smiled a beautiful, fragile smile.

I smiled back, wishing time would stop, before the world took her from me.